MW01076046

The Moneylender *of*
TOULOUSE

The **Moneylender** *of*
TOULOUSE

A FOOLS' GUILD MYSTERY

Alan Gordon

St. Martin's Minotaur ✿ *New York*

THE MONEYLENDER OF TOULOUSE. Copyright © 2008 by Alan Gordon. All rights reserved. Printed in the United States of America. No part of this book may be used or reproduced in any manner whatsoever without written permission except in the case of brief quotations embodied in critical articles or reviews. For information, address St. Martin's Press, 175 Fifth Avenue, New York, N.Y. 10010.

www.minotaurbooks.com

Library of Congress Cataloging-in-Publication Data

Gordan, Alan (Alan R.)
    The moneylender of Toulouse : a Fools' Guild mystery / Alan Gordon.
—1st ed.
        p.   cm.
    ISBN-13: 978-0-312-37109-8
    ISBN-10: 0-312-37109-8
    1. Bishops—Fiction.   2. Fools and jesters—Fiction.   3. Toulouse (France)—Fiction.   4. France—History—11th century—Fiction.
    5. Murder—Investigation—Fiction.   I. Title.
    PS3557.O649M66   2008
    813'.54—dc22
                                                                2008003450

First Edition: May 2008

10 9 8 7 6 5 4 3 2 1

To Vesta Downer,

a remarkable woman who raised

two remarkable daughters,

and graciously let me marry one

The **Moneylender** *of*
TOULOUSE

CHAPTER 1

It's up here," said the landlord, leading us up a steep flight of
steps. There was a trapdoor at the top which he pushed up.
I climbed after him, then reached back for Portia as Claudia
handed her up to me. The baby looked at everything at once
and said, "Ooooo."

"She likes it," said the landlord.

"That's a good start," said Claudia as she pulled herself
through.

"Now, this is the main room," said the landlord.

Cob walls, with a thin coat of whitewash slapped on them
sometime in the last decade. I thought that I could put my
fist through them fairly easily. I made a note to hold my temper. At least, while I was inside.

"And you got your brazier over here," he continued. "It
keeps the place nice and toasty when it's going."

We looked at the brazier, which was the size of a piglet,
and the runt of the litter at that.

"Does all right," he insisted.

He threw open shutters on both sides of the room, and
the chill wind whipped through.

"You get a nice breeze," he observed.

"Just what we want in December," I said.

"I take your point, Senhor," he said, closing the ones on the west side of the room. "But come the summer months, you'll need every scrap of air you can get. Now, here's the one room, and there's the other. You can try out the pallets if you're so inclined."

There was a rustling noise from one of them. He moved quicker than I thought he could and stomped down hard. The rustling noise stopped.

"Of course, you're free to bring in your own," he added.

"Not much furniture," observed Claudia.

"Will you be entertaining much?" he asked.

"We're jesters," I said. "We entertain for a living."

"Oh, is that what you are?" he asked. "I don't see any motley on you."

"It's Advent," I explained. "No entertainment until Christmas season."

"Then you're unemployed jesters," he said. "In that case I'll be wanting six months in advance. Two pennies a month."

"For two pennies a month, we can live in town," I said.

"Then live in town," he said evenly.

"Three pennies for two months, and I'll pay for four in advance," I said.

"Done," he said, so quickly that I regretted not haggling more. That's the problem with coming to a new place and not knowing the price of things.

I held out my hand. He looked at it curiously.

"Oh, I need you to sign an agreement," he said. "It's the way of doing business here. I'd trust you, but the wife doesn't like me to do that. You know how women are."

"I do indeed," I said, as Claudia shot me a quick smile.

We went downstairs to his rooms and he produced a document and a quill and ink.

"Just an ordinary lease," he said. "Nothing fancy. I don't even bother with it after. You can sign with an X if that's all you know, I don't mind."

He passed it to me. I looked at it, using my best puzzled expression.

"I don't know what this says," I said.

He glanced over my shoulder, then turned it right side up. "Just put your mark down there," he said.

"I'm not sure," I said. "It looks like Latin."

"Oh, that's just how they do contracts here," he said. "Like I said, nothing to worry about. I can't even read it myself."

"What a lovely hand it's in," exclaimed Claudia, looking at it. "All those curlicues. You can tell that the scribe was a learned man."

"Yes, but I don't see any numbers," I said.

"Well, that's because they're written out as words," she explained. "See there? That's a three."

"Ah, so this would bind us legally to pay three pennies a month," I said.

"It certainly would," she agreed.

"Not at all what we just discussed, is it?"

"Not at all."

"I am thinking that if I brought this document to a baile, then perhaps this landlord could find himself in a spot of legal difficulty," I said.

"I would think so," she agreed.

"Now, there's no need for that," said the landlord hastily. "We can dispense with the formalities. I'm sure your word is good enough for me."

"But is yours good enough for us?" I asked. "I think a contract is an excellent idea, friend landlord. Have your scribe draw one up reflecting the price we agreed upon. And make a copy for us."

"I might have one or two where the terms can be filled in," he admitted grudgingly.

"Eminently satisfactory," I said. "And please remember that we are fools with some education."

"So I see," he said, fetching a pair of documents from his desk. "What do I call you, Senhor Jester?"

"Tan Pierre," I said. "This is my wife, Domina Gile. The baby is Portia, and that's our older daughter, Helga, with the wain."

"My name is Honoret. Pleased to meet you, I'm sure," he said, holding out his hand.

I grasped it and pulled him to me.

"You'll find us to be reliable tenants," I said softly. "Unless crossed. See that you perform as reliably as our landlord. And get us a decent-sized brazier that can actually produce some heat."

"I will," he promised quickly.

"Then we have an understanding," I said, releasing him.

He massaged his hand, grimacing, while I signed the contracts, making sure to enter the agreed-upon price first. He added his signature somewhat shakily, and I paid him for four months, which soothed his injured pride considerably.

Helga was sitting on the wain when we emerged from the front door, holding Zeus's reins and chatting with a pair of young men.

"So, I will see you in church then," she said smoothly as I came up. "Nice to meet you."

They glanced at me and made their farewells immediately.

"New friends?" I asked.

"I have to have something to do until Christmas," she said, pouting.

"It's called training, Apprentice," I said sternly. "You have fallen behind in your studies. You will never become a jester in full at this rate."

"I was practicing my flirting," said Helga. "You told me that that was an essential tool for every fool."

"That's true enough," I conceded. "Good. You have earned the privilege of helping me unload the wain."

"We'll be living here?" she said dubiously. "Why not in Toulouse proper?"

"It's cheaper in Saint Cyprien," I said. "And it's only twenty minutes' walk to the center of the city. Less for a pair of young legs like yours. Now, take those props and instruments up."

Claudia stayed with the wain, nursing the baby, while Helga and I made several trips up the steep steps. Despite the cold air, we were both drenched in sweat by the time we had finished.

"You'll be in the smaller room," I said, pointing it out. "We'll be in there."

"And Portia will be with me," she said.

"No, Portia will be with us," I said, carrying the cradle inside the large room. When I came out, Helga was staring in rapture at the smaller room.

"My own room," she breathed. "My very own room!" She squealed and hugged me fiercely.

"Enjoy it while you can, Apprentice," I said. "Once the baby is weaned, she'll be moving in with you."

"There's no hurry on that," she said. "She's so plump and happy. I think you could nurse her until she's five or so."

"I am thinking not," said Claudia, coming through the trap. She had Portia in her right arm and a broom in her hand. She tossed the latter to Helga.

"A new broom for a new room," said Claudia. "I want this

place spotless by the time we get back. Take the pallets outside and burn them. Handle them carefully. I don't want you to get bitten. Then fetch some water up here and mop the place out."

"Yes, Domina," said Helga, spinning the broom until it was a blur.

"No fooling until the work's done," added Claudia.

"Yes, Domina," she sighed, putting the broom to its proper use.

We went back down the stairs.

"I saw a stable over by the cemetery," I said.

"It's probably going to cost more to keep Zeus comfortable than to keep us," grumbled Claudia as she climbed onto the wain.

"Well, he does eat more," I said, sitting beside her and flicking the reins.

She was silent as we rode past the cemetery.

"We could sell him, you know," she said.

"I couldn't possibly part with Zeus," I said. "I have grown too attached to him."

"He, on the other hand, or hoof, would cheerfully trample you into the grass and eat you if you gave him half a chance," she said.

"That's why I need him around," I said. "He keeps me ever vigilant."

We found the stable. I did a better job of haggling this time. A boy who didn't know any better took the reins, and we heard shouts of panic as he tried to wrestle the horse into a stall. Other boys rushed in to help, and we finally heard a door slam and a neigh of frustration.

"Anyhow, I owe him," I said. "He's earned his keep. And I want him here just in case we have to get out of town in a hurry."

"We're already out of town, so you've gotten a head start," she said. "We're supposed to be settling down, aren't we?"

"I've never been good at that," I said.

"Thank you so much, said his wife," she said.

"You're the exception that proves the rule," I said, putting my arm around her as we walked. "I need you around, too. You also keep me vigilant."

"So, I am the equivalent of your horse," she said. "The compliments never stop coming, do they?"

"I love you, you're beautiful, a goddess among mortals."

"That's it?"

"I adore the shape of your nose. I don't think I've ever told you that."

"Then because you adore the shape of my nose, I will share your bed tonight, husband," she said, leaning into me for a moment.

We located the local market and loaded up with provisions. There was a shop that sold used furniture. Claudia took over the haggling, and by the time she was done, we had a table, six stools, and some pallets that looked clean and, more importantly, uninhabited. She arranged for everything to be delivered to our rooms, then rejoined me outside.

"It's rather pleasant to be walking with you in civilian clothing," she said.

"We've been in civilian clothes before," I said.

"Only when we were pretending to be civilians," she said.

"We were wearing the same clothes we're wearing now," I said.

"Yes, but wearing them for a mission made them into disguises," she said. "Now, we're just acting normally, doing normal things in normal clothing."

"It's still a disguise," I said. "Every costume is a disguise."

"I shall go nude," she said. "It's the only way you will ever believe me."

"Fine by me," I said, hoisting Portia onto my shoulders. "I am only trying to say that acting normal is just another disguise. We are abnormal people."

"Still, it's nice to come to a new place during Advent," she said. "It takes the pressure off of trying to break in and perform immediately. We can get to know the place without people staring at our makeup and motley and expecting us to be funny."

"We should get in touch with the local fools," I said. "We need to find out how we can meet the Master of Revels."

"It's two weeks to Christmas," she said. "We have time. Now, since our clever apprentice has already brought up the topic—why Saint Cyprien? Everyone we need to know is in Toulouse proper. And the city does have those nice, big walls protecting it."

"Yes, and you remember the last time we lived in a city with nice, big walls protecting it," I reminded her. "We almost died because we were inside those walls. I'd rather be in a position to flee than be trapped inside if war ever comes to Toulouse."

"The great Theophilos, running from danger?" she gasped. "Is this the man I married?"

"The very same," I said.

"Our mission is to prevent war," she said.

"It is," I agreed.

"Then why would you run from it?"

"Because if it comes, then we have failed," I said.

It was the last day of the previous August, at the farm where the Fools'
Guild was now living in exile, hidden deep within the Black Forest.
One of the novitiates came running up to where I was playing with
Portia, who was just beginning to crawl then.

"Father Gerald wants to see you," he said, panting.

"About what?"

"I am not privy to the thoughts of the great," he said. "I am only
the messenger. I suggest that you find out for yourself."

"Seen my wife about?" I asked.

"She is out hunting," said the boy.

"Any good at minding babies?" I asked.

"Not at all," he said quickly. "The last three entrusted to my care
died horrible deaths."

"Well, little fool, I guess you're coming to see Father Gerald," I said
to Portia, scooping her up. "Don't embarrass me this time."

Father Gerald was sitting on a bench in front of the barn. Beyond
him, teams of jesters unaccustomed to real work were putting up addi-
tions to the Guildhall so that there would be solid walls and roofs when
the winter came. I hoped to Christ that they knew what they were do-
ing. Every time the wind blew, I thought the building would collapse
on top of us. But so far, so good.

The old priest had his face tilted up to the sun, his eyes closed. Not
that that made a difference at this point. I cleared my throat.

"Ah, Theophilos. Good," he said. Then he sniffed the air, and smiled.
"And you brought my favorite goddaughter. Give her here, boy."

"You're one of the few people alive old enough to call me that," I
said, carefully handing Portia to him.

She looked up at him in awe as she always did, then giggled as he
nuzzled her belly.

"I shall miss her," he said softly, and my heart leaped.

"You have an assignment for us," I said.

"I do," he said.

"Should we go somewhere private to discuss it?"

He shrugged. "At the old Guildhall I had an office, a desk, a carefully organized system of maps and files," he said. "Here at the Guildhall in exile, I only have this bench, but the good Lord has compensated me by making me blind, so one place is as good as another."

"He works in mysterious ways," I said.

"I confess that I don't always get His sense of humor," he said. "But not everyone gets mine, so I suppose that I am made in His image. Where is your wife?"

"Hunting," I said. "Hopefully just deer. Seeing her come back with that boar was terrifying."

"Terrifying, but delicious," he said. "I will miss her as well."

"You haven't said you are going to miss me, I notice."

"I was getting to it," he said, smiling beatifically.

"And where will we be when you are missing all of us?"

"Toulouse."

"Really?"

"Yes. You know the city."

"I've stopped there a few times. When King Denis returned from Beyond-the-Sea, he made the pilgrimage to Compostela to celebrate his safe return. We passed through Toulouse both coming and going."

"And that was when?"

"Sometime in '94, thereabouts," I said.

"Good enough. I am making you Chief Jester there."

"I am honored. What happened to Balthazar?"

"He died."

"Sorry to hear that. Of anything that I need to investigate? Avenge?"

"Down, boy," he admonished me. "Some jesters do live to a ripe old age."

"Or past it, in your case."

"Hmph. Anyway, Toulouse has always been in a precarious spot. Balthazar did well to keep things as peaceful as he could, given the ambitions of the counts and every neighboring monarch, and he died as he lived, peacefully."

"And why me instead of one of the Toulousan fools?"

"Because the other fools there aren't worth a sou, in my opinion," said Father Gerald, some of the old, familiar sharpness returning to his voice. "And the troubadours I assigned have become positively flighty. Peire Vidal was kicked out years ago for lusting after one of the old count's mistresses."

"Typical of him."

"Gui de Cavalhon is riding the circuit, but doesn't have the staying power of a butterfly. I had hopes for this new boy, Peire Cadenet. Tremendous talent for songwriting, but an equal talent for frivolity. He just went chasing off to Aragon after some woman or another."

"What about Raimon de Mireval?"

"He's at the court of Pedro the Second. He has a commission to constantly praise the king's current mistress."

"Sweet arrangement," I said. "All right. To Toulouse."

"There will be one stop to make along the way," he said. "Pack your gear, then stop by after the evening meal and Brother Timothy and I will give you all the details."

"Very well, Father."

He patted Portia on the head and held her up to me.

"One more thing, Theo," he said as I took her. "Two more, now that I think of them."

"Yes, Father?"

"The last time I sent you on a mission, I promised that I would be alive when you came back."

"And you kept that promise," I said.

"I did," he said. "I won't be making it this time."

I reached down and grasped his hand. He held mine tightly and pulled me down to whisper, "And I expect to hear your confession tonight. It's my last chance. And yours."

I took a deep breath.

"All right," I said.

"Tonight, then," he said, letting me go.

Our new rooms were appreciably cleaner when we returned, and Helga commensurately dirtier.

"Good job, Apprentice," I said.

"At least I wasn't wearing whiteface," she said, coughing dramatically. "How is Zeus?"

"Being fed a steady diet of stableboys," I said.

"Stableboys?" she said, brightening under the dirt. "I should visit him."

"Easy, girl," said Claudia. "They wouldn't like you."

"Why not?" she asked indignantly.

"Because you're an unstable girl," said Claudia. "It would never work. Now, go back to the well, fill that bucket once more, and wash everything on you that sticks out."

"Yes, Domina," she said, curtseying.

"Call her Maman, daughter," I said. "You must stay in character. You never know who is listening. These walls are so thin we could be overheard in Toulouse."

"Yes, Papa," she said.

The men from the furniture shop arrived. Claudia inspected the pallets carefully before allowing them to grace our rooms. Portia waved and burbled at them from her cradle. A substantially cleaner Helga returned from the well, climbing the steps with a bucket of water balanced unaided on her head, which prompted impressed exclamations from the men. She smiled at them as they left.

I got a fire going in the brazier. Claudia tossed me a sack of white beans. "Your turn to cook," she said.

"This will be our last meal of just beans," I grumbled. "Tomorrow, I will go to the market and—"

"Tomorrow is Sunday," said Claudia. "The market will be closed."

"Tomorrow will be our last meal of just beans," I said.

She produced two loaves of dark bread and tossed them to me.

"Just beans and bread," I said.

"What else shall we do tomorrow?" asked Helga.

"Well, since it's Sunday, I think we should go to church," I said.

The looks of astonishment on their faces gave me a great deal of satisfaction.

In the morning, we brushed our clothes to a close semblance of neatness. When I deemed that we were presentable, I turned to Portia, who held out her arms and chirped, "Up! Up! Up!"

"Up, up, up," I agreed, tossing her into the air and catching her. She shrieked with delight. I placed her on my shoulders, and she grabbed my hair with both hands.

"Gently, poppet," I urged her, and she loosened her grip slightly.

Some parents might look askance at a man climbing down a stairway with his infant daughter on his shoulders. But we are fools. Claudia pulled the trapdoor shut and padlocked it.

We walked past the cemetery toward the Garonne river.

"Is that the church?" asked Helga, pointing to a bell tower.

"That is a church," I said. "Saint Nicholas, the local church. I'm sure it's fine enough for everyday sinners, but I will settle for nothing less than a cathedral for my family."

"Because we are sinners on a grand scale," explained Claudia.

We had ridden to Saint Cyprien on the east bank of the river to avoid notice. As a result, we had only seen Toulouse from a distance, the view dominated by the three towers of the Château Narbonnais.

The river was wide but not particularly deep. Indeed, it was more of a marsh than a proper river on the west bank where we now lived. There was a low bridge connecting our new neighborhood with the city proper, built on hexagonal supports made largely of thin red bricks. On the other side and downstream was a narrow island, the Ile de Tounis, every foot of its shores covered with mills vying for the available currents. More mills were nestled between the arches of the bridge, perched on boats and barges anchored off the island, their wheels turning lazily in the water.

The city itself was dotted with a number of towers, indicating the locations of the wealthy and the means they took to protect that wealth.

"It reminds me of Pisa with all the towers," commented Claudia. "Only they favor brick here."

"Stone is scarce, clay is cheap," I said.

"It makes everything pink," said Helga. "It's pretty. I like it."

The bridge took us to an opening in the city wall. There were some terraced vegetable gardens descending from an abbey to our left. Beyond them, the banks of the river stopped at a low cliff which was protected in turn by the city wall. To the north, the river curved away from the city, a massive dam stretching across it to an island by the bend. More mills hugged both shores of the island and the bank north of the walls. An immense fortification loomed beyond them.

"Test time, Apprentice," I said. "We have crossed the Daurade Bridge. Where would you expect the cathedral to be?"

"To the south," she said.

"Why?"

"Because the Château Narbonnais is to the south, and you would expect the cathedral to be close to where the count lives, so he doesn't have to walk too far to church."

"More or less correct," I said. "This is the old city ahead of us. The bourg is the newer part to the north. We'll be walking through it later so you can learn where everything is. The cathedral is actually near the southwestern wall."

Saint Étienne was not huge as cathedrals go. I don't know when it was built, but at one point they had enough money to bring in some stone for its construction. At least for the front, where the paying customers could see it. There was brickwork at the sides, more of those thin bricks that were favored by the Toulousans. A large rose window dominated the front, but the main doors were to the right of center, so everything seemed thrown off as a result.

There was a cemetery in front of the cathedral, an odd location for the dead. Most churches tuck them out of sight in the rear so they won't disconcert the living, but here they served as a constant reminder of what was coming up next. To the right of the cathedral was a cloister, and a smaller church beyond that. In between the cemetery and the cathedral were statues of the Apostles, their legs crossed as if they were about to start dancing. Behind them, flanking the main doors, were two female figures bearing shields on which were sculpted the zodiacal figures of the lion and the ram. It never hurts to back up religion with a little old-fashioned astrology. Just in case.

"I wonder if there is room for us," said Claudia as we approached.

"I have a feeling there will be," I said.

The churchgoers were not exactly pouring through the

doors. It was more like a sporadic trickle, mostly elderly folk whose feet were dragging them there out of habit.

The benches inside could hold several hundred people, but only if several hundred people decided to show up. I counted the crowd—maybe eighty all told. We sat near the back.

The interior may have been grand at one time, but they hadn't kept it up. The plaster in the walls was several years away from its last coat of whitewash, much of it chipped and crumbling. The benches were cracked, with names of long-grown schoolboys carved into them dating from some other dull long-forgotten Sunday.

The choir entered and took their seats to the right. Then the Bishop came in, accompanied by three priests and some sleepy altar boys. The choir began singing without any real enthusiasm. Several of them lost their place halfway through the opening hymn and clammed up, looking embarrassed or trying not to laugh. The rest finally stopped, though not all of them at the same time.

The Bishop, suddenly aware of the silence, stood up hastily and began leading us through the service. He had a decent speaking voice and an adequate command of the Latin. However, his perfunctory readings of the text did little to keep the aging congregation awake, and those of us who were, felt like we were aging more rapidly by the minute.

His vestments were richly trimmed and must have been grand when new, but they had not been kept well in the few short years of his reign. Neither had he, if his face was any indication. He was puffy around the eyes, with a broad, florid nose dominating a tiny, thin-lipped mouth and little chin to speak of. Whoever was in charge of shaving him must not have liked him very much, for his cheeks and neck were nicked in several places. His neck seemed to wobble under the weight of his miter, or perhaps it was his state of indignation that did that.

"It is appalling that now, as we approach the holiest time of year," he began, "when we celebrate the birth of Our Savior, that His Church is in such dire straits. It is embarrassing that in these prosperous times, when the taxes have been lifted and the money is flowing everywhere, that not one trickle of it comes into our collection box. Why, there is so little in our treasury that our own sick parishioners, whom we have maintained in our hospital for years, have sought out other establishments for their convalescences, because we no longer have the means to feed them at the same level as our brethren with the Benedictine abbeys. Even our lepers have been complaining, and you know how they never complain. Now, I know that many among you have already paid for your funeral masses, and I am grateful to you, and will celebrate your eventual demises with all due solemnity. But many of you have not provided for this inevitable occurrence. Do you hope to avoid fate by postponing payment? I assure you that your days on earth are numbered, and if you die unprepared, you cannot count on your survivors, in their grief or distance or dotage, to consider your needs at that time. The proper prayers at your death may be crucial, and yet you blithely go on about your daily lives, blissfully ignoring the risks."

He stopped to swallow dramatically, his Adam's apple trembling in terror.

"Should we purchase our funeral masses?" whispered Claudia. "We might be able to get a bargain rate today."

"I am not planning to die here," I whispered back.

"That's a relief. Where, then?"

"In some other woman's bed if you do not cease this yammering."

"It is not the finances of the church so much as the appearances that concern me," continued the Bishop. "If we fail to attract the sinners, then we fail in our mission. These are dangerous times. Those heretics known as Cathars lurk in the shadows of our very doorstep, seducing the unwary with their false beliefs and their perjurious attacks on us. Will you deny yourself the Kingdom of Heaven because a false prophet denies himself meat and calls himself pure? Or because he promises salvation through the mere touch of his hand, though you have done nothing to merit it? Yet the simpleminded and the sinful have flocked to these devils as sheep would to a . . ."

He gulped, having wandered into a metaphorical dead end.

"What evil would attract sheep?" whispered Helga.

We all pondered this weighty question as the Bishop recovered and simply moved on.

"With every new heretic, the church is diminished in life, and in tithes," he said. "With every diminution in income, we become more and more of a laughingstock. We cannot demonstrate the path to Salvation when we cannot even keep ourselves in bread. Why, when our brother bishop came all the way from Osma on his holy mission, we were unable to show him the hospitality that one bishop should provide another. We could not feed and house his entourage, and they were forced to put themselves up at their own expense in a common tavern."

"Where they were forced to drink common wine and consort with common whores," I muttered.

"Poor dears," sympathized my wife.

"So I say unto you, my children, poverty of the church will mean poverty of the soul," he concluded. "We must restore this house of God to its former glory. Amen."

"I find no satisfaction in my soul today," murmured my wife as the choir stumbled through the concluding hymn. "So, that's Bishop Raimon de Rabastens. Seems like a nice fellow. I suppose he means well enough for a bishop."

"Yes," I agreed. "Too bad we have to get rid of him."

CHAPTER 2

Brother Timothy tapped me on the shoulder after the evening meal. We slipped away to join Father Gerald, who was sitting on a boulder by the edge of the stream that ran past the farm. The old priest lifted his head and cocked it toward us as we came up.

"Toulouse," he said. "It is our belief that things are building to a crisis there."

"They always are in Toulouse," I said. "What's different now?"

"The Church," he said. "If they came after the Fools' Guild after all we have done for them, then they will go after anyone they find displeasing."

"Toulouse has displeased Rome?"

"In many ways," he said. "Did you meet the current count when you were there?"

"Raimon? Yes," I said. "It was right before his father died, so he wasn't count yet. He had this very pretty wife, Bourguigne, who was from Cyprus. She was his third, as I recall, maybe fourth. I forget what alliance was being forged with the union. His father would marry him off to any woman who was useful to him back then."

"Raimon, son of Raimon," said Father Gerald. "Now the sixth count of that name, with a few more wives and territories notched on his belt since then and another Raimon of his very own, courtesy of wife number five."

"Feckless, irresponsible, and so on?"

"Surprisingly, no," said Father Gerald. "Seems to be an astute man, at least when it comes to keeping the competing powers at bay. But he's like a juggler who is tiring—you know that sooner or later, he'll start dropping the clubs."

"You want me to be there to catch them."

"Among other things," said Brother Timothy. "We also see an opportunity to help the Guild get back in the good graces of the Church."

"How? And how much do we have to compromise our mission to do it?"

"Always a problem," sighed Father Gerald. "If our mission is to continue at all, we must end this papal interference. Someone close to Pope Innocent is working against us, for whatever reasons. We have to start building up our own influence to counter it. That means getting our own people inside."

"How does sending me to Toulouse help us get inside the Church? Why don't I just go to Rome and tell Innocent a few jokes?"

"Your jokes aren't that good," smirked Brother Timothy.

"There is a bishop in Toulouse, Raimon de Rabastens," said Father Gerald. "We think he may be vulnerable. We want to replace him with one of our own people, then use the bishopric as a stepping-stone to Rome."

"Who do you plan to install?"

"Do you remember Folquet, the troubadour?"

"From Marseille. I met him once."

"He's a Cistercian abbot, now. We need you to persuade him to work for us again, and then find a way of forcing Raimon de Rabastens to resign his office and bring Folquet in to replace him."

"Is that all?" I laughed. "I was hoping for something challenging. Tell me that this isn't our only hope."

"We will be working on many avenues," said Brother Timothy. "This is just one."

"In fact, you may receive some assistance from an unexpected source," added Father Gerald. "Don't be surprised by it."

"Nothing surprises me anymore when you start making plans," I said. "Any suggestions as to where in this bishop's life I can start?"

"You'll find something," said Father Gerald, turning to listen to the stream rush by again. "Everyone has something."

Bishop Raimon de Rabastens stood in front of the cathedral, greeting the congregants as they shuffled out.

"Good to see you, good to see you," he said continuously. "How is your poor mother doing? Tell her that she is in my prayers. Hasn't that leg of yours healed yet? Did you try that balm I gave you? You did? Strange, it worked wonders for my shoulder."

As the line came to us, he looked quizzical for a moment, then brightened.

"Why, do we have some new parishioners among us today?" he exclaimed. "Welcome to God's house, my friends. I am Bishop Raimon."

"Your Holiness," we murmured, bowing.

"Yes, yes, always good to see new blood at our cathedral. Are you recently come to Toulouse?"

"Just this past week, Your Holiness," I said. "We have taken up residence in Saint Cyprien, near the Saint Nicholas church."

"Ah, lovely little church," he said. "The parish is under the aegis of the Cluniac brothers. Of course, there is nothing like coming to a cathedral to worship, and I thank you for taking the trouble to join us today. I did note your contribution at collection. And did I see you add to the poor box as well?"

"In thanks for our safe journey and arrival," I said.

"Goodness, how rude of me, I have neglected to ask your names," he said.

"I am Tan Pierre," I said. "My wife, Gile, and our daughters, Helga and Portia."

"What a lovely family!" he exclaimed, smiling at my wife and chucking the baby under the chin. "And an unusual collection of names. I take it you are not native to this region?"

"No, but we are hoping to settle and find employment here," I said.

"Well, if there is any assistance I can give you, please let me know," he said. "What is your profession?"

"We are a family of jesters," I said. "And, if I may be so bold as to take you up on your offer, we would be more than happy to perform at your Feast of Fools this season. We would offer something lower than our usual rates in return for the introduction to the city."

His smile became fixed and odd.

"The Feast of Fools," he repeated. "Yes, well, I do not think that I can help you there."

"Of course," I said. "There must be some other person in charge of that. If you could direct me to him, then . . ."

"What I mean to say is that there will be no Feast of Fools here," he said.

"There won't?" I said in surprise.

"No," he said. "But I am sure that you will find some employment come Christmas. Welcome to Toulouse, my friends."

We moved away from the entrance as he turned to the next parishioner.

"Some welcome," muttered Claudia. "How on earth can they have Christmas without the Feast of Fools?"

"There have been rumors that the Pope was going to ban the Feast," I said. "I never thought he would actually do it."

"I do not like this pope," said Claudia.

"Maybe the Bishop could hire me as a choirmaster," I sighed. "They could certainly use one."

There was a raising of voices behind us. We turned to see the Bishop, of all people, in heated argument with a man who appeared to be well-to-do based upon the richness of his garments. He stood with his hat in his hand but otherwise showed no deference whatsoever to his Holiness.

"How dare you approach me on God's day!" thundered the Bishop.

"Why, have I not approached you on all the days belonging to the rest of us?" asked the man. "And every time, I was told that you were at prayer. What a religious man you are! What an inspiration to all of us poor sinners!"

"Be careful, Senhor," said the Bishop. "There is a price to be paid in Hell for mockery such as yours."

"Yes, well, it's the price to be paid here on Earth that interests me," said the man. "Especially the interest. There is a note due that has your name on it, and I will not hesitate in showing up at the assizes first thing tomorrow morning with it if I do not receive satisfaction."

A priest who had been standing in the shadows behind the cathedral entry sidled out quietly and whispered something to the Bishop. The Bishop took a breath and gathered the remains of his dignity back together.

"Father Mascaron suggests that you wait in my office," he said stiffly.

"The question is, will you be coming there?" asked the man. "I would hate to see you suddenly all prayerful again. It would waste my time, and I have other places to go."

"One of them is to the Devil, as far as I am concerned," snapped the Bishop.

"Not on God's day, surely," sneered the man. "Besides, I have no quarrel with the Devil. He always pays his debts on time. I thought you would know that, being in the business and all."

Father Mascaron touched him on the shoulder, and he followed the priest inside. Bishop Raimon looked around to see who had observed this little scene, but we were playing with the baby at the foot of the statue of Saint Paul, oblivious to anything else. He watched us for a moment, his eyes narrow and shrewd, then flicked at his robes and went inside.

"That might be useful," commented Claudia.

"Maybe," I said. "A bishop owing money is not an uncommon thing these days. I don't know that it is something that we can use to drive him out."

"But it may be a starting point," argued Claudia.

"Agreed," I said. "Helga, take the north side and watch for that man. We'll take the other side. If he comes out your side, follow him and find out who he is and where he lives. Meet us back home by sunset."

"Yes, Papa," she said happily, and she skipped over to a group of children who were kicking a ball around.

We took Portia between us and walked her over to the cloisters, each holding one tiny hand. She was not quite walking on her own yet, finding the process much more tedious than crawling. She had proven to be a prodigious climber, however, with a sense of balance that made her quite fearless. That, combined with a love of mischief that bordered on the diabolical, left no doubt that she was the daughter of fools.

We played with her, using the pillars of the cloister arches for hide-and-seek and peekaboo as she shrieked and giggled. Then, out of the corner of my eye, I saw Helga scratch her nose and leave her game.

"She has him," I said to Claudia.

"Good," she said, picking up our wriggling child. "How much lead are you going to give her?"

"She already has the width of a cathedral," I said. "I'll give her a cloister's worth more."

Claudia kissed me, and I winked at Portia.

"Kiss Papa on the nose," I said, and she did. I kissed her nose in return, then ambled past the cemetery, keeping our apprentice in view.

Apprenticing to a master fool requires that one pass an undetermined number of arcane tests. Following without being seen is one, of course, but that isn't as hard as it might sound. Those inclined to become jesters become adept at changing appearance at a moment's notice, and the simple addition of a cloak and hat will erase any memory of motley that the quarry may have retained. When we are in civilian garb to begin with, we become even more invisible.

But the true test of a jester on the tail of her prey is whether or not she can in turn spot the jester tailing her. Helga was now being put to that test, whether she knew it or not. I thought back to my last apprentice, none other than my wife, who I trailed through the winding streets of Constantinople as she pursued a seller of spurious relics. She spotted me with alacrity, something she reminds me of periodically.

I could no longer see our man, but Helga was plainly visible as she bobbed through the Toulousans who were out visiting on this cool, sunny Sunday. I paused, keeping her in sight as she crossed the Montaygon Square, then hurried across it as she disappeared into a street on the other side, still heading north. When I reached the Montardy Square, she had increased the distance between us. I had to pick up my own pace without drawing her attention, but she was fixed upon her quarry.

Our path was taking us from the city to the bourg, I saw. That meant our unknown collector was from the new money part of town. Interesting, I thought. I wondered how far afield the Bishop had to go for his borrowing. It might be that nobody from the old town trusted him enough to loan him money anymore.

The street fetched up against the Saracen Wall which divided the old from the new. The Maison Commune, built to celebrate the union of city and bourg, was to my right, so the Portaria, the old fort that once guarded the entrance to the city when there was no bourg, had to be on the left. I stopped short of the intersection to glance cautiously around the corner. Sure enough, my apprentice was vanishing through the Portaria into the bourg. It would have been fun to quickly climb to the top of one of the lookout towers to track her, but I didn't have time to talk my way past the guards who were stationed there. I took a chance and ran to the gate, then peeked through to the other side.

She wasn't there. I had lost her.

I cursed myself under my breath, then slipped through the gate. As soon as I reached the other side, a small hand snaked out to grab my wrist.

"It took you long enough to get here," muttered Helga. "I thought you were in better shape than that."

"Congratulations, Apprentice," I said. "You passed. When did you figure out I was following you?"

"The hairs on the back of my neck were tingling about a block after I left," she said. "I got a glimpse of you at that first big square we crossed."

"The Montaygon," I said. "Well done."

"I was wondering if you were going to try that on me," she confessed. "Some of the older novitiates talked about it back at the Guildhall. But I would have spotted you anyway. I've been watching our backs ever since we left Marseille. You taught me that."

"Impressive. Now, impress me some more and tell me where our mysterious man lives."

"He went through those gates past the church with the tower," she said, indicating a cluster of large houses around an interior courtyard. "The center house of that group. I don't know if that was the master of the house I was following or just one of his men."

"It wouldn't be one of his men on a mission like that," I said. "No one would send a clerk or a lackey to accost a bishop in a cathedral. That would be adding insult to more insult. If I was threatening a bishop with litigation, I would certainly want to take that task upon myself, if only for the pleasure it would give me."

"Let me stay and find out some more," she said. "There are children playing, and there are bound to be women doing laundry."

"All right," I said, pleased. "We will have dinner waiting for you."

"And you should take advantage of my absence," she said, waggling her eyebrows. "It's so difficult for married people when there are children about."

"I will consider your advice," I said seriously.

She skipped away, looking all of ten years old. I knew her to be really twelve, verging on thirteen, with all the guile of an adult fool. But there she was, joining a group of girls who were playing tag in front of the courtyard, to all appearances just like them.

And to think that a month ago, she had killed a man for the first time.

I sighed and returned home. Claudia was unpacking our gear and inspecting it for any damage it might have sustained during our recent travels.

"Portia's asleep," she whispered, then she gasped as I picked her up and slung her over my shoulder.

"What do you think you're doing?" she asked as I carried her into our room.

"Time to put this new pallet to the test," I said.

It was a good day for passing tests, as it turned out.

We were fully dressed by the time Helga returned, her face a mask of studied indifference which dissolved into a grin as Claudia hauled her up from the last of the steps and embraced her.

Portia was awake and burbled, "El, el, el!"

Helga went over to her, squatted in front of the cradle, and said, "Hug for Helga?" Portia held out her arms and Helga lifted her into a tight embrace and danced with her around the room as the baby laughed and laughed. I quickly closed the trapdoor before any accidents could happen.

"Any luck, Apprentice?" asked Claudia.

"It's not luck, it's skill," the girl replied. "The man we saw is named Milon Borsella. According to the children who play in that courtyard, he is a mean man who lays about him with his stick at the least excuse. He has a wife named Béatrix who almost never comes out. They said she may be ill, but some think that it's because he beats her, too."

"Nice," I said. "What does he do when he's not beating women and children? Does he kick puppies?"

"I met one of his servants," she said. "She was taking down laundry from the lines, and I offered to help her. She thought I was very mature for such a little girl."

"And what did you say to that?"

"I said, 'I'm not a little girl, I'm a big girl!'" she said, thrusting her lower lip out like a little girl. "She said she could tell that I wasn't from Toulouse because of my accent, so I told her all about our pilgrimage to Rome, and that we came here to look for work, and she said there was work to be had for honest, God-fearing folk."

"That lets us out," said Claudia.

"That's a relief," I said.

"Anyhow, she told me that her master was a middle son," continued Helga.

"Those are often the ones that cause trouble," said Claudia.

"Their father made his fortune in lumber, and left the business to the oldest son, Bonet. He's on the city council. He was just elected this year. Milon was given the house and enough money to do what he wants, and there's another son who is a Benedictine at Saint Sernin."

"Well-connected family," I said. "What does he do with the money his father left him?"

"Tends it, lends it, and spends it," she said. "They say he likes wine and whores, and he trades with merchants in Narbonne. He also lends money, mostly to old families in the city. She says he likes lending to them so he can lord it over them and their fancy airs. She says she thinks he prefers it when they don't pay it back, so he can take them to court and humiliate them in public."

"Nice fellow for the Bishop to be beholden to," I said. "A good afternoon's work, young lady. You have earned yourself my very own, specially prepared—beans and bread!"

I dumped some into a bowl, tore off a piece of brown bread, and handed them to her.

"What is so special about the preparation?" she asked, looking at them dubiously.

"This time, I cooked them," I said. "I would have spent more time on the meal, but I was busy this afternoon following your sound counsel."

"Her what?" sputtered Claudia. "Fie upon both of you! Discussing such personal matters like that. I'm outraged. Oh, and grateful."

"Shall I go back there tomorrow?" asked Helga.

"Might as well," I said. "Find out what else he does for fun, and if he has any hold over the Bishop besides the money."

"I wonder if they paid him today," said Claudia. "And with what, and if there is anything left."

"We need to meet the local fools," I said. "Jordan first, I think. He's senior to Pelardit."

"How well do you know them?" asked Helga.

"Not at all," I replied.

"Didn't you meet them when you came through Toulouse before?" asked Claudia.

"No, unfortunately. I reported in to Balthazar, who was a talented jester, but I was otherwise preoccupied. Young kings on holy pilgrimage require a great deal of entertaining."

"In other words, you spent most of your time here drunk," said Claudia.

"That is a less charitable way of putting it," I said. "But my sins were absolved in Compostela."

"Have you committed any since then?" asked Helga.

"Eat your beans and bread, Apprentice."

In the morning, we rose and walked across the bridge. There was a stream of pilgrims going the other way, and we all waved to them, including the baby.

"They all look so happy to be going to Compostela," said Helga.

"More like they are happy to be leaving Toulouse," I said. "Pilgrims pay dearly for the privilege of stopping here."

We kept going straight until we reached the Grande Rue, then turned north.

"Jordan has a house on Rue de Agulhers," I said to Helga. "Come find us there if you need us. Otherwise, we will meet you at home."

"Have fun, dear," said Claudia for the benefit of anyone listening.

"I will, Maman," cried the little girl, and she skipped away.

Rue de Agulhers was where the needle-makers had their shops, and we passed by store after store with displays of needles of various kinds, made of bone, wood, and iron. Women gathered about the stores, spending half their time haggling, half gossiping.

"An excellent location for a fool," Claudia observed. "Jordan must get all his information here."

"No man is a hero to his seamstress," I agreed. "That must be Jordan's house over there."

There was a small house with a tailor's shop on the street level and living quarters above and behind it. The shop was shuttered, but there were two small boys playing in the mud in front of it, poking at a frog with a stick. On the door leading to the steps to the upper level, a white mask had been painted, with a grinning red mouth and a cap and bells on top.

The boys looked up as we approached, and the frog made a leap for freedom. I caught it in mid-hop and handed it back to the larger boy, who appeared to be about nine.

"Is this the house of Jordan the Jester?" I asked him.

He nodded solemnly, clutching the frog too tightly.

"He's my father," he said.

"Mine, too!" added the smaller boy indignantly.

"Is he at home?" I asked.

They both nodded.

"Would you be so kind as to tell him that he has company?" I asked.

"He's with Maman," said the older boy. "He told us to stay out here and play."

"I understand entirely," I said as Claudia suppressed a smile. I looked around and spotted a small tavern. "I'll tell you what. When he comes out again, tell him that some traveling friends of his are visiting, and that we may be found over there. Can you describe us to him?"

"Tall skinny man, short pretty lady with a baby," said the boy promptly.

"That should do," I said.

"And thank you for your gallant description," added my wife, patting him on the head.

We were halfway through a bowl of mussels when a rotund man entered the tavern, glanced around, then came over to us. Despite his girth, there was a delicacy to his movements, a dancing in his step. The two boys peered in at the doorway.

"I am Jordan the Jester," he said, bowing slightly, his fingers interlacing in an intricate wiggle before his chest. "Are you the traveling friends of whom my son spoke?"

"We are," I said, rising to my feet.

I pursed my lips and whistled softly. His eyes widened in surprise, then he smiled broadly and whistled the counter.

"Jordan, Guildname of Rollo," he said softly.

"Tan Pierre, Guildname of Theophilos," I said. "My wife, Gile, Guildname of Claudia, and our baby, Portia."

"You've come from the Guild!" he chortled exultantly. "I knew it! I knew this day would come. Boys, quickly."

The two scampered in and stood at attention.

"Roland, go tell your mother to prepare a welcoming meal for our friends," he ordered. "A celebration. Spare no expense. Get the good wine from the back. Oliver, run and find Pelardit. He's probably still asleep. No dawdling! Scoot!"

The boys ran out, and Jordan turned back to us.

"I thought it would be me," he confided. "Pelardit is a good fool, no mistake, but experience counts in this world, and that's no lie. It's a pity that Balthazar had to die for the Guild to make me the Chief Fool here, but that's life, isn't it?"

"Excuse me?" I said.

"Now, we are going to show you and your lovely wife a glorious time, Advent be damned," he continued. "I feel positively inspired. I may buy out a tavern and put on a special performance for the occasion."

"I think there has been a misunderstanding," I said.

"Maybe some new motley," he said. "I have had my eyes on a bolt of garance red that my wife, she's a seamstress, by the way, her name is Martine, got in from Montpellier this month. It's beautiful, a real— misunderstanding?"

In response, I handed him a small scroll from my pouch. He glanced at the seal, then at me.

"From Father Gerald himself," he whispered, holding it as if it might burst into flames in his hands.

He unrolled it, then read it over several times, his lips moving silently. His face crumpled in disappointment as he looked back up at me.

"So, you are the Chief Fool of Toulouse," he said.

"Yes."

"After all my years of service, never complaining, they gave it to an outsider," he said. "That's hard. That's very hard to take."

"It was not my decision," I said. "Nevertheless, the decision was made. So, here we are."

"Here you are, and here I am," he echoed in a tight voice. "Yes, well, as the former senior surviving fool in Toulouse, let me bid you welcome. Our celebratory meal will proceed."

"Perhaps we should—"

"Please, my house is yours. Come."

We quickly paid for our meal and followed him.

A small, pinch-faced woman was waiting at the top of the steps, wearing over her gown a many-pocketed apron containing an assortment of needles and thread. She clapped her hands in glee when she saw her husband.

"Has it happened?" she asked.

"Meet the new Chief Fool of Toulouse," he said as he reached her.

"At last!" she shrieked, embracing him hard. "Oh, bless that old priest."

"I wasn't talking about me," he said.

She withdrew from the embrace, dismay rippling across her face.

"They didn't appoint you," she said. "Is it the man or the woman?"

"This is Tan Pierre, the new Chief Fool," he said, gesturing curtly to me. I bowed. "That's his wife, Gile. She's a fool, too. This is my wife, Martine."

"I see," she said flatly. She turned to us and made courtesy. "You are welcome. Please come in."

She bustled about as we entered, preparing the meal.

"May I help?" offered Claudia.

"Certainly not," she snapped. "You are our guests."

As she turned her back on us, Portia started to cry. Claudia held her close and patted her, but the yowls did not abate. Jordan began dragging the table to the center of the room so that more people could sit around it. I grabbed a thick board that was resting against the wall and placed it across the two stools on one side of the table, making a bench for four. Jordan nodded his thanks and did the same with the other side.

There was a clatter of steps, then the older boy burst into the room.

"Pelardit is coming," he announced breathlessly.

The man who came through the door was skinny like me but slightly shorter, all bones and angles, with a hangdog expression and sleepy-looking eyes. Despite that, I noted that he looked quickly around the room, taking in my wife and myself with a single glance. He looked at Jordan inquisitively.

"Oh, my friend," moaned Jordan, bursting into tears. "The Guild has passed me over. They have sent an outsider to replace Balthazar."

Pelardit's face collapsed in a rictus of sorrow, looking like nothing more than the ancient mask of Tragedy perched upon the body of a scarecrow. He threw his arms around the other fool, his shoulder heaving to match Jordan's sobs. It was the very image of commiseration, yet as he looked over the larger man's shoulder at me, he winked.

"Thank you, old friend," said Jordan, releasing him. "What is done is done. Such a pity that the Guild does not know my true value as you do."

Pelardit nodded emphatically in agreement. Perhaps it was my imagination that detected a hint of mockery in the nod. Perhaps it wasn't. Pelardit then came over to me.

"My name is Tan Pierre, Guildname of Theophilos," I said.

He looked at me impassively, his body immobile as stone. "Of course," I said, and I whistled the password.

He whistled the counter, then reached out his hand. I shook it. He glanced at my wife.

"Gile, Guildname of Claudia," I said. "And Portia, no Guildname yet."

He reached out his hand, then pulled it back as Claudia held hers out and made a deep bow. The baby was still crying. Pelardit looked at Portia appraisingly and held out both hands. Claudia hesitated for an instant, then handed over the baby.

Portia was startled at being given to this stranger, and was fully prepared to take the crying to the next level, which was substantially louder in my experience. But Pelardit fixed his gaze on her, then suddenly mirrored her expression, his eyes scrunched, looking ready to bawl himself. The baby stared at him in shock, taken aback by this behavior. Then one of his eyes opened, saw that she was watching, and immediately snapped shut again. She caught her breath. He opened the other eye, seemingly surprised to see her watching him, and closed it again. She reached out and touched his nose, something she did to comfort us. He opened both eyes this time, his expression turning to exasperation. She started to giggle, and a small smile began on his lips that proceeded to spread across his face until Tragedy had given away completely to Comedy. He jiggled her slightly, and she laughed loud and long.

"You're hired, starting immediately," laughed Claudia, and it seemed as if all of the tension in the room had dissipated. Even Martine was smiling, which made her face much more pleasant.

"Let us dine, now that we are all here," said Jordan.

We took our places together at the table. Jordan poured cups of wine and passed them about.

"I leave the honor of the first toast to our new Chief Fool," he said.

I lifted my cup.

"To the memory of Balthazar," I said. "May he be telling a joke to the First Fool in Heaven right now."

"To Balthazar," said Jordan. "Although Saint Peter would have had to bend some rules to let him in."

"That's probably true for all of us," I said.

Pelardit rapped his knuckles on the table in agreement.

"How is he going to toast?" asked Claudia.

In response, Pelardit held his cup toward our hostess, kissed the back of his hand, and drank.

"Very gallant, I'm sure," said Martine. "And here's some stewed lamb for you in thanks."

She had just finished serving us when we heard someone burst through the outer door and charge up the steps. I was on my feet with my dagger in my hand in an instant, Claudia a second behind, when Helga tore into the room.

"He's dead!" she shouted.

"Who is this?" demanded Jordan. "What do you mean by breaking in like this?"

"Who's dead, Helga?" I asked.

"The man I was following," she cried. "Milon Borsella. He's dead!"

CHAPTER 3

"You were following Milon Borsella," said Jordan, confused. "Why? And who are you?"

"This is Helga, our apprentice," I said. "Introductions later. Who killed him?"

"I don't know," said the girl. "I was playing in his courtyard, hoping to find out more about him, but he wasn't home. He hadn't been home all night, I heard, but that wasn't unusual, according to the people there."

"That's true enough," said Jordan. Pelardit nodded, a lewd expression flashing across his face.

"Then one of the nightwatch came in, shouting for Borsella's wife. A manservant came out, and the guard said that Borsella was dead. His body was found in the tanners' quarter. I ran down there as fast as I could. We all did—there was a big crowd already when I got there, and lots of guards holding everyone back, but one of the guards was saying Borsella had been hit over the head."

"Maybe we should go take a look," I said.

"He'll keep until you get there," said Helga, giggling inappropriately. "He'll keep very well."

"Your meaning, Apprentice?"

"They found him in a tanner's pit, soaking with the hides. He should keep very well indeed."

"Oh, if I didn't know she was in the Guild before, I'd know it now," said Jordan as Pelardit winced.

"I have been working very hard on this meal," said Martine.

"No need for all of us to go," I said. "You stay here and enjoy this fine repast. I'll go with Helga."

Pelardit rose and thumped his chest.

"I would be delighted," I said.

We followed Helga out of the house and down to the Portaria. This time, we turned left after passing through it. The road took us through a marshy area, then kept parallel to the Saracen Wall until we came to the parish of Saint Pierre des Cuisines, so called because of the communal ovens that the Benedictines maintained for the area.

I don't know when or why the tanners' quarter had been given to this parish, but the arrangement had been made long before I was born. The proximity of the canal that ran from the Garonne to Saint Pierre was one reason, of course, and water was diverted to the tanners' pits by an ingenious system of water wheels and sluices. Dozens of shops were clustered together, surrounded by small sheds where hides were laid out to be scraped and dried. Barrels containing bark from oak and elder trees were stacked around them, ready to be poured into the pits to replenish their powers.

There was a growing crowd gathered by one of them. The stench was unpleasant, and many had kerchiefs tied over their mouths and noses. We did the same, but even so, our eyes stung. We were unable to shove our way to the front, so this became one of those occasions where my height was useful. Helga stomped her foot in exasperation, so I simply picked her up and sat her on my shoulders. She could have stood on them easily enough, but this was not the time or place to put on a show. Pelardit stood on his tiptoes for a moment, then looked around until he found a decent-sized rock on which to balance.

The guards were keeping the onlookers back while a baile stood cautiously at the edge of the pit, looking down.

"One of you, go pull him out," he commanded.

"I'm not sticking any part of me in there for duty or love," replied a soldier. "That stuff burns."

"Whose pit is this?" demanded the baile.

"Mine, Senhor," said a man from the other side of the soldiers. "I can get him out for you."

"Do it," ordered the baile.

The man ran to a nearby shop, and returned with a long pole with a blunted hook at the end of it. He reached with it into the pit and expertly snagged something. He pulled back with all his might, and I saw a boot heave up onto dry land. No, a leg encased in a boot. The tanner handed the pole to a soldier, pulled on a pair of thick gloves, grabbed the leg and hauled the body out of the pit.

"He's not very tanned yet," observed Helga.

"It takes a few days," I said. "And I don't think he was dressed properly beforehand. Or undressed improperly. What are they all pointing at?"

The baile, clutching his kerchief to his face, was bending over the corpse. Gingerly, he rolled it over onto its stomach, then poked at the back of its head.

"I don't see any blood, but the skull doesn't look right," reported Helga with her younger eyes. "I think somebody conked him!"

"So much for accidental causes," I said. "Unless he slipped and fell backwards, then rolled into the pit. Perhaps a fit of some kind."

"But what would he be doing at the tanners' quarter?" asked Helga.

"I have no idea."

"If there is anyone here who knows anything about this, I charge you to come forward!" cried the baile.

There was absolute silence from the crowd.

"Fine," sighed the baile. He pointed to the tanner. "Take him."

"Me?" protested the tanner. "I have nought to do with this."

"He's murdered in your pit," said the baile. "That's something. Until we know the rest, you'll be kept where we can find you easily."

A guard snatched the tanner's hook from his grasp. Two more guards quickly knocked him down and trussed him up for transport, to the glee and derision of the crowd. The tanner's howls continued unabated as they threw him onto a wagon.

"Inquest tomorrow," said the baile. "I am done here. Get the body to assizes."

The corpse was picked up and dumped next to the tanner, whose howls changed to screams as he squirmed away from his unwanted companion.

Pelardit tapped me on the shoulder and made a quick hand to mouth gesture.

"You're right, we might as well get back to our meal," I said.

We walked back toward the Portaria, Helga still riding my shoulders. As we neared the Borsella house, I reached up and lifted her off me.

"I thought we were going to our meal," she said.

"We are going to our meal," I said. "You, on the other hand, are going to perform an act of Christian charity."

"I am?"

"A household has lost their head," I said. "They will no doubt be needing extra help to prepare for the onslaught of condolence. And since you have already proved your worth to their maidservant . . ."

She rearranged her features into an expression of mourning.

"How's that?" she asked.

Pelardit turned her toward him and inspected her critically. Then his face drooped into a mask of such abject sorrow and pity that in comparison hers looked like indifference. She studied him and altered her expression until it matched his perfectly. He nodded and patted her shoulder in approval. She turned back to me.

"Don't overdo it, or you will have me in tears," I warned her. "See you outside the gate before sunset."

She trudged dolefully toward the house, in mourning for her lost chance at Domina Martine's feast.

Pelardit looked at her, then turned to me and cocked his head inquisitively.

"Yes, she's that good," I replied. "Father Gerald thinks she's the best he's seen in many years."

His eyebrows rose, impressed.

"Let me ask you something," I said as we resumed our walk to Jordan's house. "If there ever was some important information for you to convey, you do have the power of speech, do you not? I don't want to waste time playing charades when there's an emergency."

He smiled slightly.

"Fine," I said. "What if you had to warn me quickly?"

He put his two index fingers into his mouth and produced a loud, piercing whistle that startled a flock of starlings out of a distant tree.

"That works well enough," I conceded, my ears still ringing. "Save it for an actual emergency, all right?"

Martine had kept our food warm for us, thankfully, but mine cooled off as I was forced to recount the details of what little I knew. To my chagrin, Pelardit happily dug back into his meal, contributing nothing to the conversation. Oh, well, such is the price of leadership.

"Milon Borsella, murdered," said Jordan. "The only surprise there is that it didn't happen long ago."

"Not a popular man in town?"

"He has made more than his share of enemies over the years. I pity the poor baile who has to find the murderer. Which one was called in?"

Pelardit mimed what looked to me like an exasperated bulldog.

"Arnald Calvet," nodded Jordan. "Honest man, not too much imagination. I doubt he'll get very far."

"I was thinking we could lend our efforts to the investigation," I said. "Unofficially."

"Why bother?" asked Jordan. "Why is it any business of ours? Why were you having that girl follow him?"

"A chance encounter," I said. "We saw him trying to shake down the Bishop yesterday. At the cathedral, no less."

"He may have to get in line," said Jordan. "Well, not now, obviously, but the Bishop owes money to quite a few people. He just came into office two years or so ago, and found out that his predecessor had pledged most of the rents to creditors. Poor Raimon has been living hand to mouth ever since."

"Hmm. And there is no pressure being put on him because of this?" I asked.

"He has the Count's favor," said Jordan. "What is your interest in the Bishop?"

"The Guild wants me to figure out a way to replace him with one of our people," I said.

Jordan and Pelardit looked at me in astonishment, then Jordan started to laugh.

"A jester in a miter," he roared. "Well, that will make the Feast of Fools a year-round celebration!"

"It might help bring it back," I said. "But it's not a jester who we want in there. It's a troubadour, or one who was one once upon a time."

"A troubadour? Who?"

"Ever hear of Folquet of Marseille?"

"Certainly," said Jordan as Pelardit looked thoughtful. "Much despised locally, thanks to a few choice ballads commissioned by the last count's enemies that found their way to his ears. Didn't Folquet become a monk?"

"He did, and rose to become a Cistercian abbot at the abbey of Le Thoronet."

"And you think that you can persuade him to leave a quiet, God-fearing abbey to take over this noisy, iniquitous town?" asked Jordan.

"I already have," I said. "That was the first part of my mission from the Guild. This is the second part."

"And how do you plan to do it?" demanded Jordan. "Do you know how hard it is to get rid of a sitting bishop? They've been trying to throw out the Archbishop of Narbonne for years, and he's still glued to his glory."

"I don't know how yet, but that's why I am following up on this connection to Borsella. It's a place to start poking around. Anything either of you find on him, I want to know about it."

"Oh, no, not me," said Jordan.

"I wasn't asking," I said. "As the Chief Fool, I expect your cooperation."

"You do," sneered Jordan. "The Guild is cowering in the Black Forest until Rome gets weary of chasing them. If they're lying low, then why should we stick our necks out?"

"They aren't lying low," I said. "They are fighting back."

"By getting Folquet made a bishop? That's the great strategy cooked up by Father Gerald?"

"Part of it," I said. "I am not aware of all the irons he has in the fire. I do what I am supposed to do."

"And for this, I am supposed to jeopardize all that I have accomplished in Toulouse," said Jordan.

"If it comes to that, yes," I said. "That's what we do."

"There's a limit," he said.

"Not for me," I said.

"A true believer," he scoffed. "A Guild fanatic. Would you put your life on the line?"

"I already have," I said. "Many times. Have you?"

"I have a wife and family," he said.

"As do I."

"Would you sacrifice them?" he asked. "Your wife's a fool, so you'd put her in danger in an instant, but what about your daughters?"

"Helga's an apprentice, not my daughter," I said.

"And the baby?" he insisted. "Would you endanger her life? Slit her throat at Aulis for favorable winds to Troy?"

"She may already be condemned, just for being a fool's daughter," I said softly. "Do you think, do you truly believe that hiding from danger will make the danger go away? The Church is going after the Fools' Guild, all of us, whether you lay low or not. They've forced us to flee the Guildhall, they've banned the Feast of Fools. It's only a matter of time before they start coming after the individual jesters. Will all you have accomplished and established in Toulouse protect you when that happens? Will it save your family?"

"I told you it would come to this," muttered Martine. "I told you to get out years ago. You kept clinging to your little ambition to be Chief Fool of Toulouse, and now you don't even have that."

"Peace, woman," he snapped.

"Why all this ambition when you don't even want to work with the Guild?" I asked.

"Why?" he returned incredulously. "For years, I have been waiting for the golden apple of foolery to come within my grasp. Sucked up the lesser jobs, did what I was told, all for the promise that someday it would be mine."

"Promised by who?" I asked. "And what is this prized apple?"

"To perform before the Count at the court," he said, almost in tears. "All these years, and Balthazar kept it to himself. Oh, once in a blue moon, he'd bring us in as stooges, but it was always Balthazar who reaped the glory, and Balthazar who reaped the rewards. And now, with it dangling before me, I am back to the old second-rate jobs, waiting for—"

He stopped abruptly.

"Waiting for the new Chief Fool to die," I finished for him.

He turned beet red.

"I didn't mean—"

"Yes, you did," I said. "Well, that was churlish behavior on the part of Balthazar, no question. But you will find me, I hope, to be a different sort of fool. When we were in Constantinople—"

"You were in Constantinople?" exclaimed Jordan.

"I was the Chief Fool there," I said. "Long story. Many long stories, in fact, and I will happily regale you with them some other time. But there were several of us there, and we all worked the palace, we all performed for the Emperor and the Empress, we all played for the great crowds at the

Hippodrome. We all worked together, in other words. I promise that you will play before Count Raimon, as long as you prove yourself a reliable fool."

"I am a funny man, I assure you," he said quickly.

"No doubt," I said. "But a reliable fool is one I can trust in everything."

"I see," he said heavily. "Lay my life on the line for you, and if I survive, I might make some money."

"That's putting in pessimistically."

"Why shouldn't I go to the Master of Revels myself?" he said. "They know me. They don't know you."

"Because they will know me very soon," I said. "All of Toulouse will know Tan Pierre, Domina Gile and the Fool Family, as well as our superior talents. That's another reason the Guild chose me over you, and I will take any fool's challenge you have to offer if you want proof. And if you continue to refuse to help me, I will have the Guild send more talented fools who will. You may find the demand for your services to be dwindling."

Jordan looked over at his wife, but she was busying herself with wiping the faces of her two boys, taking care to avoid meeting his eyes. He looked back at me.

"You can get us a performance before the Count?" he asked.

"If I get in there, we will all be in there," I said.

"And you'll keep the life-threatening situations to a minimum?"

"In truth, he's more likely to risk his own neck before he risks anyone else's," said Claudia. "I know that from experience. Sometimes I have to beg him to put me in harm's way."

"I didn't get this far in life by making good choices," sighed Jordan. "You have my help."

He thumbed his nose at me. I returned the gesture.

"Good," I said. "Who in particular might have had it in for Milon Borsella? Someone whose debt was particularly large, or someone who had been ruined by him? Women he's used, men he's cuckolded?"

"There's his brother," offered Martine.

We all looked at her in surprise. She shrugged.

"Which one, the consul or the monk?" I asked.

"The monk, the younger one," she said. "Brother Vitalis. I was dropping off a dress I had redone for Domina Garba, who lives in one of those monstrous new houses near Saint Sernin, and I saw Milon and his brother coming out of the cloisters. Milon was laughing and Vitalis was screaming at him."

"Screaming what?"

" 'I will see you in Hell!' was the one I heard," said Martine. "And he stormed away while Milon just laughed his head off. Vitalis is such a religious man, so you can understand my wondering at what got him that way."

"Add him to the list," I said wearily. "All of you, keep your ears open, pick up any information you can. Next order of business: When is the count returning to Toulouse?"

"He always comes in the week before Christmas so he can attend Mass at the cathedral," said Jordan.

"Who is his Master of Revels?"

"His name is Oldric. Decent fellow, as a matter of fact. He and Balthazar were thick as thieves. He actually came to the funeral."

"How do you get on with him?"

"Why, the last time we spoke, I said, 'Greetings, Senhor Oldric,' and he replied in the very height of courtesy, 'Oh, it's you,' and continued on his way."

"Sounds promising," I said. "I think we should all meet him together. Could you arrange the interview since you know him so well?"

"Consider it done," said Jordan, puffing up slightly.

"Very good," I said. "Domina Martine, we thank you for the splendor of your cooking, especially on such short notice. Will you and your family do us the honor of joining us for dinner next Sunday after Mass?"

"Why, yes," she said, startled and pleased. "Thank you."

"Then we will bid you farewell. We need to collect our apprentice from her spying."

We bowed to Martine, thumbed our noses at Jordan, and left.

"Good meal," I said.

"She's a good cook," commented Claudia as we walked down the street. "She barely ate anything herself, though. I hope she wasn't too upset over Jordan's not getting the job. You handled that most diplomatically, by the way. I'm more used to seeing you ruffle people's feathers than smoothing them. I didn't expect coming in as Chief Fool in Toulouse would be more difficult than it was in Constantinople."

"That's because there were no other fools in Constantinople when we came in," I said. "I only had you to argue with."

Someone cleared his throat behind us. We turned to see Pelardit standing there. He looked around to make sure no one was close by, then beckoned us toward him. When we did, he pointed at us, then raised each finger in turn and put them to his chest.

"You're saying that we can count on you," I guessed.

He nodded.

"Thank you, Brother Fool," I said.

He bowed, then sauntered away.

"He does speak," I observed as we resumed walking. "But only when he has something to say."

"Which makes him unique among fools," said Claudia. "Unique among men, for that matter."

We arrived at the entrance to the courtyard in front of Milon Borsella's house and waited for Helga to emerge.

"We could pay our respects to the family, I suppose," I said, watching the stream of the sympathetic, the curious and the freeloaders pouring through the main door. "There might be some food left."

"We don't know her, so it would be rude," said Claudia. "Besides, I am sure Helga saved us a few choice morsels."

There was a sudden commotion at the door of the house, then the crowd scattered like chickens as two pairs of men bowled through them, shouting at each other.

"Isn't that the Bishop?" asked Claudia.

"Certainly looks like him," I said.

The Bishop, with a priest flanking him, was backing fearfully away from a pair of men, one of whom was wearing the black cowl and robe of the Benedictine order. The other, who was older, was wearing a dark red coat trimmed with fur and had some kind of official looking chain dangling from his neck. Despite the tonsure on the monk, the two appeared like enough to be brothers, both in face and build. And the build in each case was impressive—for all the niceties of their costume, they had the burly mien of a pair of tavern brawlers, and the looks on their faces would have been equally at home in that setting.

"Have a care, sinners," shouted the Bishop. "Show the respect due to my office."

"Show the respect due to the house of the dead," the older brother shouted back. "If I catch either of you in here again, miter or no miter, I will horsewhip you out of this courtyard and into the street."

"And you, my good monk?" snarled the Bishop, looking at the monk. "Do you join in your brother's perfidy?"

"I won't bother with the horsewhip," said the monk, pounding his fist into his palm. "Get out, and take your lackey with you."

He took a step toward the Bishop, but the priest glided in between them, his hands up, palms outward.

"No need for this," he said placatingly. "The embarrassment is sufficient for the day. Come, Your Holiness."

With that, he took the Bishop by the elbow and escorted him from the courtyard. By the time they passed through the gate to the street, the Bishop had regained his composure and assembled his face into the proper expression of ecclesiastic dignity.

As they passed us, the priest glanced for a moment in our direction, then back to his master. He stayed a step behind the Bishop, his hands folded and covered by the voluminous sleeves of his black robes, the very picture of humble obedience. I wondered if he, like me, kept a dagger up his sleeve, just in case.

"If this sort of thing happens often, then we will have quite a lot of competition for entertainment," observed Claudia.

"They didn't even collect from the crowd," I noted. "Amateurs."

The battling brothers watched their adversaries retreat with smug satisfaction, then turned and went back inside. As they did, Helga emerged from the house, bowing to them as she did.

"Helga, come play with us!" cried a girl with a group of children in the courtyard.

Helga look toward the gate, saw us, and shook her head.

"I can't," she replied. "My parents are here."

There were groans of disappointment from the children, and Helga trudged toward us, her head down.

"She can come back tomorrow," I called, and the children cheered.

Helga grinned at us as she reached the gate.

"Did you see the fight?" she asked excitedly.

"We saw a great deal of masculine posturing," said Claudia. "No actual blows."

"That would have been so funny," said Helga wistfully. "All those holy costumes getting torn and shredded while they rolled through the dirt."

"What started it?" I asked as we walked back home.

"I was helping serve the guests," said Helga. "They put me in an apron and handed me a pitcher of wine, so I walked around and filled every cup I could see. Béatrix, the new widow, was in the main parlor, and the two brothers were standing by her."

"Those were Milon's brothers we saw?"

"Right, Vitalis and Bonet. Anyhow, the Bishop was announced, and that surprised the brothers. They actually whispered to each other for a minute before they let the Bishop come in."

"Why would a condolence call from the Bishop be so surprising?" wondered Claudia.

"It's not his local parish," I said. "Everything in the bourg is under the dominion of Saint Sernin. You would expect the parish priest from the Taur, even the abbot from Saint Sernin, but not the Bishop of Toulouse."

"I think that's what surprised them," said Helga. "So, in comes His Holiness, making a very grand benediction that took forever. I had to go refill my pitcher, so I slipped out. Then I saw that priest slip off into another room."

"Had he come into the parlor with the Bishop?"

"No, and that made me suspicious," said Helga. "I think he's the same priest we saw on Sunday when Milon had the argument with the Bishop."

"Interesting," I said. "What was this room?"

"I peeked through the door. It looked like it was an office where Milon conducted business. There were a lot of ledger books and papers stacked around. This priest was going through them like a burglar. I thought that since I was now a loyal servant of the household, I had better tell someone. So, I went and told the cook, and she ran and got Evrard, who's the keykeeper, and he went and told the Borsella brothers, and they came pounding into the office, screaming at the priest."

"What was he looking for?"

"I don't know," she said. "Bonet sees that there is a drawer open in the desk, and he looks in and starts yelling, 'It's gone! What have you done with the book?' And the priest starts saying, 'What book? What are you talking about?' And the two brothers grab him and flip him over so that his robe falls all around his head."

She started giggling.

"He has the scrawniest legs," she said. "Good thing he's a priest and you don't have to see them. So, he's hollering, and the two brothers are searching him and yelling, 'Where is it?' and then the Bishop comes in and yells at them to stop, and they drop the priest on his head because they had finished searching him and whatever they were looking for, he didn't have it. So, the priest gets back up and dusts himself off, then he looks at the Bishop and shakes his head, and that sets the brothers off again, and they start shoving the priest around, and the Bishop is shouting at them to stop, and that's when things got out of hand and spilled out of the house."

"So the Bishop was creating a diversion for his holy burglar," I mused. "Nice plan, thwarted by a pesky little apprentice fool. Did you get a good look at the drawer where this mysterious book came from?"

"Of course," she said proudly. "It was a small drawer, and it had a lock on it."

"But it was open," I said.

"Yes, and it didn't look forced," she said.

"Either someone picked the lock, or someone had a key," said Claudia. "Would Borsella's keykeeper have one?"

"Maybe," I said. "But for a desk drawer in his private office? That sounds like something Borsella would keep to himself."

"That could be what he was killed for," said Claudia. "To get the key to get the book."

"The key for the book, and the book is the key," I agreed. "But the key to what? And why would the Bishop want to steal the book? If it contained a record of his debt to Borsella, then stealing the book wouldn't erase the debt. And most debts, while embarrassing, are not worth killing for."

"Even for a bishop?" asked Helga.

"Especially for a bishop," I said.

We got up at the unfoolish dawn so that we could get decent seats at the assizes. For all that, there was a good-sized crowd of the curious and the unoccupied waiting at the gates of the Château Narbonnais. A guard let them in in groups of ten, his lips moving as he counted.

The château was actually a group of connected buildings, holding the courts, the consulate, and the Count's residence. Three towers dominated the rest of the complex. The Tower of the Eagle and the Round Tower flanked the gate through which we passed, while the Grand Tower, presumably the bastion of last resort, was set back in the interior. Crenelated walls, maybe twenty-five feet in height, enclosed the rest.

"What's interesting about this place is that it seems intended more to withstand an attack from within the city than it is to defend it from without," I observed. "That says something for the confidence of the counts over the years."

"Some of those walls look ancient," said Claudia.

"They say one section goes back to when Julius Caesar conquered Gaul," I said.

"He should have stayed here," said Claudia. "It's much nicer than Rome."

The Palace of Justice contained both the courts of assizes and appeals. The benches in the courtroom were set up rectangularly so that everyone was faced toward the center of the room. A coffin holding the late Milon Borsella rested on a pair of trestles.

Jordan was already inside, and waved us over to a section of empty bench beside him. We squeezed in, Helga sitting on my lap.

"Thanks," I said. "I didn't expect to see you here."

"It's the major gossip in town," he said. "I need to keep up. Besides, you've aroused my curiosity. Look, there's Calvet coming in. Ah, and there's the family. We should be starting soon."

The Borsella brothers entered, the widow Béatrix between them. She was in black and veiled, leaning on Bonet for support. We all stood in respect until they sat down on a front bench directly by the coffin. Béatrix took a handkerchief from her sleeve and pressed it to her mouth.

"By the door," whispered Helga.

A priest was entering as the crowd settled back into their seats. He took a bench by the far wall, pulling his cowl down. It was the first time that I got a good look at his face, which was slightly reminiscent of a greyhound, but he was the one who had been with the Bishop.

"The priest by the door," I murmured to Jordan. "Know him?"

"Father Mascaron," replied Jordan. "The Bishop's right-hand man. Why?"

"He and the surviving Borsella brothers nearly came to blows in public yesterday."

"No!" exclaimed Jordan, and people turned to shush him.

A pair of guards holding halberds took up position on either side of the coffin, then thumped the floor for silence.

"In the name of Raimon the Sixth, Count of Toulouse, I open these proceedings," said Calvet, standing by the coffin. "An inquiry into the death of Milon Borsella. Who found him?"

"I did," said a man wearing mail over a leather coat, an iron hat plopped atop a thick, round head.

"Approach and give your name," said the baile.

"Stephen de Villanova," said the man. "Member of the nightwatch."

"Take the oath," ordered the baile, and the soldier was sworn in. "Report."

"I was making my rounds, walking along the canal, making sure no one had fallen in, which is what I usually have to do," began de Villanova. "There are taverns near the Bazacle, and those coming home can't always tell the path from the water, or go off the path to relieve themselves, so I'm half the night hauling them out and pointing in the right direction."

"Shouldn't you be locking them up?" asked the baile.

"Not enough jails in Toulouse for all the drunks out after gates close," said the soldier, and there was a quiet, amused murmur of agreement from the room.

"Fair enough," said the baile. "Continue."

"Well, right around dawn breaking, I heard a splash off to my left, and I thought, here we go again," said de Villanova. "Then I realized it wasn't from the canal, and I hurried, because I figured someone went into one of the tanning pits, and that could blind a man if he doesn't get help. But there were a lot of pits to check, and it wasn't until I got to the fourth one that I saw him."

"How did he appear?" asked the baile.

"He was floating face down," said the soldier. "I could see he was dead right away. The back of his head was caved in, you can see it right here."

"And you didn't try and remove him?"

"Not if he was dead," said the soldier. "I sounded my horn and waited for help. We kept everything as it was until we found you, Senhor."

"When you first saw him, did you see blood?" asked the baile.

"Back of his head was covered in it," said the soldier, and there was a brief sob from Béatrix. "Begging your pardon, Domina. The waters in the pit washed it away by the time he was pulled out."

"And you heard no outcry?" asked the baile. "No blow being struck? No one fleeing into the night?"

"No, no, and no, Senhor," said the soldier. "Whoever did it was a quiet one. Might have been watching me the whole time, for all I know."

"If he was floating facedown, how did you know it was Milon Borsella?" asked the baile.

"That's what I wanted to know," muttered my wife.

"I knew him," said the soldier. "I recognized his clothes. And I saw him walking the other way early evening, when I was beginning my rounds."

"Was it unusual for him to be out in your vicinity?"

"Oh, no, your honor," said the soldier. "He lives in the bourg, not too far away, and, like I said, there are taverns out the other way. Begging your pardon again, Domina, but he liked his taverns."

"That will be all, good soldier," said the baile. "Bring in the tanner."

The poor fellow was in shackles now, a modest improvement over the hog-tying of the previous evening. He did not seem to appreciate his good fortune. He shuffled into the center of the room between two guards.

The baile made him take the oath, then the two guards held him against the open coffin. The baile stepped forward, grabbed the back of his head and forced him down until his face was inches away from that of the dead man.

"Did you see him last night?" asked the baile.

"No," whimpered the tanner. "I never did."

"What time did you leave your shop?"

"I locked up just before sunset, like I always do, and went home to my wife. She's here, she'll tell you."

"On pain of death, is he telling the truth?" asked the baile of a woman sobbing in the second row.

"He is, I swear it!" she blubbered.

The baile looked back and forth at the two of them, then sighed.

"There is no reason to suspect you of this," he said. "Release him."

The tanner was unshackled and fell into his wife's arms, the two of them wailing.

"You'd do the same for me, wouldn't you?" I whispered to Claudia.

"Tell the truth under oath? Or lie?" asked my wife.

"Whichever would get me out of whatever predicament I was in."

"I would consider it," she said.

"Evrard of the Borsella household, step forward and take the oath," said the baile.

A handsome man in his late twenties dressed in black walked to the center. A large bunch of keys rattled faintly at his waist.

"You are the keykeeper of the Borsella household," stated the baile.

"I am, Senhor," he replied. "Eight years in their service, and with his father before."

"Will you formally identify the man lying in the coffin before you?"

Evrard bent forward, the same formal bowing motion that he might have made had his master still lived. He straightened and nodded.

"That is my master, Milon Borsella, and never was a man sorrier to say it than I am," said Evrard.

"Your sentiments and loyalties are admirably expressed, good Evrard," said the baile. "When did you last see your master?"

"It was the night before last, or rather, the late afternoon," said Evrard. "He came home, changed, and left shortly before sunset."

"Did he advise you where he was going?"

"He did not," said Evrard.

"Did you know where he was going?"

"No, Senhor."

"As keykeeper, you were entrusted with the security of the household, were you not?"

"I was, and I am, Senhor," replied Evrard with dignity. "And I hope that I always will be."

A murmur of approval from the onlookers, most of whom I guessed were not as trustworthy when it came to other people's keys. The baile, on the other hand, seemed less satisfied with that answer.

"My point, Senhor Evrard, is that it seems somewhat surprising that your master, who entrusted you with his keys, did not confide in you his destination."

"It was not within the purview of my duties," replied Evrard. "I was responsible for the household, not for the master's business affairs outside of it."

"And if there had been an emergency in the household, how would you have contacted him?"

"If there had been an emergency in the household, I would have taken care of it," said Evrard. "No need to be disturbing him about it."

"Prior to his death, had you observed him in any situation that might have suggested to you a threat?" asked the baile.

"No, Senhor," he said firmly.

"Any arguments with anyone? Anything out of the ordinary?"

"No, Senhor," replied Evrard, yet I thought, though it

might just have been my imagination at play, that there was a moment of hesitation this time.

"Is there any knowledge that you possess that might in any way help this court determine who killed your master?"

"I can think of none," said Evrard. "If I remember anything else, I will bring it to you immediately."

"Thank you," said the baile. "You may stand down."

The baile walked over to the Borsella family.

"Forgive me, Domina, but it is my duty," he said, holding his hand out to her.

Trembling, she took it and rose to her feet. She came to the edge of the coffin and broke down, sobbing.

"Surely there is no need—" protested Bonet, but the baile silenced him with a gesture.

"Please, Domina," he said. "I will not ask you to take the oath. But can you tell us if you know anything of how or why he was killed?"

"Nothing," she managed to get out.

"Then I will not question you further," said the baile gently. "My sympathies for your loss."

He escorted her back to the two brothers. Vitalis embraced her as she sat.

Calvet looked around the room.

"Is there anyone here who knows of any enmity held toward this man?"

"Half the town owed him money!" shouted someone from the crowd.

"Then we will question all of his debtors," said Calvet. "I call upon Bonet Borsella to preserve his brother's accounts and ledgers until such time that they may be examined."

Bonet gave a curt nod.

"Will he tell him about the one missing?" I wondered.

"I doubt it," said Claudia.

"Before I make my preliminary ruling, I call upon all present to rise and take the oath," said Calvet.

We all did, our hands raised.

"If there be any among you who has any knowledge that will assist this court in its inquiries," said Calvet, "I charge you under your oath to step forward now."

I glanced around the room, just to see if anyone would. Many were doing the same.

And Father Mascaron was staring directly at me.

CHAPTER 4

I returned his glance boldly, not breaking it. It was like a children's game, seeing who would blink first. Finally, I gave a minute shrug, and he smiled slightly, then looked away.

"What was that all about?" whispered my wife, who misses nothing.

"I don't know," I said. "We will have to find out."

"Anyone?" asked the baile.

There was no response. He turned to a scribe who had been recording the statements of the witnesses, and was about to say something when a voice screeched, "I saw it done!"

There was an immediate uproar, and a disturbance among the sea of bodies to our right. A man was struggling to get through, his clothes in disarray, his nose carbuncled.

"I saw it done!" he kept shouting.

"Armand, please," said the baile.

"Who's this, the town drunk?" I asked Jordan.

"It's not an official position," he replied. "Nor is he the only contender for the title. But he certainly deserves consideration for it."

"Armand, if you continue to interrupt official proceedings, I will have to lock you up again," said the baile.

"But I did see it, your eminence," said Armand. "I really did."

"You were drunk last night," said the baile. "You're drunk every night."

"Not yesterday!" said Armand triumphantly. "Yesterday, I was drunk in the afternoon!"

"Get out of this court," said the baile.

"I was sleeping it off in one of the tanners' sheds, and I was woke during the night by the sound of two men arguing," continued Armand. "It was that Borsella fellow and someone else."

"Do you expect me to give someone like you any credence?" asked the baile.

"Swear me in," growled Armand. "Put me to any oath you like, to the Count, to Mother Mary, to the Devil himself, but I swear to what I saw."

"And you saw who killed Milon Borsella," said the baile.

"Not his face," said Armand. "I was lying down. I could only see part of him through a crack in the shed."

"Then of what use are you to this investigation?"

"Because I saw his feet," said Armand as if that settled the matter.

"His feet," repeated the baile wearily. "And I suppose that you can identify whose feet they were?"

"Well, no," said Armand as people started to laugh. "But they were wearing sandals, weren't they?"

The room abruptly went silent.

"Oh, no," groaned Jordan.

"Sandals, you say," said the baile, suddenly interested.

"As sure as I am here," said Armand. "He was one of them Cathars, he was, and that's my testimony."

"Well, well," said Calvet, almost as if he was talking to

himself. "Well, well, that is interesting. Very interesting indeed. Armand, forgive me. You may have proved yourself invaluable today."

Armand bowed clumsily, looking quite pleased with himself.

"Anyone else?" asked Calvet, looking around the room. "Very well. It is my preliminary ruling that Milon Borsella is the victim of foul and loathsome murder by a person unknown, but very likely one of the Cathar cultists. We will adjourn until such time as enough information has been gathered so as to bring the guilty party to justice. In the name of the Count, these proceedings are ended."

The two soldiers thumped their halberds upon the ground, and we all filed out.

We conferred under the cover of the general hubbub.

"How could he allow that to happen?" fumed Jordan. "To let all of the Cathars come under suspicion because of one drunk's story? This is terrible."

"Helga, follow Evrard," I ordered. "If he goes back to the Borsella household, get back inside, see what you pick up. Dearest, are you up to the task of tailing a priest?"

"I don't follow the Church as much as I used to, but in this case I'll make an exception," she said. "And you?"

"My inclination is to imbibe," I said. "I will follow the drunkard. Brother Jordan, see what you can find out about this new outbreak of Catharist violence."

We walked with the crowd back through the Porte Narbonnaise into the city.

"Our good Father is hanging back," said Claudia. "I am going to fuss over our daughter for a few minutes."

"Evrard is in a hurry," observed Helga.

"Which is why God gave you young legs," I said. "Go."

We separated, each after our various targets. The crowd was still abuzz over the court proceedings, distorting them into stranger and stranger accounts and rumors and spilling them down the gutters of every street and alley in the city.

Meanwhile, either the source of the truth of the murder or the propagator of a base and dangerous lie was walking quite happily along the Grande Rue. He turned left at the Rue de Comminges, which took him toward the river. The neighborhood he was aiming for had its share of taverns, not to mention more than its share of prostitutes, so it was not a surprising choice for a man like him. He appeared to be in no particular rush, nor was he paying any attention to anyone else, which made my job easier.

Except that Father Mascaron was following me, and being rather obvious about it. I doubted that he knew I was following Armand, but I couldn't risk pursuing the drunkard with the priest hot on my heels. My best chance was to allow Mascaron to waylay me and hope that my wife would switch to Armand.

I stopped and bought a bag of roasted chestnuts from a stall, then tossed one over my shoulder. There was a brief yelp of surprise and, I hoped, pain.

"Careful, Father, they're hot," I said without turning.

"Not as hot as Hellfire," he said.

I turned to face him, and grinned.

"Have you come to save me?" I asked.

Out of the corner of my eye, I saw Claudia walking past us and down the street, bouncing Portia in her arms.

"You were heading toward drunkenness and lechery," said Father Mascaron.

"Was I?" I exclaimed. "How delightful! I thought that I was just wandering aimlessly. Thank you for that information. I should hire you as my guide."

"Insolent cur," he said. "Have you no respect for my office?"

"Respectful jesters don't get much work," I said. "I'll stay insolent and well fed, if you don't mind. Why are you following me?"

"What makes you think I was?" he asked.

"The cathedral is in the other direction," I said. "I may be a fool, but I know when I'm being followed. And I don't like being followed by anyone who isn't female, pretty, and of age. You fall short on two of those counts, although you compensate by being three times too old."

"I marvel that you talk so much here, yet were so reticent in the courtroom," said Father Mascaron.

"No one asked me to testify," I said.

"Calvet charged us all upon our oaths to come forward with information of relevance," said the priest. "Yet you remained where you were."

"What information does a worthless fool like me have that could have assisted the mighty baile?"

"You saw the late Senhor Borsella arguing with my most holy master," said the priest calmly.

"Yes," I said. "But I saw nothing there that I believed of value to a court."

"That is what I wished to hear," said Father Mascaron.

"Nothing of value to a court, certainly," I said. "Yet not without value. At least, not without value to someone."

"What are you talking about?" he asked warily.

"Well, as you said, I am a talkative man," I rattled on. "A most voluble fool, but is being voluble valuable? I know fools who think they must be paid by the word, and who will as a result pad their loquacity with excessive eloquence, who will persist and persevere in pursuing this persiflage until the purses of their patrons are penniless."

"Are you performing right now?" asked the priest, scowling. "You know that such entertainments are forbidden during Advent."

"Am I being paid for this stream of amusing banter?" I asked. "Not a sou. For that matter, are you even being entertained? That sour expression suggests not. Therefore, I conclude that my soul is safe enough for the moment, although I am intruding upon your territory with that reasoning."

"You have certainly strayed from your own territory," said Father Mascaron. "You were speaking of the value of your knowledge."

"Well, as to that, some of the time I'm paid to talk," I said. "And some of the time, as the old adage goes, silence is golden."

"Golden," he repeated.

"Or silver," I said. "Silver is good, too."

"You are asking me to pay you to be silent," he said.

"I am doing nothing of the kind," I said. "I would like to be paid to talk, but Advent turns my world topsy-turvy. Perhaps being paid not to talk is part of the natural order of things."

"What do you consider this silence to be worth?" he asked.

"There's a quandary," I said. "I haven't tested the market. Yet. What is the going rate in Toulouse?"

"What would the rate be for you to be going?" he returned.

"Oh, I plan to settle here," I said. "Even without the Feast of Fools, a man with half his wits could make twice the living here as elsewhere. No, good priest, my silence is not for sale just yet."

"What about your loyalty?" he asked.

"Can you afford the loyalty of a fool?" I asked.

"You need work at the moment," he said. "Unfoolish work that pays."

"Work for the Church?" I laughed. "Sounds too much like an honest living, and that, Senhor, is something I have spent my life avoiding."

"I am not necessarily offering honest work," he said.

"Senhor Priest, you have just piqued my interest. Go on."

"Not here, not now," he said. "Come by the northern entrance to the cathedral at vespers, and we will discuss your employment."

"Vespers? That's when the gates are closed," I said. "I'll be trapped inside the city. That's a long night for one conversation."

"I will make it worth your while," he said.

"What makes you think I'm the man for this type of work?" I asked him.

"Because you didn't come forward when the baile called," he replied, and with that, he turned and walked away.

Neither did you, I thought. And you are the one who is supposed to respect an oath.

I ate a few chestnuts, watching him until he was safely out of sight. He did not turn to see if I was following him. That meant either he was an amateur at the cat-and-mouse, or absolutely confident that he was safe from such games.

Or that he had someone watching his back. Or watching me.

I sighed and walked toward the river, then ducked into a narrow alleyway that led me into the Jewish quarter. I quickly moved into the shelter of a doorway and waited until I was sure no one was following me. Then I waited some more to quell the second-guessing.

By this time, I had small hope of finding my wife or Armand, but I walked down to the riverside and back to the quarter that took its name from the Rue de Comminges. I saw half a dozen taverns, and decided that it would be worth my while to investigate all of them, if only to fulfill my mission for the Guild.

"Did you know that the consulate passed an edict banning prostitution from the city three years ago?" said my wife, appearing at my side and taking a chestnut from my bag.

"I knew you were there," I said as Portia clambered into my arms.

"I learned this from a pair of prostitutes," continued Claudia. "They were plying their trade quite openly, despite this edict. They explained to me that since prostitution no longer existed in the city, they must have been figments of my imagination. They asked me if I was interested in supplementing my meager income by becoming an imaginary being like them. I declined."

"How much of a supplement?" I asked.

"You're a pig," she said. "Armand went into that tavern over there. I peeked inside, but it isn't a place for a woman to enter alone."

"Was he with anyone?"

"No," she said. "And there aren't many others in there. I imagine it fills up once the mills close for the day."

"Daylight frees the tavern for the true wastrels," I said.

"Then you won't appear out of place," she said. "I will leave you to him. You'll tell me about your chat with Father Mascaron at dinner."

"I'll be missing dinner tonight, I'm afraid. He's offered me employment."

"As a fool?" she asked, surprised.

"Something shadier," I said. "So shady, it must be done after sunset. See if you can find Jordan or Pelardit before you head home and have him keep an eye on the northern side of the cathedral at vespers."

"Wouldn't you rather have me?" she asked.

"In many ways," I said. "But I want to find out how good they are at this."

"You sound like a Chief Fool," she said. "Very well. I will see you in the morning."

I kissed Portia on the nose, Claudia on the mouth, then handed the baby back to her mother. Portia started mewling.

"Hush, dear," whispered Claudia. "Papa needs to go to a tavern now."

The tavern was called the Miller's Wheel, and had a sign showing a waterwheel like those nearby on both sides of the channel running between Ile de Tounis and the city. This waterwheel, however, was scooping up ale, as far as I could tell. An encouraging sign. I went inside.

Armand was seated at a low table, a pitcher of ale in front of him, watching the door. He looked disappointed when he saw me, and looked past me at the door again. I ignored him and went up to the tapster. There were beef ribs roasting behind him in the fireplace. I bought two along with a small pitcher of ale and some bread and carried the mess over to a corner bench where I could watch Armand watching the door.

It was a long wait. I was forced to maintain my cover by purchasing another small pitcher of ale, while Armand lapped me several times in this race. Then a woman I took to be one of the area's nonexistent prostitutes came into the tavern and whispered something in his ear. He grinned lewdly, slapped some coins down on the table, and walked out with her.

I followed after a moment, not having much hope of success at this point. If everything was what it appeared to be, then I would be treated to the sight of a drunk and a whore copulating in an alley, something that no longer held the thrill that it once did.

On the other hand, if all he was looking for was a few moments of illicit love, he had had ample opportunity before this, given where we were. Unless this lady was a particular favorite, in which case . . . I decided to stop guessing and just follow them.

She led him to the door of a two-story house, the second level hanging over the first and sagging dangerously. They went inside. I waited for a beat, then burst through the doorway.

"Where is she?" I shouted drunkenly.

I was in a parlor where a number of bored young women in linen shifts reclined more or less decorously on cushioned chairs. A man with well-oiled curly hair and a red-brocaded doublet rose quickly.

"May I help you, Senhor?" he asked.

"Where's my wife?" I shouted.

"I fear that there's been some mistake," he said, stepping toward me.

I shoved him aside and barged through the halls.

"Sophie, you whore!" I shouted. "Where are you?"

I kicked open one door after another, gathering enough indecent sights to make a highly successful volume of pornographic illustrations, had I any talent for drawing. In the fourth room, I struck gold.

Armand was in there, but not with the lady who enticed him from the tavern. Turning toward the door, sword in hand, was Bonet Borsella.

"Looking for my wife," I muttered.

"As you can see, she is not here," said Borsella.

"Sorry for the intrusion," I muttered, and I pulled the door shut.

I kept shouting and kicking in doors after that one until a pair of large, muscular men caught up to me.

"You are disrupting our master's business," said one of them.

"I want my wife," I moaned, weeping sloppily.

"There are no wives here, my friend," said the other man, not unsympathetically. "This is where men come who don't want wives. We must, perforce, escort you from the premises."

"Does it have to be perforce?" I whined.

It was per quite a lot of force. I was grateful that my rampage hadn't taken me to the upper floor, as the velocity with which I was thrown out of the building might have carried me into the Garonne from that height. As it was, I soared a good fifteen feet before the earth reclaimed me. Around me, people were laughing as I picked myself up and brushed myself off.

It was nice to hear people laughing at me. It had been a while.

The sun was beginning to set. I hurried to reach my appointment with Father Mascaron.

The north side of the cathedral was all brick. A pair of round windows called oculi looked out from it, each ringed with red and white bricks, giving the observer the feeling he was being observed in turn. Did God need the Church to watch us? I wondered.

Vespers sounded, and a door opened. A cowled figure

beckoned to me, and disappeared inside the darkness of the doorway.

I had not lived this long by walking into darkened doorways at the behest of cowled figures. I stood where I was, my arms folded.

After a minute, Father Mascaron peeked out.

"Aren't you coming in?" he asked.

"Why don't you come out?" I replied.

"You don't trust me?"

"Two nights ago, a man was killed and tumbled into a tanner's pit," I said. "I don't trust anyone after sunset, and damned few in the light."

"In here, you will find safe haven," he said, his hands out.

"Maybe," I said. "But first, step outside and let me search you for weapons."

He came out into the open. I stepped forward and patted him thoroughly.

"This is the second time I've been searched in two days," he sighed. "As you can see, I am unarmed. Now, let us . . ."

He stopped as I pulled out my knife.

"As you can see, I am armed," I said. "We will enter the cathedral together. So closely together, in fact, that anyone waiting for me with a blade on the other side of that door had better be quite sure which man he is cutting."

"There is no one there," said Father Mascaron.

"Then there will be no problem if we do it my way," I said, grabbing him by his cowl and turning him toward the cathedral. We walked inside with my knife pressed firmly against his neck. I kicked the door shut behind us. No assassins lurked in the shadows.

"My office is to the left," he said, nodding helpfully in that direction.

"After you," I said.

His office was small, enclosing a scratched oaken desk that barely left enough room to maneuver around it. I stayed right with the priest as we awkwardly negotiated the corners, then stopped him while I checked under the desk for weapons.

"The haven looks safe enough for now," I said. "Please, sit down."

"I thank you for your hospitality," he said, sitting behind the desk. "Of course, all I have to do is raise the alarum and accuse you of burglary, and you'll be swinging from a gibbet in a day."

"This blade would be in your heart before you finished drawing breath," I said. "If I'm going to swing, it will be for something worth swinging for. No more threats, Father. They don't get us anywhere."

"Agreed," he said. "Put your knife away."

"Employment," I said, sliding it back into my sleeve.

"And now you're a fool who doesn't waste words," he said. "Good. To the point. I need to find something. A small book, the size of my hand, bound in black leather."

"Have you looked under everything?" I asked.

"Needless to say, it is not my book to possess," he said. "But I would possess it."

"Whose house shall I find it in?" I asked. "And how will I know which book it is?"

"It was secured with a gold clasp," he said. "The front cover was decorated with four golden crosses on each corner, and in the center was the name, 'Milon Borsella.'"

"He may have had a dozen such books," I said. "How should I know which one is yours?"

"He only had one," said Father Mascaron. "I know that for

a fact. He kept it in a locked drawer in a desk in the office he kept at his house."

"And you tried to find it there yesterday," I said. "That's what the fight was about, wasn't it?"

"I'm ashamed to say so," he said, looking not all ashamed. "Unfortunately, someone beat me to it."

"What's in this book?" I asked.

"Accounts of debts owed," he said.

"By the Bishop?"

"Yes," he said.

"But aren't those debts a matter of public record?" I asked. "Won't there be other ledgers recording them as well?"

"There are some debts beyond the public ones that Milon kept in that special book," said Father Mascaron. "Debts beyond what would be approved of the cathedral if they were made public."

"And which could not be proved without this book."

"My point exactly," beamed Father Mascaron.

"Why trust me with this task?" I asked. "There must be some appropriate people who know this city much better than I do."

"Frankly, I don't trust the local talent," said Father Mascaron. "Those who run to sin in this city work for some men who are most particular about controlling their activities. And I would prefer that this book not fall into their hands."

"Or they may become the ones to collect these special debts," I said.

"That is my fear," he acknowledged.

"Have there been any attempts at collection?" I asked.

"Not as yet," he said.

"If there are, you must alert me," I said. "They would most likely send an intermediary, but I could trace him back to his source. That might be the most direct way of finding the book."

"I would prefer that we not let things progress that far," he said. "Find it for me, and there will be a reward."

"And my pay for searching?" I asked.

"A penny a day, and a report of your work each morning," he said. He reached into a purse at his waist. "There's three pennies to start. Two for tonight, one for tomorrow. Will that suffice?"

"Until Advent is over," I said. "At which point I resume my foolish ways."

"Fair enough," he said. "If it isn't found by then, we will abandon the effort and await the extortionists."

He held out his hand. I took it.

"You may leave by the door you entered," he said.

I pulled my knife out.

"You first," I said.

He sighed, and got up.

We walked to the north entrance. He opened the door and looked out cautiously. I gave him a gentle shove and he stumbled outside. No one attacked him. I slipped past him into the darkness as he stepped back into God's house.

As I reached the next corner, I heard a dog growl at me briefly from an alleyway.

"Make sure I'm not being followed," I said softly in that direction. "Meet me at the Miller's Wheel."

I turned left, and walked down toward the Comminges quarter. The tavern was much livelier now, filled with millers, the boatmen who rowed to the Ile de Tounis with empty barrels and sacks of grain and returned with empty sacks and barrels of flour, and those who sought to part these hardworking men from their hard-earned pay. I did not see Armand nor, to my relief, the burly men who had turned me into a projectile a few hours earlier. I bought a large pitcher of ale, picked up two cups, and sat at a bench at the side of the ruckus, keeping an eye on the door.

Pelardit wandered in about ten minutes later. He caught my eye and gave me the all clear signal. I held up one of the cups and he was at my side in an instant. I poured, and we bumped cups. Gently, so as not to lose a precious drop.

"I am working for Father Mascaron now," I muttered.

His eyebrows rose so high, I thought they might reappear on the nape of his neck.

"I'll tell you all about it later," I said. "You can put me up tonight? I missed the closing of the gates. One disadvantage to living in Saint Cyprien."

He nodded.

"But first, let us finish the contents of this pitcher," I said.

He nodded more happily.

One pitcher was not enough. By the time we finished the third, the place had begun to clear. It was only Tuesday, after all, and a working man has to pace his drinking. We staggered back to Pelardit's place. which was a single room over another tavern in the Daurade parish. He had constructed a system of broad shelves on which he kept dozens of props and costumes, neatly folded and organized. He pulled out a bedroll from one and tossed it to me, then sat down on a pallet in the corner and pulled off his boots.

"Thanks," I said, unrolling the bedroll. "Let me tell you about today."

He nodded and looked at me expectantly. I told him everything, from the court proceedings through my transactions with Father Mascaron. When I was done, he looked thoughtful, then held his arms over his head, curving them and bringing his hands together so that they outlined the shape of a miter.

"I don't know how much the Bishop is involved in this yet," I said. "Mascaron could be following his orders, or taking the initiative in protecting him. Certainly, they were working together when Mascaron tried to loot Borsella's office."

He pretended to read something.

"I don't know what's in that book," I said. "I doubt that it's merely an account of secret debts owed by the Bishop. That hardly seems worth the trouble that they are going to. A brazen burglary is the mark of desperation."

He pointed to me, then rubbed his thumb and forefinger together.

"Yes, hiring an untrustworthy lowlife like me seems even more desperate," I agreed. "And it's very convenient that he is employing me to find something that would help me in my own mission. But I don't think he really hired me because he wants me to find the book."

Pelardit looked at me quizzically, then his eyes widened in comprehension.

"Right," I said. "He hired me so that he could keep an eye on me."

He stood and walked a few steps. Then one of his legs was yanked into the air by an invisible rope.

"That occurred to me, too," I said. "It could very well be a trap."

CHAPTER 5

As I came up through the trapdoor into our rooms, a trio of small, unidentifiable objects came flying at my head. I caught them, one after the other, and juggled them in a basic pattern until I recognized them as fresh biscuits. I started taking bites out of each, still juggling them as I did.

"Good morning," said Claudia. "We have some grape compote to go with them."

"Compote is too hard to juggle," I said. I caught the half-eaten biscuits and carried them over to our table. She placed the compote before me, and I spread some on the biscuits.

"Much better," I said.

"How was your evening?" she asked.

"Eventful," I said, and I recounted it to her.

"Some men do get killed over debts," she said when I was done. "Maybe that's all this is. Not the Bishop, necessarily, but some other secret debtor."

"Maybe," I said. "Although I wouldn't put it past Mascaron to have it done. Or to do it himself, for that matter."

"Only then he wouldn't have been searching for the book afterwards," she pointed out. "He would have had the key to the drawer, and gone right to it."

"True enough," I said. "But if it was some other secret

debtor, I would assume that he would simply destroy the book."

"Unless he saw a way to use it for profit," she said. "A man desperate enough to kill for a debt might commit other crimes for money. He could have seen all of the names as an opportunity for extortion."

"So we would need a list of secret debtors who are now candidates to be extorted," I said. "Which means our best leads are the Borsella household and those of his brothers. Where's Helga, by the way?"

"Already gone to Milon Borsella's house," said Claudia. "She said Evrard went straight there after the inquest and waited upon the widow for the rest of the day. The two brothers escorted Béatrix home, stayed for a few minutes, then went their different ways."

"Why don't you pay your respects to Béatrix?" I suggested. "Bring your lute, offer to provide some comforting music."

"All right," she said. "Where are you off to?"

"I am going to poke around Bonet Borsella's life," I said. "Maybe track down Armand and get him drunk and talking. He probably has a head start on the first part."

"How was Pelardit last night?"

"He did fine. He's going to trail me again today. I am glad that you got him rather than Jordan."

"I thought that a silent man would be a better shadow than a noisy one," she said. "Be home for dinner tonight."

"I will," I promised. I swallowed the last of the biscuits and left.

Bonet, as the inheritor of the bulk of his father's estate, lived in a fortified château near the Montardy Square. While it lacked the tower that showed true wealth along with the fear of suddenly having it taken away, the house was still impressive, looming over a row of street-level shops. The shops here sold silks and spices, high quality merchandise that must have brought in a nice bit of change, although they weren't doing much business when I walked by them.

The courtyard gate was closed, and a single guard stood in front of it, leaning on a spear and trying to look alert. I approached him.

"Is your master at home?" I asked.

"Not likely," he said. "No money to be made at home."

"It depends on your business, I suppose. If he is not here, where am I most likely to find him?"

"Lately, he's been spending all of his time at the new sawmill," said the soldier. "Just finished building it, and he runs to it every morning when a sensible man of wealth would be looking to his mistress."

"A man of wealth who looks to a mistress rather than his business will usually end up without wealth, business or mistress," I said. "Where is this new sawmill?"

"At the Bazacle dam," he said. "You can't miss it. Just listen for the sound of trees screaming their last."

I thanked him and left, passing by Pelardit, who was engrossed in examining some silks at one of the shops.

At the northern end of the bourg, where the walls reached the river, the Garonne makes a dogleg to the left, sending part of its waters coursing through a channel between an island and the banks. It was shallow enough at that point that you used to be able to walk across, but thirty years ago the millers built a dam across it. They said it was the longest dam in Christendom, and I believed them. A double row of pilings, smeared with pitch and filled with rubble. The river butted its head against this wall over and over again, surging with frustration, seeking a way through, finding itself at the beck and call of the puny two-legged creatures who clung to its shores and reined it in.

And once they had enslaved the river, they forced it to do their bidding, diverting it through sluices and canals, spinning waterwheel after waterwheel, their shafts turning complicated arrangements of gears, cams, belts and millstones. Freed from the uncertainties of their floating counterparts, the millers ground grain for flour, bark for the tanners, and most importantly, what made me kneel before them and give my most fervent blessings for their existence, malt and beer mash for the brewers.

The new sawmill was perched on the mainland, near the top of the island. On the other side of the sluice gates, barges carrying denuded trees floated gently to a wharf, where teams of burly men waited to wrest them onto land, after which several boys would simply roll them through the last leg of their journey.

The sawmill itself was a giant shed, open at both ends. The roof at the far end projected over a pair of waterwheels, one set lower than the other to tax the water a second time as it charged through the mill run. The upriver one was twenty feet high, the second maybe fifteen, and they both turned lengthy oak trunks, each bedecked with several large gears that spun smaller gears that were attached in turn to saw-wheels, bright spinning steel discs that spat yellowed dust through the air as they screeched through the logs.

The men who shoved the logs into the saw-blades were large of limb and short on fingers. I found myself doing a quick count of my own, and was relieved to find exactly ten, neither more nor less. Either of the latter results would have proved disturbing.

At the end closest to me, other sawyers were shaping the planks with two-man blades or planing them to more uniform smoothness, activities I found enjoyable to watch, especially since I didn't have to do any of them. I have nothing but respect for those lumbering men who reduce logs to more manageable shapes. During my last sojourn at the Guild haven in the Black Forest, I had taken my turn with those who were building the new Guildhall. We had no waterwheels turning blades, so were forced to make do with two-man saws. Several days of that made me grateful that my regular profession just involved falling on my face, juggling knives and avoiding the occasional death threat.

Bonet Borsella was down by the lower waterwheel, supervising a pair of men who were constructing a curious contraption. A vertical gear linked to a horizontal one that turned a stout pole. Mounted at the top was another wheel that had short rods projecting diagonally from it. The two men were trying to wrestle a pole of young, green wood into a bent position just below the upper wheel. I went over to get a closer look. Despite their best efforts, it kept springing back upright.

"I was like that when I was young and green," I remarked to Borsella.

"Weren't we all?" he said. "Make yourself useful and help them."

I went over and added my weight to the pole as the other two brought it carefully down.

"Over to the right," directed Borsella, and we eased the end of it to a point just under the upper wheel on the vertical shaft.

"Good," he said.

He took a rope and looped it over the end of the bent pole, then tied it to a metal hook set into the floor. One of the other men wedged a prop under the spring-pole and secured it.

There was a hole, about two inches in diameter, bored through the upper end of the spring-pole. The two men picked up a straight saw-blade that had a long wooden handle at one end. They raised it vertically and slipped the handle through the hole, then fastened it in position with pegs. The handle poked about six inches through the other side of the spring-pole, and the blade was now dangling freely underneath.

"Carefully now," said Borsella.

He and one of the men held onto the rope holding the end of the spring-pole while the other one loosened it. They allowed the spring-pole to rise until the handle of the saw came up against the upper wheel.

"Right there! Tie it off quickly," said Borsella.

The other man retied the rope at the hook, then stood back expectantly. Borsella and the man holding the ropes let go.

As the upper wheel turned, the projecting rods forced the saw-handle down. When the rod passed, the handle was released, and the spring-pole snapped back to the upper limit of the rope, putting the handle in line for the next rod to repeat the process.

In other words, as the wheel turned, the saw-blade moved back and forth in midair without the aid of a single man.

"Marvelous," I said, applauding. "If you were a Roman emperor, you could justly say, 'Veni, serra secavi, vici' at this moment."

"What does that mean?" asked Bonella.

"I came, I sawed, I conquered," I replied.

"We'll see," said Bonella, smiling. "I saw this arrangement at a mill up north. I am not convinced that it's stable enough to be of use, but it looks worth the experiment."

"I am for anything that takes the place of me doing actual work," I said.

"Since you don't actually work here, your desires have been achieved," said Borsella. "Thank you for your assistance, but who are you?"

"My name is Tan Pierre," I said. "At the moment, I am an unemployed jester waiting for Christmas."

"And you've come looking for employment to tide you over?"

"Not in a sawmill," I said. "But I am a musician and singer as well. I have come to offer my services for your brother's wake. My condolences, by the way."

"It is not my family's custom to have music at the wake," he said. "I am afraid that you have wasted your time. But if you need help—it is the season, after all."

He reached for his purse. I held up my hand.

"Please, Senhor, I do not seek charity," I said. "I ask for honest pay for honest work, and nothing more."

"Well said. Forgive me for my impertinence," said Borsella. "Let me walk you out."

"On the contrary, I thank you for your intended kindness," I said. "Now, if you would like entertainment during the Twelve Days, or anytime after, we are available. That is, if the period of mourning will be over by then—I do not know the local custom as to that."

"You are not from Toulouse," he observed as we left the mill for the sunshine.

"No," I said. "I had heard that a jester here had passed away, and thought there might be some opportunity."

"Balthazar," said Borsella. "Funny man. So he dies, and you try to move in on his territory. My brother dies, and you try to pry some silver out of my hands. You are quite the scavenger of the dead, aren't you?"

"Every profession has its competitors, Senhor," I said. "You are trying to outdo other sawmills, I am trying to outdo other jesters. Should I mock you for employing these wonderful wheels that take the place of a dozen men? As for prying silver from your hands, if it is the expense that concerns you, I will make you a better offer. I will perform at your house gratis."

"You will?" he said in surprise. Then his eyes narrowed in suspicion. "What favor would you request from me?"

"Only that your favor fall upon me," I said. "We are new to your town, and seek the influence of the mighty. To have the patronage of a consul and a wealthy businessman such as yourself would be most advantageous."

"I see," he said. "My brother is dead but two days, and you are here turning this sad occasion into a business proposition."

"No disrespect intended, Senhor," I said. "His death does not stop you from attending to matters in your own profession."

"I should have my men throw you out on your ear," he said.

"That's not where I usually end up landing," I said. "Why, just yesterday, when I was thrown out of that bordel in Comminges, I did a most elegant pair of somersaults at the far end of my trajectory."

He looked at me, his eyes suddenly widening in recognition.

"Of course, we all mourn in our own way," I said. "I know many who have sought comfort in such establishments after the loss of a family member. Usually in the arms of women, but I do not judge you for your particular tastes."

"You were the man who was breaking down doors looking for his wife," he said. "Or was that just a ruse?"

"Not my concern if two men have to meet in a bordel to satisfy their illicit lust for each other," I continued. "I had a cousin who was that way, and still just the nicest man . . ."

"I should have cut you down on the spot," he spat. "So your true purpose in coming here is to offer your silence for sale."

"Gossip is a sin," I said. "Among the vast panoply of sins, one of the lesser, but still one that I indulge in. I am seeking to mend my ways, but it's difficult."

"You are wasting your time, Fool," he said. "That man and I are not lovers."

"There, see how a simple misunderstanding can cause so much trouble?" I said. "I am glad to hear it. No doubt that there was a perfectly legitimate reason for the two of you to be meeting in a bordel, and you have nothing to fear from such knowledge being let loose."

"It was about a business arrangement," he said carefully.

"Then that clears up everything," I said cheerfully. "Who would doubt that a man like you would not want to have a business relationship with a man like him in a place like that? Why, I am certain that the baile investigating your brother's death would have no interest in your clandestine business arrangement with the man who supposedly witnessed it."

"How did you . . ."

"So much idle time for a jester during Advent," I said. "Having nothing better to do, I seek what entertainments this town has to offer during this holy season. I attended the inquest, and saw Armand's performance. Unconvincing, I thought, but I am a professional, so I tend to judge amateur theatrics harshly. Lucky for him his audience had lower standards. It certainly bodes well for my success once I start up again."

"You have a vivid imagination, Fool," he said. "To suppose that anything between Armand and myself had anything to do with my brother's death . . ."

"I do have a vivid imagination, Senhor," I said, "but a man of none, say, for example, our esteemed baile, would still be struck by the coincidence."

"What would it take to prevent him from being struck?" asked Bonet.

"Your patronage would go a long way toward soothing my restless mind," I said. "And if you have any influence over the Bishop, I would dearly love to see the Feast of Fools restored."

"I am a man of business, not religion," he said.

"In Toulouse, the men of business approach business with religious devotion, while the men of religion run the Church like a business," I said. "I have heard that you are not without influence in these matters. A younger brother who is a Benedictine, yes?"

"A monk at Saint Sernin," he said begrudgingly. "But Saint Sernin and Saint Étienne are two different worlds. The Bishop takes his orders from Rome, not from my brother."

"He doesn't take his orders from the order? Pity," I said. "All I can say then is that a church that is more favorably disposed to fools will find this fool more amenable to amending his sinful behavior."

"Will that be all, milord?" he said with a sneer.

"Now that you mention it, could you spare a bag of saw-dust?" I asked.

"What?"

"All this talk of silence put it in my mind," I said. "I have use for it, and you do provide it, do you not?"

"You are a strange man," he said.

"I have been known to act irrationally upon occasion," I admitted.

He went inside the mill, then returned a few minutes later with a sack about the size of a loaf of bread. He tossed it to me.

"How much?" I asked.

"Helping bend that pole is worth a bag of sawdust," he said. "Consider us even."

"For now," I said.

"For now," he agreed. "We will speak again."

I bowed and walked away. I knew without turning that he was watching me, so I did not give him the satisfaction of looking back. At least, not until I had passed out of his sight. Then I doubled back and kept watch on the sawmill, waiting to see what he would do next.

I did not have to wait for long. Bonet bustled out of the mill minutes later, barking orders over his shoulder. He was not worried about being followed, being one of those men who saw only his own path. I could have walked one step behind for the entire journey in safety, but I chose to honor my training and stay unobserved.

His path led east, and as I drifted along behind him, I saw him dwarfed by the bell tower of Saint Sernin directly ahead.

His brother. Of course.

There was a ring of fortified houses and towers surrounding the church, each a formidable display of new money. In the city, one was forced to confine one's building to the lot defined by one's neighbors, but in the bourg, construction was unfettered by such petty problems. Each house competed with the others in height and ornament, and it would not have surprised me in the least to see trebuchets installed on the roofs just in case the neighbors got feisty.

The church itself made the cathedral look like a dog-house. They had started with a mix of brick and stone when they built it, but must have run short of funds, for they continued with just brick after they reached the top of the doors. Nevertheless, the entrance was a grand double-arched affair, surmounted by a rose window that must have been twenty-five feet across.

North of the church were its cloisters, and it was to them that Bonet proceeded. I was forced to hang back, given the large open space surrounding them. As I watched, Pelardit joined me.

"Anyone meeting there would easily see us coming," I said. "No doubt that is why he chose that spot.

Pelardit nodded.

A monk emerged from the church and walked slowly toward the cloisters, head bowed, for all appearances deep in contemplation. From this distance, I could not make out his features, but he had the burly build of the belligerent Benedictine I had seen in the Borsella courtyard.

The two brothers walked together while engaging in a conversation that quickly became heated. I would have given a week's worth of drinking to know what transpired between them, but could not see any way of doing that undetected. Whatever the subject, it was clear that Bonet was the more agitated of the two. He began gesticulating angrily, pounding his right fist into his left palm several times. The monk responded by holding his palms up, placatingly. Bonet glowered at him, then made one brief statement, pointing at the monk's chest. The monk put his palms together and nodded. Bonet nodded back, then stormed off in our direction. The monk disappeared back into the church as the bell started to ring for noon prayers.

"I'll take the merchant, you take the monk," I murmured.

Pelardit nodded and slipped away.

I stepped into an alleyway to let Bonet pass, then back into the road behind him. But all he did was go back to the sawmill, where he spent most of the rest of the afternoon. Then he went home. So much for that.

I stopped by Jordan's house before going home. Martine was in her shop, adding a brocaded piece to a gown of light blue. She did not look pleased to see me.

"Your husband about?" I asked.

"Not yet," she said. "He was doing something for you, he said. That is what he's doing, isn't it?"

"It should be," I said. "Very well. Tell him I came by, if you would be so kind."

"Oh, and he said you all have an appointment with Oldric tomorrow afternoon."

"Excellent," I said, pleased. "We will rendezvous here late morning. Now, I was wondering if I could commission a small project from you."

"Me?" she said suspiciously. "What do you want me to do?"

I plunked down the bag of sawdust on her worktable. She looked inside, then back at me.

"What am I supposed to do with this?" she asked.

I told her, and she softened immediately. We agreed upon payment, and I left for home, just making it out of the city before vespers.

Helga and Claudia were already home, my wife supervising the girl as she stirred something in a pot on the brazier. Portia was asleep.

"That smells delicious," I said.

"Helga has profited from her time with the Borsella cook," said Claudia.

"It's a chicken stew," said Helga. "At least, it's supposed to be chicken stew. With fennel, parsley and almonds."

"I'm glad that somebody learned something useful today," I said.

"No luck with Bonet?" asked Claudia.

"I'm not sure," I said, and I told her about my encounter with him and his meeting with Vitalis.

"You're going to have quite the reputation as a ruffian before people even learn that you're a fool," commented Claudia. "Do you think the two brothers did in the third?"

"I don't know," I said. "Did either of you get any sense from the household that there was that kind of enmity among them?"

"Cook said that Milon always envied Bonet getting the family business," said Helga. "He always thought he had the best chance of making a go of it. He always talked about Bonet throwing money away on big, impractical machinery when there are plenty of men who will do the same thing for cheap."

"Sounds more like a reason for Milon to want Bonet dead rather than the other way around," I said. "What about the widow? Were you able to pay your respects?"

"Lute in one hand, baby in the other," said Claudia. "Béatrix was grateful for both. She held Portia while I played."

"How did she seem?"

"Very subdued," said Claudia. "I think that they have

been giving her something in her wine to soothe her. Vitalis came to visit for a while. He held her hand and prayed with her."

"When was that?"

"Late morning. He had to leave in a hurry when the bells sounded for noon prayers. I heard nothing useful from either of them."

"What about Evrard?"

"He waited upon his mistress for the most part," said Claudia.

"He did go out in the afternoon," volunteered Helga. "For about an hour. Told the cook he had an errand, but didn't say what it was."

"You didn't follow him?"

"I couldn't," she said, feeling my disappointment. "I was in the middle of helping the cook prepare the evening meal."

She finished stirring, and tasted the spoon.

"At least I got this recipe," she said, ladling the stew into wooden bowls and handing them around.

It was the best meal we had had in weeks.

After dinner, I moved the table against the wall.

"Rehearsal time," I said. "We have an audition tomorrow."

"With the Master of Revels?" asked Claudia.

"Oldric himself. Jordan came through. At least on that count."

"Hooray!" cried Helga. "It's fool season at last!"

"Only for the seasoned fools," I reminded her. "You are still an apprentice."

She picked up a sprig of dried parsley and tucked it behind her ear.

"I'm seasoned now," she declared defiantly. "Do I qualify?"

"That's good," said Claudia. "We should work that into the act somewhere."

"We will," I said. "In the meantime, let's work on our short routine."

About halfway through the juggling, it hit me. I grabbed the clubs as they came at me and put them down.

"What's wrong?" asked Claudia.

"If Vitalis was comforting the widow before dashing off to noon prayers, then who was Bonet talking to at the cloisters?" I asked.

"Oh," she said. "I should have thought of that."

"Damn those cowls," I muttered. "He had the same build. I just assumed it was Vitalis."

"So we have to find another burly monk at Saint Sernin," she said. "There can't be that many."

"Unless it was someone else disguising himself as a monk to meet with Bonet," chirped Helga.

"Wonderful," I said. "I followed the wrong man. I hope Pelardit learned something."

"Nothing to be done about it now," said Claudia. "Let's keep working."

We were doing our exercises at Jordan's the next morning when Pelardit arrived.

"What happened with the monk?" I asked him.

He dropped to a kneeling position with his hands together in prayer.

"How long?" I asked.

He stayed there, a statue. Then his eyes slowly shut and he toppled to the side, the praying hands making him a pillow.

"Nothing else?"

He shook his head.

"Well, I have some news for you," I said. "He may have had Vitalis's burliness, but that wasn't Vitalis."

Pelardit remained on the floor, but his eyes popped open in surprise.

"A burly monk, but not Vitalis?" repeated Jordan.

"Yes," I said. "Know of any?"

"I don't frequent Saint Sernin," he said. "Pelardit?"

The other fool shrugged.

"Pelardit attends the new Dalbade Church, and we're in the cathedral parish," explained Jordan. "So we go to the cathedral."

"When we bother going at all," said Martine. "Ever since that bishop took over, it's become a weekly haranguing for money."

"So, you don't go to Saint Sernin," I said. "Do you have any contacts there? Any sources of Benedictine gossip? It is the major church for the bourg. That makes it the church for half the consulate and all of the new wealth in Toulouse."

"Balthazar had some contact with them, I think," said Jordan uncertainly.

"A name, Fool, can you give me that?" I said, almost shouting.

"I wasn't preparing for all this," he whined. "Had I known that you were coming in hellbent on intrigue, I would have concealed myself in the baptismal font breathing through a hollow reed and eavesdropped for the last three months."

"Fine," I said, taking a deep breath. "What have you heard from the Cathars?"

"Now, them I know," he said confidently.

"And?" I prompted him.

"And they have all clammed up," he said. "They are terrified that this baile is going to whip up the church-fearing part of the population against them. They don't believe that anyone will believe them if they deny involvement in Milon Borsella's death, so they aren't saying anything."

"Do you think someone from the cult was involved?"

"No," he said. "But that doesn't mean I'm right."

"All right," I said. "Let's eat, then it's off to see Oldric."

We were in motley today, at long last, but in deference to the season kept ourselves covered by cloaks and left the makeup off until we reached the Château Narbonnais. Oldric had an office in the Count's palace. When we reached it, we waited in the hallway and quickly applied our whiteface. My wife and I added the finer details to each other's faces, finishing with the green diamonds below the eyes that had been my trademark but had been adopted by her. Helga, as an apprentice, was not in motley. We had left Portia with Martine, to the consternation of both.

A servant admitted us to the office. Oldric was seated behind a desk, a tall, thin graying man whose eyebrows sloped down to the sides, giving him a perpetually sad look. He was writing something, ignoring our entrance. When he was done, he blotted it, then looked up at us.

"Let's see it," he commanded.

We bowed, and Jordan stepped forward.

"Greetings, milord," he said. "The season of joy is nigh, and . . ."

"Just get to the entertainment without preamble," said Oldric.

"Very good, milord," said Jordan. "A song to begin. Pelardit, if you will?"

The other fool stepped forward with a tiny viol that he handed to his rotund partner, while keeping an oversized lute for himself. They made a fussy display of tuning the instruments, after which Jordan gave an elaborate flourish of his bow, nearly decapitating Pelardit who ducked just in time. As he straightened back up, the backswing of the bow hooked his ear and slammed his head into Jordan's shoulder. Jordan, oblivious, bowed back and forth, whipping Pelardit about helplessly. Finally, the fat fool stopped and looked at the silent one.

"You aren't playing," he complained.

Pelardit disentangled himself from the bow and nodded, then walked to the other side of Jordan, out of harm's way.

"Let's try that again," said Jordan.

He gave the elaborate flourish again while Pelardit watched it, smug in his safety. Then Jordan swooped the bow across the viol's strings, and on the upswing poked Pelardit in the eye. The latter dissolved in an exaggerated display of pain.

I glanced at Oldric. He was watching wordlessly without a trace of a smile.

"That's all very well and good," he said finally, interrupting as Pelardit was about to brain Jordan with his lute. "But we've seen it before, haven't we?"

"The Count hasn't," said Jordan.

"Nor will he, if that's all there is," said Oldric. "Let's see what these new people have brought along."

We had devised a routine involving a family on a pilgrimage, where the holy purpose becomes undermined by their squabbling with each other. As the father, I was provoked from slow burns of anger to outright flare-ups of rage, proving the desperate need for absolution. Ultimately, objects were thrown, which turned into a juggling match.

We performed it flawlessly, then launched into song, with Jordan and Pelardit accompanying on their instruments.

Oldric had yet to smile, but he didn't interrupt, and he nodded when we were done.

"I suppose that is acceptable," he said. "And the woman is pretty enough—the Count will like that. Let me see—Advent is over on Sunday, and Christmas is the Saturday after. We are expecting the Count to return in two days. He usually invites the more influential members of the community to dinner the Monday before Christmas. You will perform then."

We bowed.

"May I ask you something, milord?" I said.

He looked surprised, but indicated that I could speak.

"You know that the Feast of Fools has been banned from the Church," I said.

"I had heard," he said. "A foolish decision by the Pope. It shows fear."

"I agree entirely, milord," I said. "Would there be any way of bringing your influence to bear in changing this?"

"You must take up your quarrel with Rome, I'm afraid," he said.

"Then what would you say if we were to hold it in public instead?" I asked. "It would not be the same thing—we couldn't ape the Mass, for example—but it would be a glorious occasion. The Montaygon Square would do nicely."

"I shall discuss it with the Count," he said. "The Feast has always been a favorite of the citizens here. I would like to see it continue in some form. Now, there are musicians to hire, so I must get on with my day."

"Thank you, milord," we said in unison.

We bowed as we walked backwards out of his office. Not an easy thing to do, and we ended up jammed together in the doorway, finally falling over each other into the hall. I glanced back into the office as the door closed.

There. A smile. At last.

CHAPTER 6

L et us give thanks to the First Fool that you are pretty enough," I said to Claudia as we walked away.

"Just think, if I was slightly less pretty, we would have lost this chance," she said.

"You had it by an overwhelming margin, my love," I said, and Pelardit nodded emphatically.

"We did it!" chortled Jordan, grabbing the silent fool in a bear hug. "The Count's dinner at last!"

"We will rehearse at our place on Sunday when you come over," I said.

"No need to rehearse," scoffed Jordan. "Pelardit and I know this routine down to the last flick of an eyebrow."

"How long have you been doing it?" I asked.

"Oh, ten or eleven years," he said.

Pelardit stretched the air with his hands.

"Maybe longer," conceded Jordan.

"Then maybe that's why you haven't gotten into the Count's dinner before," I said. "They want fresh material."

"This routine never fails to get its laughs!" insisted Jordan indignantly.

"It failed with Oldric," I said.

"He's a professional stoneface," said Jordan. "Your lot

didn't make him laugh, either, and the material was new to him."

"True enough," I admitted. "Tell you what—let me see the whole routine on Sunday, and we'll discuss it then. You're not too old to learn some new tricks, are you?"

"I—well, no," he said. "Very well. Must keep an open mind, right?"

"Absolutely," I agreed cheerfully. "Now, let's all wash our whiteface off before we go back outside. We don't want to get fined by the baile for being too amusing before Advent is over."

"But I will only be prettier with my whiteface off," protested Claudia. "My throngs of admirers will be driven to a frenzy of adulation."

"I'll chance it," I said.

A few minutes later, the flour-chalk coatings had been scrubbed away, and five relatively normal people walked out of the château. Claudia caught me looking at her and smiled.

"I can't help it," I said. "That's the face I fell in love with."

"Can't blame you," commented Jordan jovially. "Although for the life of me, I can't see what she saw in you."

"It wasn't his face," she replied.

"We don't need to hear more," Jordan said hastily as Pelardit sternly clapped his hands over Helga's ears.

"'Twas his wit, his agile mind that inspired my passion," Claudia said airily.

"Of course, of course," said Jordan as Pelardit removed his hands from the giggling girl's ears.

"Plus he's a stallion in bed," concluded my wife, a lewd grin on her face. "What woman could resist?"

"None that I have ever met," I said.

"Oh, dear," said Jordan as Helga snickered. "We fall short of you in so many ways, don't we, Pelardit?"

Pelardit shook his head in disagreement.

"Right, back to work," I said. "Helga, back to Milon's house. Find out if Evrard has been seeing anyone on the outside."

"Yes, Papa," she said, and was off like a shot.

"Wait!" I called.

She skidded to a halt and ran back.

"Find out if anyone had been in Milon's office that morning before the Bishop arrived," I said.

"Yes, Papa," she said, and she took off again.

"Helga?" I called.

She stopped short, and trudged back to us.

"What?" she said.

"See if any of the servants noticed whether or not that desk drawer had been opened before Mascaron was in there."

"Fine," she snapped, and stood stock still.

"Well?" I said. "What are you waiting for?"

"Right," she said, and left at a moderate trot.

"On three," I said. "One, two. . ."

And Claudia, Jordan and I all shouted, "HELGA!"

Without turning, she made a gesture that would have been excessive even for Pelardit and continued without breaking stride.

"La Vache used to pull that one all the time when we were apprentices, remember?" Jordan said to Pelardit.

The latter nodded, rolling his eyes.

"You apprenticed with La Vache in Paris?" I asked. "When were you there?"

" '79 to '81," he said. "Pelardit came a year later after training at the Guildhall. Why, were you there?"

"Just for a few months at the end of '75," I said. "Then things got complicated, and it was a while before I came to the Guildhall. Marvelous juggler, La Vache."

"The best I've ever seen," agreed Jordan as Pelardit nodded.

"All right, the two of you keep listening around, see what you can find out about anyone who may have owed Milon."

"What about you?" asked Claudia.

"I should check in with Father Mascaron," I said. "He'll be wanting a report on my progress."

"So do we," said Claudia. "Let us know if you make any."

I thumbed my nose at them, and took the next street going east.

Father Mascaron was in his office, reading some correspondence. The door was open, but I knocked respectfully before entering. He waved me in.

"Payment first," he said, handing over a few pennies. "This will take you through Sunday."

"I don't have much worth paying for," I said, sitting down.

"I am paying for your efforts," he said. "If you retrieve that book, then I will pay extra for the results."

"Fair enough," I said. "Tell me about when you were in Milon's office."

"How did you know I was in there?"

"I have been making inquiries of the household," I said.

He sighed.

"While the Bishop was consoling the family, I slipped inside the office," he began.

"Had you ever been there before?"

"Yes, with the Bishop," he said. "On church business."

"But it's not your parish," I said.

"The Bishop of Toulouse—" he started in lofty tones.

"Has no say in the bourg," I said. "The Benedictines are not beholden to him, are they?"

"No, not at all," he admitted. "They are rather smug about it, too."

"Nothing like a little Christian competition," I said. "Milon's office was unlocked?"

"Yes," he said.

"And the desk as well?"

"Yes," he said. "That surprised me. And then to realize that the book was gone—I went through the entire desk, everything on it, looking for it. Then the household descended upon me, and things became—embarrassing."

"I hear you have scrawny legs," I said, and was pleased at his look of chagrin. "Why did you think the book would still be there?"

"Why wouldn't it be?" he asked.

"It could have been on Milon's body," I said.

"It wasn't," he said with certainty.

"How do you know that?"

"I have my sources within the guard," he said. "I was waiting at the Palace of Justice when they brought Milon's body in. I administered the last rites, which was more than . . ."

He caught himself. It was a brief flash of anger, still sharp even though its target was three days dead.

"More than he deserved?" I said. "Don't we all deserve the same treatment from God's house?"

"I ask His forgiveness," he said. "I have no sympathy for—blackguards like Milon Borsella."

"Understandable," I said. "So, under the cover of seeing to his final needs, you searched his body."

"Yes."

"Resourceful. You're in the wrong profession," I said.

He glared.

"Or maybe the right profession," I continued. "One that gives you such ready access to the dead. My friends who have gone into grave-robbing would be envious that you can get the same results with so little work. And you didn't find the key on him, either?"

"None of his keys were there," he said. "They must have been stolen by the man who killed him."

"Very like, very like," I said. "Has anyone attempted to get money from you or the Bishop in exchange for the book?"

"Not yet," he said.

"He must be waiting for the dust to settle before he makes his next move," I said. "Tell me, you are familiar with the brothers of Saint Sernin, aren't you?"

"The monks?" he said in surprise. "Yes, of course. Why do you ask?"

"The problem with a book of secret debtors is that they are secret," I said. "But why is a debt something to be concealed? It's a normal part of doing business in Toulouse or anywhere else. That's why Milon prospered."

"But the monks?"

"I am thinking that there must be other men in the same position as your bishop," I said. "Men who were not supposed to be incurring debts of this nature or size, who perhaps have pledged properties that were entrusted to the church, not for their personal frivolities."

"That's not why . . ." he protested.

I held my hand up.

"I am sure that the Bishop incurred this embarrassing debt for the best of reasons," I said. "Although . . ." I paused as if a thought had just struck me. "If there was a particular weakness that he had succumbed to, for which he was forced to borrow these sums, then someone else privy to that information might have had the idea to steal the book from Milon."

"If that was the case, and I assure you that it is not," said Mascaron calmly, "then I would have no need of you. Nor do I trust you enough to discuss such matters."

"But there are none to discuss, so there is no point to discussing my trustworthiness," I said. "I am wounded, I must say. Have you heard anything of what I know or saw from anyone other than me? I have been the very soul of discretion, and for just a penny a day."

"You must be waiting for the dust to settle," he said.

"You know, you really are in the wrong profession," I said. "You might have made an adequate fool."

"A lost opportunity," he said. "I will take that as a compliment. I don't think that you are particularly suited for the priesthood."

"And I will take that as a compliment," I said. "Now, let's say that I am right about the other debtors being from the religious community. Who among the monks of Saint Sernin would be a likely candidate for secret depravity in your opinion?"

"It's a ridiculous idea," he said.

"Those are frequently the kind I have," I said. "But I don't have the same idealistic view of abbeys that you might. What about Vitalis Borsella?"

"Vitalis kill his brother? Absurd," said Father Mascaron.

"Brothers do kill brothers," I noted. "The very first murder was a fratricide. But you knew that."

"Why Vitalis?"

"He has a temper," I said. "But you knew that as well."

"His anger at me was justifiable," said the priest. "I have already forgiven him."

"But Milon wouldn't be able to forgive him now, would he?"

"I don't think this is a profitable direction for you—"

"There is another monk there, a bruiser like Vitalis. Know him?"

"A— Do you mean Brother Donatus?"

"I don't know anyone's name. Is the abbey known for its muscular approach to God? As opposed to the scrawny-legged entry requirements of the cathedral?"

"Apart from Vitalis, only Donatus would meet that description," said Mascaron. "A former soldier who turned to silent contemplation after returning safely from Crusade."

"What else do you know about him?"

"Why do you consider him a suspect?" asked Mascaron.

"I saw him with someone else I don't trust," I said. "But it's still speculative."

"I know of nothing to tarnish his reputation," said Mascaron.

"Then his vice must be a great and secret one," I said, getting to my feet. "Good. Something to look into."

"It sounds like a fruitless effort to me," grumbled the priest. "The abbey of Saint Sernin is hardly lacking for funds. All the new money is in the bourg nowadays. As soon as anyone makes their fortune, they grab a large piece of land near the abbey and heave up some new monstrosity of a house. On Sundays, they make a show of who can give the most to the collection while wearing the gaudiest outfit. It's all done in the worst of taste."

"And none of it comes to the cathedral," I said. "Too bad. You come from old money, don't you?"

"I do," he said. "But I did not join the priesthood because I was the least-favored son, if that's what you're thinking."

"Why did you join?"

"For the love of Our Savior," he said. "Why did you become a fool?"

"Because I wasn't particularly suited for the priesthood," I said. "My efforts on your behalf continue through the end of Advent, then it's back to my fooling."

"It's hard to distinguish them at times," muttered the priest.

I waved and walked out of his office. There was no one praying in the cathedral, so I took advantage of the solitude to throw my civilian clothes on over my motley. Then I turned toward the altar and knelt, praying to the First Fool to forgive me for my use of His house as a changing room. I didn't consider it to be a great sin. After all, was I not His guest?

And on the list of sins in my life, this one would barely raise an angel's eyebrow.

So, Brother Donatus. He did not seem given to silent contemplation when I saw him with Bonet. I wondered what their connection was. And what it meant.

The sun was nearing the horizon, so I walked quickly to Milon's house to pick up Helga. Just as I arrived, I saw Bonet Borsella coming through the gate. I stepped into a doorway to let him pass. I did not want him to make the connection between Helga and me just yet, as that would have ended her access to the household.

She emerged a few minutes later with, to my delight, Claudia and Portia. Claudia had her lute slung behind her. She spotted me immediately and smiled.

"Well met, husband," she said as they came up to me. "Take this."

Portia reached for me, and I put her up on my shoulders. Tiny hands seized my hair and held on tight.

"How goes your life of crime?" asked my wife.

"With the Church on my side, how can I fail?" I asked.

I recounted my conversation with Father Mascaron as we walked home.

"Do you know what strikes me as odd?" I asked when I was done.

"What?" asked Claudia.

"If he didn't have Milon's keys, what made him think he could get into the locked drawer in Milon's desk? Why would he even try?"

"Desperation," guessed Claudia.

"Maybe they taught him to pick locks when he trained for the priesthood," said Helga.

"No, we do that," I said. "Which reminds me, I have to add that to your studies soon."

"Oh, good," she said, brightening.

"What strikes me as odd," said Claudia, "was that Mascaron was trying to discourage you from looking into the monks of Saint Sernin."

"Which means that may be the best place to dig up some dirt on the Bishop," I said. "Now, report, Apprentice."

"Evrard has been wooing a maidservant from the Château Bazacle named Audrica," she said. "Cook thinks they'll be getting married soon. Cook thinks this is because they have to get married soon, or there will be a little boy running about with no official father but who looks a lot like Evrard."

"Anything about Milon's office?"

"No one was allowed in there if Milon wasn't there," she said. "He was very particular about that. The maid would go in first thing in the morning with him and do a quick dust and sweep while he watched."

"Was it locked when he wasn't there?"

"Yes, but Evrard had a key to the door."

"Which makes him more powerful than Béatrix in the household," I mused.

"Except that she would have had access to Milon's keys at night," said Claudia. "They did share a bed, after all. At least, during those hours of the night after he finally came home from his carousing. She could have made copies of his keys. All it would take is some wax for making an impression and a pliable locksmith."

"Then that could also be said for any number of prostitutes in this city, if his reputation was deserved," I said. "I wonder if he went to anyone in particular. What about his business? Who's taking care of it?"

"Big brother Bonet," said Claudia. "He came in to pick up the ledgers, and has started collecting the overdue debts. Béatrix wanted to send Evrard as her representative, but Bonet wouldn't hear of it."

"What about a will?" I asked.

"There is one," she said. "I don't know all of the details, but apparently the bulk of the estate goes to the family, with some going to local hospitals."

"He took care of the widow at the last," I said. "Something to be said for that."

"The funeral is tomorrow," said Claudia. "At Saint Sernin."

"I think we should attend," I said.

The next morning, we left Helga at the Borsella house where she had promised to help the cook with the funeral meal.

"We shouldn't let her spend too much time there," remarked Claudia as we walked to Saint Sernin. "She is supposed to be apprenticing to a jester, not to a cook. We don't want to lose her to the wrong profession."

"Gossiping with household cooks is an essential skill for any fool," I said. "It brings you information and sustenance at the same time. Here we are, my love. Let's not be seen arriving together."

I hung back as she went through the front doors, then followed her inside. She was already at the front, paying respects to the widow, who was seated between Bonet and her four children.

I took a moment to glance around. I had forgotten what an enormous place this was, with its brick and stone columns shooting fifty feet or more to the vaulted ceiling. The capitals were sculpted into scenes of demons devouring sinners, while the floors were of intricate traces of black and white tiles. Mosaics of Our Savior looked down at us from above the altar, glittering with gold leaf.

New money had done well for the Benedictines.

The monks were filing in, a cloud of black-garbed silence, taking their seats on benches on either side of the altar. I spotted Vitalis on the right, and on the left was the man I had mistaken for him, Brother Donatus, his cowl back so that his face was finally visible. A former soldier, Father Mascaron had said, and I could see that in the firm set of his jaw, a muscular hardness in his arms that made him stand out among identically clad men. There was a sense of precision in his movements that suggested absolute control. While Vitalis looked like he could be a brute in a fight, my money would have been on Donatus should they ever be matched. I had the feeling that he would methodically destroy his opponent in a matter of seconds.

Not that monks ever fight, of course.

Most of the household servants were present, seated behind the family with Evrard at the head. Claudia took a seat on the bench just behind them, while I joined the sparse group of people that had come to see the moneylender buried.

"Small crowd," I remarked to the man sitting next to me.

"Not the most popular of men," he said. "Most of us are here to make sure they bury him deep enough."

The abbot stepped forward and led us through the mass most economically. When it was over, Bonet stepped up to the coffin with two other men who wore the chains of office indicating that they were also consuls, while Vitalis, Donatus and another monk came to the opposite side. They lifted the coffin onto their shoulders, and exited through a smaller set of double doors on the right. We followed.

The cemetery was behind the church. Milon was lowered into his grave. Then his family, one by one, shoveled dirt onto the coffin.

The abbot spoke to the family first, patting the heads of the children and speaking softly to them. None of them were crying, I noticed. The consuls followed, particularly attentive to Bonet. Then came the monks, many of whom embraced Vitalis, who was standing by his brother.

When Brother Donatus reached the Borsellas, he too embraced Vitalis, then clasped hands with Bonet. I caught a glimpse of something passing between them in the handshake, then Donatus moved on, his hands disappearing into the sleeves of his robe.

If Bonet was surprised to see me come up, he concealed it well. I merely muttered, "My condolences, Senhors," and moved on. Perhaps he was more surprised that that was all that I did. But he concealed that as well.

With Vitalis remaining with the family, there was only one burly monk to distinguish from the pack. As the monks followed a path that took them to their dormitorium, I trotted over to the side to watch the black parade. Sure enough, one monk detached himself from the line and drifted through the cloisters and walked west. It was Donatus.

Monks are even easier to follow than self-important merchants. The cowls block their peripheral vision. I could have walked at his side unobserved. While juggling cats. Reluctant cats, ones who are naturally averse to being juggled. But lacking any such flying felines, I chose to tail him from a distance.

He passed by the Fountain of Gatlepa, another display of too much money set by a crossroads. His path seemed to be taking him toward Saint Pierre des Cuisines, and I wondered if he would pass the tanner's pit where our recently buried moneylender had met his end. But the monk skirted the tanners' quarter by a wide margin, passing on the other side of the brick church instead.

He turned north once he reached the river, passing through the Bazacle Gate. A meeting at the sawmill, I guessed this time, but he fooled me again, marching steadily like the soldier he had been, veering from the river road only when the Château Bazacle came into view.

This was more of a small castle than a château, not deigning to partake of the bourg life. It had not existed when I was first in Toulouse. I had the vague memory that this had been grazing land for cattle then, but I couldn't be sure. It had been built very high very fast, that much was clear, probably with money so new that it made the new money in the bourg seem ancient. It was surrounded by walls that rose about twenty feet, and described an immense octagon in shape. They were built of sandstone, and looked impressive, but were maybe a foot thick. Not that I could get through a foot of stone, despite my wife's general assessment of my thick skull and its abilities, but they were not built to withstand a lengthy assault by a decent trebuchet.

And it was to this fortress that the monk made his pilgrimage. He pounded on the wooden gates, then said something to whoever was on guard. The gates swung open to admit him, then closed behind him. And at that point, it didn't matter how well I had followed him, because there was no way I was going to get through those gates without a good-sized battering ram and a good-sized army to go with it. I waited a couple of hours for him to come back out, then I gave up and walked back to the Bazacle Gate.

There was a cluster of inns and taverns just inside the wall, catering to the trade and pilgrimage coming from the north as well as the mill workers and tanners who worked at this end of town. I decided to scout out a few to see where we might be able to pick up some work for our jesterial side. At least, that's what I tell myself every time I go into a tavern.

There was one called the Tanners' Pit that sounded like it had some life to it despite its being midday. I walked in to find a decent crowd, many of them tanners if the smell was anything to go by. A competing stench rose from a foul-smelling fish stew simmering in a cauldron at the end of the bar. Not wanting to eat anything that swam near where the tanneries discharged, I settled for some bread, some cheese, and a pitcher of ale, and carried the lot over to a bench by the wall.

Tanning is a profession that allows for drinking, I observed. You prepare the hides, shove them into the pits, weight them down with stones, and leave them to their fates. When they are ready, you pull them out again. I suppose there is more to it than that, but here were all the tanners, pouring wine down their gullets as if the constant exposure to tannins had made each of them into a wineskin. I spotted the one who had pulled Milon from his pit, downing one cup after another, regaling his comrades with tales of his night in chains, the experience becoming more absurdly ghastly with each recounting.

Having upon occasion spent considerably longer periods of time in considerably worse prisons, I was less than impressed with his story, but it was not the right time for me to be competitive.

The door opened and Armand staggered in. It was clear that this was not his first stop of the day. He looked blearily about the room, then lurched up to the bar and pounded his fist on it.

"A pitcher of ale!" he bellowed.

"Let's see your coin first," said the barkeep.

Armand dug into his pouch, then started patting his clothes.

"I'm out," he said. "Give me one on credit."

"Not a chance," said the barkeep.

"Anyone buy a decent Christian a drink?" shouted Armand to the assembly.

"If we ever see one, we might," someone shouted back, and the room erupted into laughter.

Armand looked back and forth, trying to locate the offending voice. Then his gaze came to rest on the tanner whose stories had been interrupted by the drunk's entrance.

"You," muttered Armand. "You should buy me a week's drinks. Wasn't for me, they might still think you did Milon."

"No one thinks that," said the barkeep, and there was a chorus of agreement.

"I owe you nothing," said the tanner. "I am an innocent man, and I hope to Christ will always be so. It was my faith that protected me."

"Your faith," sneered Armand. "If they couldn't go chasing after Cathars, they would have made you swing for him, faith and all, then sold your guts for relics."

"And you think you're such a God-fearing man, selling out the Cathars like that," spat another man. "What have they ever done to you?"

"I know what I saw, and I did my duty," muttered Armand.

"You saw nothing!" shouted the man. "You're a fool, and your drunken ramblings are going to get people killed!"

"Maybe you're one of them Cathars," snarled Armand. "Maybe I should be telling the baile about you."

"You son of a bitch!" roared the man, hurling himself on him.

Armand, despite being drunk, put up a pretty good fight, and the two of them were quickly on the floor, rolling around and pummeling each other. Others joined in, whether out of principle or for the love of fighting, I could not say. The barkeep came around the bar with a club in his hand and started laying about the group, finally reaching the original parties. He grabbed Armand by the scruff of his coat and pulled him up.

"You. Out," he growled. "You are banished from my establishment until you show me something round and shiny to assuage my humors. Now, go!"

He shoved Armand out the door, then turned his attentions to the other man.

"Pay your bill now," he said. "All of what you owe me. I don't want them throwing you into prison owing me money."

"I'll settle that bastard," said the man.

"You'll settle with me first," said the barkeep. "When Judgment Day comes, there will be a great reckoning, but until then, you pay the gods of ale and wine or you will never see Paradise."

The man handed him some coins.

"Te absolvo," intoned the barkeep. "Go and sin no more. Go scrape a hide, or something."

That seemed to be a general signal for the tanners to return to work. I finished my meal and joined the crowd filing out.

Armand was standing in the middle of the road, a lost look in his eyes. I walked over to him.

"No money left?" I asked.

"What's it to you?" he asked me.

"Just surprised, that's all," I said. "I would have thought Bonet had paid you enough to last you for a while."

"What do you know about that?" he whispered, looking around hurriedly.

"I know lots of things," I said. "I would like to know more. Maybe you could help me with that, and I could help you with a few coins. How much did he pay you?"

"Not enough," said Armand. "I owed people. I still owe people."

"Shall we go somewhere quiet to talk?"

He looked at me cagily, then glanced around.

"I talk better when I'm drinking," he said.

"We could be brothers, we are so alike in that regard," I said. "Where?"

"Not here, not now," he said. "Too close to the sawmill. You know the Miller's Wheel?"

"In Comminges."

"That's the one. Meet me there after sunset."

Another night in Pelardit's room in exchange for this, I thought.

"I'll be there," I said.

He walked away.

I found Jordan in the tavern near his house. He waved when he saw me, still in high spirits from our successful audition of the previous day.

"Cat's piss for my friend," he shouted, pounding on the table.

The barkeep ladled out a healthy dose of ale into a mug and handed it to me. I took it over to Jordan's table and tapped it against his.

"To our wives, who are pretty enough," I toasted.

"To our wives, who deserve better than us but are too good to complain about it much," he said. "How go your inquiries?"

"I ask questions, and receive more questions in response," I said. "What do you know of the Château Bazacle?"

"Belongs to Arnaut Guilabert," he said. "He built it almost ten years ago."

"Who is he?"

"The richest man in town outside of the Count," he said. "Everything that goes into the Bazacle mills or comes out of them, he gets a piece. And the tolls from the river traffic, and the northern road."

"And no title to go with the money?"

"He was a miller's son," said Jordan. "But he saw the future."

"A seer?"

"A speculator," explained Jordan. "When the millers banded together to build the Bazacle dam, they sold shares in the mills to raise the funds. People who owned the shares could resell them if they needed money, or thought they could make a profit. Guilabert started buying up as many as he could, and when the project was finally completed, he was in control of the whole thing."

"And it was that profitable?"

"Beyond what anyone but Guilabert dreamed, which is why he was able to buy so much."

"How rich is he?"

"You saw all of the new money maisons around Saint Sernin? Each bigger than the next? He decided that they were all mere trifles, and that the only way to show everyone up was to build a castle instead."

"Too much to dust if you ask me," I said.

"He didn't ask you," he said. "He doesn't ask anyone anything anymore. He tells them."

"Is he connected to the Borsellas in any way?"

"Well, he was a consul for a couple of years, so he knows Bonet," said Jordan. "Guilabert basically bought his way into the consulate. I guess he was bored just collecting money all day, but he found consul matters even more boring, so he didn't run again. I'm sorry he didn't."

"Why?"

"Oh, with the last election, the bourg seized the balance of power, and they've been dragging Toulouse from one war to another ever since. They're taking over the countryside, town by town. Guilabert thought that was a waste of time and money. So did the Count, for that matter, but the consuls ignored him. Why the interest in Bazacle?"

I told him about Brother Donatus, and he frowned.

"I can't think of any likely reason for it," he said. "It could simply be a matter of private religious instruction. Rich men still want to get into Heaven at the end of the day. But it bothers me, no question. Donatus, Donatus—there's something about that name. Former soldier, you said?"

"That's what Mascaron told me."

"Balthazar mentioned him once," said Jordan. "But I can't remember about what."

"If you think of it, let me know," I said. "All right, I'm off."

"Regards to the wife," he said.

"You may see her before I do," I said. "I'm going drinking with Armand tonight. The Miller's Wheel after sundown."

"Don't get competitive," he warned. "He's a consummate consumer. Do you think he might let his guard down?"

"He seems to want to," I said.

"May I come along?" he asked. "You haven't had me doing anything other than collect gossip. I'll be your watchdog."

"I accept," I said, pleased.

"Let me just tell my just pretty enough for everyday purposes wife that I am galloping off into danger," he said. "That way, when I safely return, her relief will turn into amorous appreciation."

"See? You've discovered the hidden benefits of being a true jester," I said.

Martine was in her shop. I stayed outside and waved while Jordan went up to her, his face serious. He knelt before her and took her hand between his own. She immediately looked worried. He whispered something in her ear and she looked horrified. He swept her into his arms, kissed her long and hard, then came back to me.

"Come, my friend," he said in stentorian tones. "Let us go bravely into the night, though it be our last!"

We marched away.

"I might have oversold it," he said, glancing over his shoulder.

"Maybe a little," I said.

"We have a fair amount of time until sundown," he said, looking at the sky. "Good. We can walk off the last drink in readiness for the next. Frankly, I could use the exercise if I'm going to be keeping up with you. How would you like a tour of the old money?"

"It would be very useful," I said.

He took me around the town, pointing to fortunes kept and fortunes lost, towers built and towers crumbling.

"Do you think the bishopric could be shifted over to Saint Sernin?" I asked as we passed the cathedral.

"That would be up to Rome, I suppose," he said. "But the counts of Toulouse have always prayed at the cathedral, even though the abbey has that fancy entrance on the side just for their personal use. The current bishop does enjoy the current count's favor, so that should keep him safe for a while."

"Except from us," I said. "The sun is starting to set. Let's get to our meeting place."

We came up along the riverside, downstream from the Comminges quarter. There was a line of waterwheels on the bank by us, turning without purpose now that the millers had left for the day, spinning like toys for a giant child. Except for one, which was stuck in position, shifting slightly back and forth.

"Looks like that one got jammed," observed Jordan. "Something must have drifted into the sluice."

I glanced where he was pointing, then took off at a dead run.

A man was floating facedown in the sluice, his head caught

under one of the blades of the waterwheel, which kept mashing it into the riverbed over and over.

"Call for the guards!" I shouted to Jordan.

I jumped into the river and waded into the sluice. He was heavy, his clothing waterlogged, and as soon as I pulled him back, the freed wheel started turning again, the river loosed around me. I felt my boots skidding along the muddy bottom as the current pushed me toward the wheel, the wooden blades slicing through the water ahead of me. I tried to heave him onto the bank, but he slid back against me. I lost my footing, and suddenly found myself sliding toward the wheel.

A hand clamped down on my shoulder, grabbing a handful of cloak.

"Hold on!" shouted Jordan. Other men were clambering down the bank, holding ropes which they looped around the body. One of them was kind enough to throw an end to me, and he and Jordan managed to haul me up.

"No guards when you need them," Jordan gasped, more winded than I was. "Found some mill workers."

"I don't find it in my heart to be choosy at such moments," I said.

They succeeded in getting the other man out of the sluice and rolled him onto his back. The waterwheel had played havoc with his face and head, but there was enough left to recognize him.

"It's Armand," said one of the mill workers.

"Always knew he'd come to a bad end," said another.

"Cathars got him, I'll bet," said a third.

"Let us go bravely into the night," muttered Jordan, "though it be our last."

CHAPTER 7

We stood in a line, our backs against the city wall while Calvet the baile stood over Armand's body, deep in thought.

"His usual method of investigation involves a dark, damp cell," muttered Jordan. "Moldy bread and filthy water."

"One night won't kill you," I said.

"The moment he asks who found the body, we're done for," he moaned.

"Who found him?" asked Calvet.

"We did," I said as Jordan winced.

He stood in front of us, giving me a thorough once-over while barely giving Jordan a second glance.

"I know this fool," he said to me, "but I don't know you."

"Tan Pierre," I said. "Also a jester, recently arrived."

"How did you happen to find Armand?" he asked.

"We were walking around, preparing the routines that we are to perform at the Count's dinner on Monday," I said. "As we—"

"The Count?" he interjected.

"Count Raimon the Sixth?" I explained. "Count of Toulouse and about thirty other places, I can't remember them all. Why, do you know him?"

"Of course," he barked. "Don't be impertinent!"

"My apologies, it's what I do," I said. "Anyhow, we were walking along the river, and Jordan said, 'That's curious,' and I said, 'What's curious?' Didn't I say that, Jordan?"

"Those exact words," said Jordan. "Or words to that effect. Certainly, you have the gist of it."

"And he said, 'That waterwheel—something's jamming it,' and I went to take a closer look and saw that man in the sluice, so I did what any good Christian would do and jumped in to help him."

"Jumping into a mill-run is quite dangerous," said Calvet. "Near suicidal, in fact."

"Well, I know that now," I said. "But I am not from here. I didn't think, I just jumped, which is a bad habit of mine. I'm only sorry that I couldn't save him, but my guess is he was murdered before he went into the river, so there wouldn't have been anything I could have done, anyway."

"Aha, so you knew he was murdered!" he pounced. "You admit it."

"Well, it was the knife wound in his back that clued me in," I said. "Surely you noticed it."

He started, and glanced nervously back at the body, which was still laid out faceup. He signaled the guards, and they rolled Armand over. Sure enough, there was a single wound in the middle of his back. Calvet squatted down and examined it.

"Knife, possibly a dagger," he pronounced. "A single, quick thrust. The killer knew what he was about."

He turned back to us.

"You saw that while he was still in the water?" he asked. "The blood was washed away."

"I saw it as they dragged him out," I said.

"You have sharp eyes, Senhor Jester," he said. "Did you know him?"

"I have seen him around," I said. "He apparently liked taverns. I like them, too."

Calvet looked upriver toward the Daurade Bridge. The arches between the supports were each filled by more waterwheels, except for the two outer ones.

"If he was killed by the riverbanks and fell in, he could have passed under the bridge without hitting any of the mills there," he mused. "He could even have been dumped into one of the canals flowing into the Garonne. And there is no telling when it happened. Senhor Jordan, you can vouch for this fool's veracity?"

"As I would my own," said Jordan smoothly.

"Where do you live?" Calvet asked me.

"In Saint Cyprien, at the house of Honoret."

"You mentioned the Count's dinner thinking that would influence me to let you go," said Calvet, softly so that only the two of us could hear him.

"Yes," I said.

"It worked," he said. "I expect both of you at the assizes in the morning. You are free to go."

We bowed and left.

"Those damn Cathars will pay," I heard him say as we walked away.

"I'm afraid they will," said Jordan.

"He could be right about them," I said.

"No," he said, shaking his head.

"Why not?" I argued. "Armand was the one who started stirring up trouble against them. They have ample reason for wanting him to shut up."

"But the Cathars are not violent," he protested. "Not the ones I know."

"Do you know them all?"

"No, of course not. But Armand was a loudmouthed,

foulmouthed drunk. There's plenty who might get mad enough to do him in on any given day."

"Actually, I saw him get into a brawl with a bunch of tanners earlier today."

"There you go," said Jordan. "And that's a profession prone to proficiency with knives. A quick thrust through untanned flesh would be nothing for one of them."

"Point taken," I said. "Reach out to your Cathar contacts. Find out if anyone knows anything."

We came to the gate to the bridge.

"I appreciate your help with the baile," I said.

"Self-interest," he grinned. "I didn't want to spend the night shackled to you. One wife is enough."

"Right. See you at the assizes."

"Such an annoying inconvenience," he sighed.

"On the contrary, a tremendous boon," I said.

"How do you figure that?"

"Why, consider what it will do for our notoriety," I said. "All of Toulouse will know that there are new jesters in town, teaming up with you and Pelardit. The scandal will make us the most wanted entertainers for miles around. We couldn't do better for ourselves if we led a parade down the Grande Rue."

"When you put it that way—Huzzah! Our fortunes are made!" he cheered unenthusiastically.

We thumbed our noses at each other and parted ways. Vespers was sounding in the distance as I passed through the Daurade Gate, the last person to be waved through before it closed. I glanced toward the mills by the Ile de Tounis, and saw the guards lifting Armand's body onto their wagon. The wheels, indifferent to the spectacle, kept turning.

"Your clothes are wet," observed Helga when I climbed into our home.

"I aimed for the bridge, and missed," I said, closing the trapdoor behind me.

"You don't look any drunker than usual," said Claudia, eyeing me critically.

I sat on a chair and stuck my legs straight out.

"Boots," I said to Helga.

She stood at my right foot and tugged mightily until the boot abruptly came free, sending her into a series of fast backward somersaults until she fetched up against the wall in a headstand, which she held for a moment before toppling slowly back onto the floor.

"Not bad," I said. "Try it again, only play up the effort more."

She picked herself up, stood at my left foot and pointed at it sternly.

"You're coming off," she growled. She spat into her hands and wrapped her arms around my foot like she was hanging onto a ship's mast in a tempest. She braced her feet and arched her body away. When the boot finally came off, the resulting tangle of arms, legs and boot spun across the floor in a blur. The resulting collision of Helga and wall had me fearing for the wall.

"I think that should be the maximum speed," suggested Claudia. "Any faster, and she'll end up crashing into the street below. Dinner's almost ready."

"I'll go get my clothes off," I said, heading into our room.

"I could help you," offered Claudia slyly.

"Later for that," I said.

Portia was asleep. I kissed her nose, and she smiled without waking. I stripped my clothes off and hung them on a line we had strung across the room for costumes. I found myself shivering, and I don't think it was from the cold.

I grabbed my motley and put it on. Hell, if a jester couldn't wear motley in his own home, then there was no point in being one, Advent be damned.

"Why, there's a fool here," exclaimed Claudia when I came in.

"A hungry one," I said.

"Feed us the gossip of the day, and we will feed you in turn," said Claudia.

"There's been another murder," I said.

"You have my attention already," she said. "Who?"

"Armand," I said, and I told her what had passed.

"Sounds like he had served his purpose, and was no longer of use," she said.

"Harsh treatment for mere uselessness," I said. "Who among us shall escape?"

"He gave his testimony and put the hounds of the law on the wrong scent," she said. "If he lived, sooner or later he would have ended up bragging about how he pulled the wool over the baile's eyes."

"That makes Bonet the likeliest suspect," I said. "With Brother Donatus as my second choice."

"There is one more obvious explanation," she said. "The one you are refusing to talk about."

"Why bother?" I said. "I knew you would bring it up."

"Someone saw you talking to him, and put two and two together," she said. "They killed him to keep you from finding out what he knew."

"But for all they know, he had already told me," I said.

"In which case, they may be coming after you next," she said.

"So I should constantly be on the lookout for someone trying to kill me"

"There's a thought," she said, placing a bowl of stew in front of me.

"As opposed to my normal behavior, which consists of constantly being on the lookout for someone trying to kill me," I said.

"Which may be me if you persist in being contrary," she said. "Just be a little more wary than normal."

"I will not be contrary, I'll persist in being wary, for my wife is very scary," I sang.

"Not scary, Theo," she snapped. "Scared. There are two men dead, and I'd rather you not be the third. Or the fourth, or any number in single, double or triple digits."

"Only if you grow old along with me," I said, taking her hand.

"Some days, I already have," she said.

"Speaking of widows, how was Béatrix today?" I asked, clumsily changing topics.

"She managed very well," said Claudia. "The usual swarm of locusts came for the funeral feast. The Borsella brothers stayed by her throughout. When the crowd left, Bonet mentioned something about going over the books with her tomorrow, then left. Vitalis stayed on to pray with her."

"Bonet didn't leave right away," said Helga.

"He didn't?" I asked as Claudia looked at her in surprise.

"I was watching Evrard while I was serving the guests," said Helga. "When Bonet left Béatrix, Evrard slipped out a moment after. I followed him. Bonet was standing by Milon's office. Evrard unlocked it, and they went inside together and closed the door after."

"What did you hear?"

"As a faithful servant of the household, it would have been wrong for me to listen at keyholes," she said haughtily.

"But you're not a faithful servant of the household," I reminded her. "You're an apprentice fool."

"Which is why I listened at the keyhole," she said. "Bonet said, 'Any luck?' and Evrard said, 'None. I've turned the place upside down. It isn't here, it isn't anywhere in the house.'"

"They're working together," said Claudia. "And they're still looking for the book."

"And they haven't found it yet," I said. "Unless one of them is lying to the other. Good work, girl."

"I wasn't finished," she said indignantly.

"There's more?"

"Bonet said, 'We have to find it before he does. Are you sure no one came in that night?' And Evrard said, 'I can't be certain. You know my situation.' And Bonet said, 'A fine time to be visiting your little maid.' And Evrard said, 'How was I to know your brother was going to get himself killed? For all we know, he may have had it on him then, and we're just pissing in the dark.' What do men mean when they say that?"

"I'll tell you when you're older," I said. "Was there anything else?"

"Evrard asked him, 'What about the ledgers? Any luck there?' And Bonet said, 'I report to one man, and you're not him. You just worry about your end of it.' And Evrard was silent after that. Then I heard them coming to the door, and I ran back to my duties. The end."

She bowed.

"Bonet is another man's lackey," marveled Claudia. "He's a consul, and a wealthy man, yet beholden to someone else."

"But to whom?" I asked. "Who is more powerful than him?"

"The Count?" guessed Helga.

"Not from what I hear," I said. "The consuls are more powerful than the Count in Toulouse, even though he reaps the benefits."

"That may be true of the consulate as a whole," said Claudia. "But not of any single member."

"So, I keep looking into Bonet's business," I said. "Frustrating. With every day, we stray further from our mission to unseat the Bishop."

"You could always just kill him and blame the Cathars," said Claudia. "It seems to be all the rage in Toulouse these days."

"Where is your sense of style, woman?" I asked. "Much too crude. Besides, I like the Cathars."

"Better not brag about that," she said.

I had a much better seat at the inquest this time. Odd, with all of the violent deaths I have seen, or for that matter inflicted, that I would be called to testify about one that I had nothing to do with. At least, I hoped I had nothing to do with. I looked at Armand, lying in the open coffin in the center of the room, and hoped he would have the decency to just lie there without saying anything troublesome.

Smaller crowd for this inquest, which was a bit of a disappointment. Portia had been fussy, so Claudia stayed behind to pay her some added attention. I had sent Helga, to her chagrin, back to the Borsella house. Jordan, of course, was seated next to me, and Pelardit had managed to find a seat where he could face us. He amused himself by catching our eyes with bizarre expressions, snapping back to normality if anyone else glanced in his direction. It was all we could do not to respond in kind, curse him.

The halberds thumped, and Calvet came in.

"You," he said, pointing at me. "Take the oath."

I did.

"State your name."

"I am Tan Pierre, a new jester in town," I said. "Head of the Fool Family, recently come to Toulouse to entertain everyone from the Count on down for the joyous Christmas season. Reasonable rates, no gathering too small."

"Long name," he said, and there were a few chuckles from the assemblage.

Damn, he got a laugh at my expense.

"You found the deceased," he said.

"Yes, Senhor. I was walking with my brother fool, Jordan, along the riverbank, planning the festivities for our performance before the Count at the dinner he's throwing on Monday. Jordan pointed out that something was jammed into one of the waterwheels. On closer look, I saw a man there, and jumped into the mill-run to try and save him. Alas, my efforts, though valiant, were to no avail."

"You observed the stab wound in his back."

"I did, Senhor, when he was dragged out of the river."

"Had you seen him at any other time?"

"Well, in here, of course, when he testified. And I've seen him in taverns around town a couple of times."

"What about yesterday?"

"I saw him earlier at a tavern up near the Bazacle Gate," I said. "There was some kind of fight, but I was not a part of it."

"Who was?"

"I don't know their names, Senhor, but there were many people fighting. I was more intent on keeping my cup from spilling than from figuring out who was doing what to whom."

"Is that all you know about this?"

"It is, Senhor, and I swear to it," I said.

Yes, it was perjury. Yes, one more black mark in the divine ledger that will add up to damnation when my time comes. There was no rectifying that balance in the long run, so no point in fretting over it now.

"You may stand down," said Calvet.

"I'm not sure how to do that," I said. "May I sit down instead?"

"Just move out of my way," he said, and then he pointed at Jordan. "You."

Jordan testified as I had. The men who helped us came next, then the barkeep from the Tanners' Pit, who managed to see all of his regular customers in the brawl, yet recognize none.

"It was confusing," he protested.

The baile sighed.

No one brought up my brief conversation with the deceased outside the tavern. That was lucky.

When all the testimony had been taken, Calvet looked around the room, his visage stern.

"This man lost his life because he had the courage to testify against the Cathar scourge," he said. "I suspect that he was killed by the same man who killed Milon Borsella, but there may be a larger Cathar conspiracy at hand. I call upon every true Christian to come forward if he knows aught of such things."

The room was either filled with false Christianity or true ignorance. In any case, no one came forward.

"Death by person or persons unknown," pronounced the baile. "Get out of here. All of you."

Pelardit joined us as we walked out of the château and back through the Porte Narbonnaise. As we came into the city, I noticed a small, dark object flying toward the general vicinity of my head. I reached up and caught it, then dropped it like a hot chestnut, which was exactly what it was.

"Where did he go?" I demanded.

"He scurried around the corner," said Jordan. "Like a rat in a cassock."

"Father Mascaron is stealing some of my moves," I said, rubbing my palm where the chestnut had stung it. "I had better go see what he wants."

He was in his office, looking expectantly at the door. I held up the chestnut, which had cooled down.

"I should not have enjoyed that, but I did," he said, smirking like a naughty child. "No doubt it will cause consternation when I bring it up in confession."

"I suppose that makes us even," I said. "I didn't see you at the inquest."

"I didn't want to give that wastrel any more importance in death than he had in life," he said. "I take it that your testimony omitted our little arrangement?"

"No one asked me about it, so I didn't say anything about it," I said.

"And if they did ask?"

"We'll never know," I said. "What do you think about his death?"

"I think that it's worth looking into," he said. "Don't you?"

"It could be coincidental," I said.

"Neither of us is fool enough to believe that," he said, his earlier humor vanishing like a dove under a conjurer's silk. "Find out who he was working for, and you will find who killed Borsella and stole his book."

"As far as my time permits," I said. "Remember, my services will be subject to demands of the season after tomorrow."

"I shall have to find a way of extending Advent," he said.

"I will trade you for bringing back the Feast of Fools," I replied. "What about Saint Sernin?"

"Not worth pursuing," he said, shaking his head. "Armand is your best lead."

"Then I shall follow the dead man," I said. "I doubt that he will prove a fast quarry."

I started to leave.

"One more thing," he called.

"Yes?"

"I hope that we may count on seeing you at Mass tomorrow," he said piously.

"I understand the Count will be here," I said. "If it's good enough for him, I suppose it's good enough for a fool."

When I came out, I saw Claudia playing with Portia in front of the cathedral. I swooped in and snatched my daughter up, throwing her into the air and catching her as she shrieked in terrified delight.

"Hello, my loves," I said as I nuzzled her, then kissed my wife. "How did you know to find me here?"

"I ran into Pelardit," said Claudia. "He told me."

"He told you? How?"

"Well, in his own way," she said. "Either he was saying that you were at the cathedral speaking to Father Mascaron, or that the city was being attacked by fish."

"And you came here first?"

"No, I checked the river," she admitted. "Everything appears safe—for now. But we should be careful crossing the bridge."

I hoisted Portia onto my shoulders, and we walked toward the Grand Rue as I filled Claudia in.

"He might be right about Armand," she said when I was done.

"Which is why I am going to look more closely into Saint Sernin," I said.

A normal wife might have questioned me at this point, but Claudia simply looked thoughtful.

"Let me see if I can follow the twisted path your mind has taken," she said. "We want to bring down the Bishop. Father Mascaron is the protector of the Bishop. Therefore, since he wants you to concentrate your efforts on Armand and drop your pursuit of the abbey, the abbey must hold something that would present a threat to the Bishop if revealed. So we must do the exact opposite of what Father Mascaron wishes to achieve our goal."

"Thank you for putting my instincts into a form that almost sounds like they make sense," I said.

"Years of practice," she said, squeezing my hand. "Now, say Father Mascaron has been on to us from the start. Maybe he knows of the true purpose of the Fools' Guild, maybe he butted horns with Balthazar in the past and finds our recent arrival suspicious."

"All right. Where does that lead you?"

"What if he doesn't even care about this mysterious book? What if there was something else in Milon's office that he was searching for?"

"But the whole fight between the Borsella brothers and him was over the missing book."

"The brothers brought it up, not Mascaron," she said. "At least according to what Helga heard. He could have then used it as a plausible diversion, and a way of finding out what you were doing."

"Dear me. Deception on both sides of our arrangement. What is the world coming to?"

"A bad end," she said. "At least, if those fish have something to say about it. Keep an eye on the river if you value your life."

"I need one of those Benedictine outfits," I said. "We don't have any, do we?"

"Alas, our cassocks only come in brown," she said. "But I will bet that Pelardit has one."

"Good thought. I'll—"

A horseman came galloping down the road, shouting, "Count Raimon approaches. Get yourselves out to greet him! They'll be throwing gold!"

"Pennies, more the like," I said. "Shall we?"

"Let's. Portia should enjoy it immensely. All those magnificent horses."

There was a gradual flow of people trudging toward the Château Narbonnais including, I noticed, a goodly number of the town prostitutes, vying to show the brightest colors in their wardrobes or the most skin under them.

There was a group of musicians hastily setting up outside the outer walls of the château. I handed Portia to her mother and went over to the leader.

"I'm Tan Pierre, the new fool," I said.

"I'm Egidius, the old trumpeter," he said. "Nice to meet you."

"Could you use an extra player?"

"Depends," said Egidius as he puffed air through a long trumpet. "What do you play?"

"Lute, flute, and tabor, mostly," I said.

"First two are useless outside," he said. "But if you are possessed of any rhythm at all, you'd be more proficient than half of the idiots I'm fielding today. Grab that side drum. Bartolomeo will tell you what to do."

I picked it up and joined Bartolomeo, a cheerful stripling strapped to a drum as large as he was.

"Right, it's fanfares, naturally," he said after I introduced myself. "Trumpets go blat blat ba blatty blat, we go tum tum terrumti tumtitty tum, whole thing repeats twice, then a big long roll when the Count dismounts and if you could just reach over and whack this cymbal at the moment he kisses the ground, that would be terrific. Otherwise, just improvise off my beat."

"Easy enough," I said. "How far away is he?"

"About that far," he said, pointing.

A squad of armed horsemen was coming around the tip of a copse of oaks that swallowed the road as it went south.

"Give them a good marching beat," directed Egidius.

"Right, that's a barrump bump bump bumpity bump bump bump and repeat," said Bartolomeo.

He counted off the beat, and I launched into my barrumps, throwing the occasional roll or flourish just to keep it interesting.

"Good!" shouted Bartolomeo, pounding both sides of his drum energetically.

"Better start cheering," a guard advised the crowd. "Louder you are, the more you get."

They got very loud very quickly, driven by hope and greed. I could see Portia perched atop Claudia's shoulders, bouncing gleefully as she saw the horses approach.

I had met the current Raimon during his younger years and mine. He didn't make much of an impression, especially since his father, Raimon the Fifth, tended to dominate whatever room he was in. The older man was ill at the time but concealed it by booming heartily at the king who I served, commending him on his holy pilgrimage and his part in the Third Crusade. Raimon the Fifth was a Crusader himself, a warrior and a leader of warriors. The future Sixth was a skinny, unimposing man in his thirties, finally with a wife he liked to all appearances. The two sat off to one side, gazing adoringly into each other's eyes. She was the daughter of the King of Cyprus, so there were political implications to the marriage, but it appeared to be a love match all the same.

It was she that Raimon, as count, would repudiate two years later so he could marry Jeanne, the sister of Richard the Lionhearted, to stave off the latter's claims to Toulouse. So much for love matches.

And now there was a new wife, Jeanne having departed this earth after producing an heir, which is all she was supposed to do. Raimon the Sixth, combining the instincts of a savvy politician with the rutting desires of a middle-aged goat, negotiated with King Pedro II of Aragon for one of his spare younger sisters, which the latter hoarded and traded with all the shrewdness of a Venetian merchant. Her name was Éléonor, and she had just come of age for marriage earlier in the year.

The Count and his wife rode side by side on matching white stallions. He had filled out since I last saw him, the stoutness of prosperity settling about his midsection. His glances toward his young wife were proud and proprietary, her dark beauty and youth on display, showing all the world that he was still in command of his potency. His hair was suspiciously black, tied into a long braid that bounced behind him. He rode easily, flicking pennies through the air to the crowd with a hand encased in dark red leather, the plumes in his cap dyed to match. The crowd scrambled to grab the coins, trampling and clawing each other in their frenzy while he watched them in amusement like a man at a cockfight.

A tall, gaunt man stood before the outer gates to the Château Narbonnais, wearing dark blue robes trimmed with ermine, a chain of silver coins across his chest. The Bishop joined him in full regalia, solemnly blessing the Count and Countess as they approached.

"Who's that with the Bishop?" I asked Bartolomeo.

"Peire Roger," he replied. "He's the viguier. Manages the Count's holdings when he's making the rounds. Here comes the fanfare—get ready!"

The trumpets sounded, more or less together, and we followed with our pounding. This continued until the viguier stepped forward and took the reins of the Count's stallion. Raimon stepped down, and we launched into a long roll.

"All hail Raimon the Sixth!" shouted the viguier. "Count of Toulouse, Duke of Narbonne, Marquis of Provence, conqueror of Carcassonne . . ."

The list went on for a while. My arms were starting to ache from the constant drum roll.

A silk square was placed before the Count. He knelt upon it and kissed the Bishop's ring, then brought his lips to the ground.

"Now!" cried Bartolomeo, and we struck a pair of cymbals that were suspended from a wooden frame.

The Count stood and plucked his girlish bride down from her mount as she simpered and beamed with all the arrogance of one who thinks she was the first to discover sex and was the sole possessor of its secrets. He took her arm, and they strolled through the gates into the Château, the Bishop and the viguier following, the rest of the entourage behind them.

Oldric, the Master of Revels, came up to Egidius and gave him a small pouch of coins.

"Good show, everyone," he said. He spotted me among the musicians and waved. "Senhor Fool, I see that you have other talents."

"Since I cannot pay tribute to the Count in my own fashion until Monday, I must do what I can to laud him in the meantime," I said.

"Well spoken," said Oldric. "We will see you at noon on Monday."

I bowed.

Egidius tossed me a penny.

"Next time we're shorthanded, we'll send for you," he said.

"I enjoyed it," I said, shaking my arms to get them loose again.

The crowd, its enthusiasm abating, trudged back into the city to resume their lives. Claudia came over with Portia, and I introduced them to the musicians.

"How did you do?" she asked.

I held up my penny. She held up three.

"The Count threw them quite hard," she said. "I really had to move to keep them from hitting Portia."

"All my hard work, and you made three times as much just standing there," I grumbled.

"Where to now, good husband?"

"To find Pelardit," I said. "I want to borrow his Benedictine outfit. It's time I paid a more thorough visit to Saint Sernin."

CHAPTER 8

Pelardit opened his door and stared at us in surprise. Portia pointed to him and said, "Ba!" He looked for a moment as if he was considering what she had just said very deeply, his brow furrowed, his hand on his chin. Then he looked back at her, opened his mouth as if he was about to reply. Then he shrugged, thought better of it, and waved us in.

"I guess 'Ba' is the password," I said.

He nodded seriously.

"You should change it," advised Claudia. "If Portia knows it, she'll be telling everybody."

He nodded again, then turned to me, a question in his eyes.

"I was wondering if you have something in a black cassock, size tall," I said.

He turned to his shelves of props and costumes, studied them for a moment, then snapped his fingers and swept his hand across until it came to rest on something black. He held it up. It was a Cluniac robe, complete with cowl.

"A loan for a few days, and I promise to wash it before I return it," I said.

He tossed it to me.

I practiced getting it on and off quickly. The rope at the waist presented a problem, but I figured out a way of knotting

it that would pass quick muster while still able to come un-
done in a moment.

"You're a little taller than him, so your boots can be seen,"
observed Claudia. "I think some of them wore boots, so that
isn't necessarily a problem."

"Unless someone is using my boots to identify me," I said.
"I'll have to get my own robe in the future. Did you make this
one yourself?"

Pelardit shook his head, swelled up and held out his arms
to indicate a fat man, then shifted to a feminine demeanor
and mimed sewing frantically.

"Martine," I said.

He nodded.

"When there's time, I shall commission her," I said. "Now,
I'm off to join some monks."

I folded the costume up neatly and placed it in my pack.
There was ample space, as my juggling clubs were back in our
rooms. One more day of Advent, then I could be a jester
again. I couldn't wait. Prancing about as a normal person for
so long was getting on my nerves.

"What exactly is your plan?" asked my wife as we walked
to Saint Sernin.

"Plan is too exalted a word for what I am doing," I said. "I
want to get a closer look at a pair of burly monks when they
are not on public display."

"Do you expect them to speak to you?"

"People speak to you when you poke them with sticks," I
said. "Even if it's only to tell you to stop."

"This is why I never let you play with hornets' nests," she
sighed.

The monks were performing the Office of None as I slipped into Saint Sernin. I had the black robe in my pack, but I doubted that I could safely mingle with them in mid-song. Nor could I fake my way through the entire service, although I have always liked the 127th Psalm, especially the part that says, "It is vain for you to rise up early." Any sacred admonition to sleep in is fine by me.

They sang the Kyrie in two parts, the harmonies echoing off the gilded mosaics and the intricate stone carvings, soaring to the vaulted ceilings high above us, though still far below God's Heaven. I waited patiently for the concluding hymn, *Rerum Deus tenax vigor,* and joined my voice with theirs. It felt good to sing at full throat, letting all my cares and troubles slip away in a moment of pure music offered to Our Savior.

But the hymn ended, and I was back to my earthly pursuits, scanning the crowd of monks for Vitalis and Donatus. Here inside the church the monks kept their heads uncovered, so I would not make the same error of confusing the two. The question was which one to approach, and how to do it.

I was about to flip a coin when they made the choice for me. It was time for afternoon chores. Donatus headed toward the dormitorium with most of the brothers, but Vitalis separated from the pack and went out the south entrance. I followed him.

He went to the cemetery behind the church and stood before the grave of his brother, his hands clasped before him, his lips moving rapidly. Suddenly, he threw himself prostrate on the grave, his hands clawing at the dirt, crying.

I came up to the grave and knelt beside him.

"Is there anything I may do, Senhor?" I asked softly.

"Go away," he moaned, his sobs muffled by the newly turned earth.

"I am sorry for your loss, Senhor," I said. "But this display is unseemly. Your brother is in Heaven now, as you should know better than anyone."

"I know better than anyone that he is not," he said, the tears subsiding somewhat. "And I shall follow him to Hell."

"That is no talk for a man of God," I scolded him. "I am not the one to tell you that, being a layman, but if you suffer for the loss of a brother, surely you have this entire community of brothers to sustain you."

He looked at me, and a bleaker expression I have not seen on a man in many a year.

"There is no comfort for the damned," he whispered.

"If I cannot console you, let me at least get you to your feet," I said, holding my hand out.

He took it, and let me pull him up. He wiped his eyes with the sleeve of his robe.

"I must look an idiot," he said.

"You looked like a man struck down by grief," I said. "No one seeing you would condemn you for that."

"Do I know you, Senhor?" he asked. "I think that I have seen you before."

"I happened by chance to be at the funeral service," I said. "I am a recent arrival to Toulouse, and wanted to see Saint Sernin, and be in the presence of the holy relics. I heard you have most of Saint George and a decent chunk of Saint James."

"A pilgrim, then?"

"No, I have come to stay, I hope. My family and I have taken up rooms in Saint Cyprien, but we may move into town someday. I have been going to services at different churches just to compare."

"You came to my brother's funeral," he said, an odd expression appearing on his face. "You stood in line with the others. I remember now."

"Yes, you were standing with your other brother, of course," I said. "It's easy to see the kinship despite the different professions. Why, when I saw the two of you in the cloisters the other day . . ."

"The cloisters?" he interrupted. "When was this?"

"Oh, three or four days ago, just before midday," I said carelessly. "I happened to be passing by and saw the two of you walking together."

"You are mistaken," he said.

"Well, I don't know why I would be," I said. "How many monks can there be with your build? I have seen wrestlers who seem scrawny by comparison."

"Donatus," he muttered.

"Excuse me?"

"It must have been Brother Donatus," he said. "But why was he with my brother?"

"I'm confused, Senhor. Are you saying that there is another such muscular monk?"

"Yes," he said. "His name is Donatus."

"My word, two giants in black robes," I said. "You should consider putting on wrestling exhibitions and charging admission. You could raise a considerable sum for the order."

"But why would he and my brother . . . well, it's of no importance," he said.

"So which of you did I see going into that big fortress of a château after the funeral?"

Large men tend to be florid, so when they turn pale, it is quite a dramatic effect.

"Donatus went to Bazacle?" he whispered, the fear written

across his face. "What was he doing there? What could he possibly want?"

"Senhor, what has caused this distress?" I asked. "It was not my intention to bring you bad news, yet I cannot see how this counts as news at all. What would you have me do to ease your troubled mind?"

He shook me off.

"My apologies," he said. "This is none of your concern, and you are blameless. In fact, it is good that you have told me. You must excuse me, Senhor . . . I don't even know your name."

"Tan Pierre, Brother Vitalis," I said. "You see? I already knew your name."

"Then, Senhor Pierre, go with God," he said, crossing himself.

He left me standing by his brother's grave and rushed away.

"I'll do my best," I called after him.

I waited until he was about to round the corner of the church, then I quickly followed. He was walking briskly toward the dormitorium, pounding his fist into his palm. I wondered if I had started a fight between him and Donatus. Maybe charging admission wouldn't have been such a bad idea after all.

There were other monks filing in and out of the building. I watched for a few minutes. Whatever sent Vitalis there so quickly, it did not bring about any disorder in the order. Brother Donatus emerged from a side door, helping another monk carry a cauldron of stew from the kitchen to wherever they dined.

After a while, Brother Vitalis came out, an expression of relief on his face. He joined the other monks going in for their evening meal. And that was that.

Claudia and Portia were waiting for me in front of Saint Sernin.

"How did the stick-poking go?" she asked.

"I'm not sure," I said. "I terrified Brother Vitalis, but only for a while. Something happened when he went inside that eased his fears."

"He must have talked to someone," she said.

"Maybe," I said. "I wish I could have gone in there. Robe or no robe, it was too risky with all of those monks wandering around."

"Let's go home," she said. "Soon, we get to put on our motley and makeup again."

"We've done all we can as normal people," I said. "Let's put our real talents to work."

We went to Mass at the cathedral that Sunday. The Count and Countess sat in the front pew, their entourage clustered about, chattering away during the service.

Yet beyond this privileged group, the cathedral held the same sparse crowd that had been there the previous week. The place was as dilapidated as before, the Bishop as threadbare, the choir as dissonant. I found the chattering by the Count's followers offensive, even for one as disrespectful of the Church as I am.

The Bishop approached the lectern for the sermon, quivering slightly as he glanced in the direction of the Count's party. The noise from that direction continued unabated. The Bishop placed his hands on either side of the lectern and swallowed hard.

"Two dead men!" he suddenly bellowed.

The shout echoed around the cathedral. There was absolute silence when the reverberations died out.

"Good opening," I muttered to Claudia.

"Two dead men!" he thundered again, more confident in the attentiveness of his flock. "One struck down in the dark, the other stabbed in full daylight. Both left to float in waters contaminated by the foul stench of iniquity. Two men murdered, and have the murderers been brought to justice? No!"

He looked directly at the Count, who was leaning back in the pew, his chin resting on one fist.

"And if they are caught, will there be justice for them to be brought to?" asked the Bishop. "For there cannot be justice where there is no order, and there cannot be order where there is sin. And there is sin everywhere. Everywhere that shuns Our Savior, that provides the shadows for evil to slink about, tolerated, protected, even encouraged. Why preach of Hellfire to come after death when it is already here among us, and no one lifts a finger to quench it? When Jews are openly employed in our government, and heretics meet freely in public and mock true Christians with their very openness? How long will the word of Christ, as sent through his chosen ministers on earth, be ignored?"

Father Mascaron sat quietly off to one side, nodding in approval.

"The Holy Season is upon us," continued the Bishop. "Advent ends, and the Twelve Days are nigh. A joyous season, and a festive one. Yet every man, woman and child who lifts a glass, who eats a pie, who gives a token to a beloved in the name of this season, yet does nothing to eradicate sin in the name of He who died for all of our sins spits upon the Cross with every sip taken, curses the name of the Holy Mother with every bite, and takes another step toward the eternal fire with every trinket bestowed. I say there will be no more toleration. There cannot be forgiveness of sinners until there is acknowledgment of sin. There cannot be peace until those who fight in Satan's name shall be sent to join their cold master, once and for all."

He glowered about the room, trembling in righteous indignation.

"Peace be with you, amen," he said, and subsided.

"And a happy Christmas to us all," muttered Claudia.

The closing hymn was subdued and blessedly short.

We stood and waited for the Count and his people to leave, then slipped into line behind them. I was interested to see what his reaction to the sermon would be. The Bishop stood by the door, gnawing on his lower lip as the Count approached him. Finally, the two Raimons stood face to face.

"Small crowd today," said the Count. "Disappointing. I would want to see that sermon reach more people."

"Yes, well . . ." stammered the Bishop.

"Maybe you could take your message to the streets," suggested the Count.

"That would hardly seem appropriate," said the Bishop. "If they will not come to God's house—"

"Jesus had no house to preach in," said the Count. "Just a big pile of dirt to stand on, and He did all right, didn't He?"

"Um, yes, but—"

"So, Raimon, we're still on for dinner tomorrow, aren't we?" the Count finished blithely.

"Of course," said the Bishop.

"Good," said the Count, clapping him on the shoulder, almost knocking his miter off in the process. "See you then."

He walked out, pursued by his entourage, most of whom did not even acknowledge the Bishop as they passed by.

"I like this count," commented Helga.

We drifted back to the end of the line to let the rest of the congregation exit. The Bishop was still distracted by the Count's behavior by the time we reached him.

"Good sermon, Your Holiness," I said as I shook his hand.

He looked at me blankly, then recognized me.

"Yes, thank you," he said. "Good to see you again."

"I'm sorry that my own search for sinners on your behalf has yet to bear fruit," I said softly.

He glanced quickly at Father Mascaron, who was standing impassively at his shoulder, then back at me.

"I appreciate your efforts," he said. "There is only so much one can do."

"Oh, but I haven't given up looking," I said. "I am a very bloodhound when it comes to sniffing out evil. I promise you that I will not rest until the threat has been extirpated."

"Thank you again," he mumbled. "Blessings upon your head."

"Thank you," I said, and we walked out of the cathedral and into the daylight.

"Poke, poke, poke," said Claudia. "What were you doing just then?"

"Letting Mascaron and his master know that I am still on the hunt, whether they want me to be or not," I said. "Let's hurry. We have a dinner to prepare and fools to rehearse."

We had laid in provisions the day before, so we sent Helga running up and down the ladder, fetching buckets of water from the common well.

"I'm still thinking about what you told me about Vitalis," said Claudia as she chopped up onions for the stew. "He was concerned about Donatus meeting his brother, and about

Donatus going to Bazacle, yet as far as you can tell, he didn't confront Donatus."

"No, Donatus came out earlier, doing his chores, and Vitalis came out later. I heard no fighting, no arguing from outside, not that that's conclusive."

"Then Vitalis must have gone into the dormitorium to check with someone else," said Claudia. "And this other monk was able to allay his concerns."

"Which narrows it down to the rest of the chapter, including the abbot," I said. "Too many to investigate."

"What if it wasn't a person at all?" suggested Claudia. "What if it was a thing, something he doesn't want found?"

"Especially by Donatus," I speculated. "And he went in to check that it was still safe, and it was. Hence the relief. You think it might be this missing book of his brother's?"

"He had access to the house," said Claudia. "And we know that he had some falling out with Milon because Martine saw them."

"Interesting," I said. "Maybe I can sneak into the dormitorium while they are all at prayer. I can put Pelardit's robe to the test."

"That's poking at the hornet's nest from the inside," she said. "If you're caught, they'll hang you as a common thief."

"Then I won't do it until after our performance before the Count," I said. "I would hate to miss a paying job because I was dead. Now, let's say Vitalis has the book. Does it follow that he killed his brother to get it?"

She threw the onions into the cauldron, then took a pair of skinned rabbits and started chopping them up.

"It doesn't mean that he did, and it doesn't mean that he didn't," she said finally.

"Wonderfully elucidating, my love," I said.

"It would account for his behavior at the grave," she pointed out. "Maybe . . ."

There was a clattering from the steps below.

"We will continue this later," I said. "Let's greet our guests."

She added the hacked rabbits to the stew, then went to wash the blood from her hands.

A hand clutching a full wineskin popped up through the trapdoor, followed by the rest of Pelardit.

"You are welcome, and your offering even more so," I said. "Happy end of Advent."

He grinned and stripped off his cloak to reveal his motley, much of it in mesclati, a blue and red weave that was a local specialty. He looked at my civilian clothes and wagged his finger at me sternly.

"Give me a chance," I said. "I just got back from church and have been cooking."

"Watching me cook, mostly," corrected Claudia, emerging from our room in her motley. "We don't have any makeup made up yet, but we are rehearsing at home, so that should be all right. Hello, Pelardit."

He bowed until his nose was touching his shin, then daintily kissed her hand like a bird pecking at its feed. Helga came up with another bucket of water.

"I think I have brought enough to start our own lake," she said. "May I stop now? Oh, what lovely motley!"

Pelardit stuck a pose, and turned gracefully so that she could see all of it.

"I hope I make jester in full here," she said. "I would love to have motley like that."

"Prospects are good, Apprentice," I said. "Why, we've been here over a week and haven't been run out of town yet."

"You can't be run out of town when you're already out of town," wheezed Jordan as he pulled himself up. He had a sack of instruments and props in his free hand, which explained the effort. "Sorry I'm late. The baile has his men everywhere, and I couldn't take ten steps without one of them making me empty my bag for them."

His two boys scampered up behind him, followed by Martine.

"Right, you get into your motley," said Claudia to me. "Welcome, everyone."

I changed quickly and came back to the sarcastic applause of the room. I made my most dignified bow, and toppled over into a pair of somersaults leading to a flip.

"You can still do that at your age?" marveled Jordan.

"Could you do it at any age?" I asked.

"Many years and many pounds ago," he sighed, putting his arm around his wife. "Then I married a wonderful cook."

"Well, I'm sure that my efforts are not up to Martine's level," said Claudia. "But we have nuts and dried plums and apricots, and a rabbit stew for the main course."

"Just some fruit and bread for me, if you please," said Martine.

"Are you all right?" asked Claudia.

"A touch of stomach," said Martine apologetically. "It generally afflicts me this time of year."

"I could steep some rue if you like," said Claudia.

"That would be most kind," said Martine.

We sat down to a proper dinner, with Jordan, Claudia and me trading stories while Pelardit caused Helga and the two boys fits of giggling with various bits of sleight of hand and some droll expressions.

We finished with some lemon cakes that we had purchased

from a local baker, and downed some more wine, feeling fat and happy.

"Well, as loath as I am to work after all that, we must," I said. "Let's see that routine again."

The two fools grabbed their instruments.

"Pelardit, a song if you will," started Jordan, and they began tuning their instruments.

"Stop there," I said. "The joke of that routine is that every time Pelardit gets his string in tune with yours, yours slips to a different tone, right?"

"Right," said Jordan.

"If that's going to work, Pelardit has to get angrier," I said. "He has to be on the verge of braining you with his instrument when you launch into the song."

"I'm not sure . . ." said Jordan, but Pelardit nodded immediately and gestured for him to start over.

The timing was better, and Pelardit's rage more extreme. Helga and the boys started to laugh.

"Better," I said. "Now, Pelardit—you have to let the anger build until you are about to lose control, but then the music starts and soothes you. Let yourself get completely carried away by it each time."

He nodded, and when Jordan began bowing away, Pelardit's face slipped into swooning, swaying rapture.

"That's good," I said. "And when that's interrupted by him poking you—"

Jordan's bow jabbed at the unsuspecting fool's eye, and he flew into silent paroxysms of rage and pain.

"That's all well and good for him," said Jordan, "but where are my laughs?"

"Yours come from being completely oblivious to what he is going through, even though you're the cause of it," I explained.

"We have to increase the danger level, so that every time he seeks revenge, you do something to thwart it while remaining blissfully ignorant. It's all in the timing—"

We worked on several bits of physical business, culminating with a now-homicidal Pelardit swinging his lute at Jordan's head right as the other ducked to retrieve his fallen bow, the momentum of the swing carrying the instrument around to strike the mute fool in the back of his head. He stared for a moment, then his eyes rolled upward and he sagged into the straightening body of Jordan.

"Never could handle his wine," sighed Jordan, looking fondly at his partner.

"Not bad," I said. "Don't anticipate the reactions as much. Let's run the whole thing."

And they did, even getting a laugh from Martine, a sound so novel that both of them broke character to look at her in amazement.

"It was funny," she protested. "I'm supposed to laugh when it's funny."

"But I told you that years ago," fumed Jordan in mock marital exasperation. "It took you this long to get the joke?"

"It's funny, now," she said. "Well done, both of you."

"I agree," I said. "Let's work on the group material."

And we rehearsed, and we drank, and rehearsed a little more, and drank a great deal more.

"I must stop," said Jordan finally. "Wine, my bulk, and those steps are not a combination conducive to a long life on unbroken limbs."

"Very well," I said. "I think we can keep things lively at the Count's dinner. They want us there at noon."

"Then noon it shall be," declared Jordan. "Any other foolish business to discuss? Any luck on your investigation?"

"No progress," I said. "On the bright side, no one else has been killed for a couple of days."

"That we know of," added Claudia. "Sometimes the bodies don't turn up immediately."

"Please, not in front of the children," said Martine hastily, looking pale.

"Forgive me," said Claudia. "The wine has loosened my tongue, which was never that tight to begin with."

"We had better be off before we get locked out of the city," said Jordan. "Thank you for the meal."

Pelardit bowed low again. This time, his head hit the floor, and his legs kicked straight up so that he was upside down, balanced on his cap and bells.

"No hands," I observed. "Impressive."

He rolled into a standing position, then pulled off the cap and showed it to me. Concealed within it was a small board, flat on top and curved to fit his head on the other side.

"That's cheating!" accused Helga.

"There's nothing wrong with cheating if it gets a laugh," I said, tossing Pelardit's cap back. "Until tomorrow, fellow fools."

They clattered down the stairs safely, and we cleared the dishes. I pulled out a large ceramic bowl and a pestle and put them on the table in front of Helga.

"First batch of the new season," I said, handing her some chunks of chalk.

She started grinding them down, white powder floating up gently about her. I tossed our flour onto the table, and she mixed it in.

"How is that?" she asked.

I licked my forefinger, dipped it into the mixture, and

dabbed it on her nose as she wrinkled it. It left a bright, white streak.

"Advent is over," I said. "Here we come."

We had found a woman who would take care of Portia for the day, so we were able to travel somewhat lighter than normal. We met up with Jordan and Pelardit at the Porte Narbonnaise. A small crowd of children were scampering around them, and when the three of us appeared, their excitement knew no bounds.

"A fool family!" "Look, a girl fool!" and "Give us candy!" rang out in rapid succession.

I pulled a handful of sweets from my pouch, juggled three, then tossed them all to the children.

"We'll be in Montaygon Square on Christmas Day after Mass," I announced. "Come see us."

"We will!" they promised.

"And bring your parents," added Jordan.

"And your aunts and uncles," called Claudia.

"And your single male cousins!" shouted Helga.

I smacked her gently on her head, which sent it wobbling back and forth as the children laughed.

Through the Porte Romaine into the interior courtyard, with the Grand Tower looming over all. The Grande Chambre, where the dinner was to be held, was to our left. Pit fires were already burning, with sides of cattle being roasted in them while men collected the drippings in long-handled pans and poured them back over everything. My stomach began rumbling immediately.

"They will feed us," said Jordan confidently.

"When we have earned it," I reminded him.

He sighed.

We saw the musicians who I had supplemented before trooping into a side door. Bartolomeo was bringing up the rear, pushing a cart full of percussion ahead of him. He looked at me for a moment, then shouted, "Our drummer is a fool! Look!"

Egidius came out and greeted us.

"Made it here at last, have you?" he said to Jordan. "About time. You doing the old duet bit with Pelardit?"

"New and improved," said Jordan. "It may even be funny now."

"Then that would be a Christmas miracle, wouldn't it?" jibed Egidius.

"Right up there with you getting through a fanfare without cracking a note," agreed Jordan.

"Now, now, let's be friends," I said. "If all goes well, we may be finding work for each other."

"I hear you're the new Balthazar," said Egidius.

"No one could replace him," I said modestly. "I merely hope to do his memory justice."

We entered the Grande Chambre, which had already been set up for the feast. Tapestries and drapes of escarlati interwoven with silver threads adorned the walls. A single table seating about twenty faced us from the end, while two long tables extended out on either side, leaving the central space available for food to be served and jesters to caper about.

Oldric came up to us.

"Timely, and thank you for that," he said. "You lot up there."

He pointed to a balcony, and the musicians groaned and started lugging their instruments up the steps.

"Now, fools, could there be juggling and quiet amusements until after the main course?" he asked.

"Of course, Senhor," I said.

"Have your wife juggling closest to the Count," he suggested. "Though not so close as to displease the Countess."

"I leave the calculation of that distance to you," I said to Claudia.

"A fresh young girl like her versus an old married woman like me?" laughed Claudia. "I could be leaning over his plate and he wouldn't notice me."

"You underestimate your charms, Duchess," I murmured in her ear. "She wouldn't stand a chance."

"This is why I keep you around," she said, and danced away, four clubs spinning about her.

"And who will be going first in the fooling?" asked Oldric.

"Jordan and Pelardit," I said. "And they'll introduce us."

"Very well," said Oldric. "Here come the guests."

I was not yet acquainted with all of the rich and powerful men and women of Toulouse, but there were many that I had met already. In came some who were clearly consuls by their chains of office, Bonet Borsella among them. He glanced at me and sneered. I gave him my best smile and kept juggling.

Calvet came in with a group of bailes, and was soon engrossed in conversation with Bonet. The Bishop entered in full regalia, but unaccompanied by any of his priests. Despite the miter bobbing over the assemblage like a cork on a rough sea, he was ignored by most of them.

A group of ladies were exclaiming over the prodigious talents of Helga, who had retreated into little girl mode again while keeping three balls in the air, a look of innocence on her face. I knew that she could do five just as well, but no point in bringing out your best tricks before the show has even started.

Pelardit, in the meantime, was doing slight of hand and close-up magic that brought oohs and ahs from the people around him.

I wandered over to Jordan, who was carrying on a lively conversation with a group while keeping a wooden ball rolling over the varying curves of his body.

"Hey, fat man," heckled one of the younger men. "Why aren't you juggling like that little girl?"

"If I juggled like her, I would be fending off your attentions for the rest of the evening," retorted Jordan.

The man's companions started laughing and elbowing him. He looked angrily at Jordan.

"Let's see you juggle, you tub of lard," he said.

I stood back to back with Jordan, still juggling my clubs, and muttered, "Spread your arms."

He stood with his hands extended outward, and I turned and slipped my arms under his, the clubs continuing in front of his ample girth. He clasped his hands in back of me, and we became a four-legged, two-headed fool.

"Behold my mastery!" he chortled as I kept the pattern going, popping my head back and forth over his shoulders. The group, which was growing in size, applauded.

"But it still isn't you," protested the heckler.

"Will you settle for half of me?" asked Jordan.

"They should, since half of you is as big as one of them," I said. "One, two, go!"

Jordan brought his right hand back to join mine for some three-handed juggling. It actually looked more difficult than it was, since we had three hands going for four clubs, but it was a nice effect, and even the heckler gave up and joined the applause.

We concluded the routine and bowed.

"Thanks for lending me a hand," I said to the groans of the crowd.

"My pleasure," replied Jordan.

We were about to move on when he nudged me. A couple had arrived whose finery stood out even in this gathering. She was wearing silk, bolts of it, gathered, flounced and beaded to an inch of its life, dyed a delicate sea-mist green that marked it as Byzantine in origin, while her hands and throat glittered with jewels. His surcoat was trimmed with ermine of the purest white, with more shiny rocks hanging from thick silver chains. He was a stout man in his late forties. Not fat, but powerful, with legs like tree trunks. He looked like he could have toppled the Grand Tower had he found a spot to brace himself against it.

"There's your master of Bazacle," muttered Jordan. "Arnaut Guilabert, and his wife, Gentille. Those jewels she has on are worth more than the rest of this room put together."

"They took care to make their entrance after everyone else," I said. "Except for the Count, of course."

There was a sudden pounding of drums, and people scurried to their places at the side tables. The five of us gathered under the balcony and grabbed instruments. Then Peire Roger entered and took a deep breath.

"Rise and give homage to Raimon," he shouted. "Sixth Count of Toulouse . . ." and there came that list of towns again.

We added our instruments to the fanfare, and filled the room with music. The Count and Countess entered, her ring-encrusted hand resting on his offered arm. The entourage followed, many of them already holding goblets of wine which they heedlessly let splash about.

Jordan took advantage of the music to point out some of them to me.

"The fellow in the escarlati cape is Bernard, Count of Comminges," he said. "Raimon's cousin, pretty much his best friend. The woman with him is Indie, Raimon's sister—well, half-sister—well, illegitimate half-sister."

"His father was quite the huntsman, as I recall," I said.

"Oh, you have no idea. Balthazar used to say that Raimon was always put off from taking a local mistress because he was probably bedding someone who his father had had first. And he didn't want them making any comparisons."

"I can certainly understand that," I said. "Who are those two following?"

"Raimon Roger, Count of Foix, and Rostaing, Baron of Sabran, both in Raimon's inner circle. They were all guarantors of the wedding contract when he finally married Éléonor. The priest is Frére François. He's with the chapel here at the château, so he's the Count's confessor when he's in town."

And so they marched in, taking their places at the center table. The Count held a golden goblet before him.

"My friends, the season of abstinence is ended," he pronounced. "The season of joy is upon us. Let prosperity flow like water through a mill-run, and may it spin all of your dreams into gold."

He drank, and there was another fanfare.

The servants swarmed in, carrying platter after platter piled high with food which the guests tore apart like wolves almost before it hit the tables.

"I so enjoy watching others eat," sighed Jordan.

"Oldric's getting up," I warned him. "Be ready."

Oldric strode to the center of the room, carrying a long oaken staff. As he did, a pair of servants brought in a wooden frame, about fifteen feet in length, from which hung a pair of scarlet drapes. They placed it about ten feet in front of us.

"A curtain for entrances," said Claudia. "Very helpful."

We heard a thumping noise as Oldric banged his staff on the floor.

"Dominus and Domina," he cried, addressing the Count and Countess. "We give thanks to Our Lord for your successful journey and your safe return."

Polite applause from the assemblage.

"Honored guests, I bid you joy and blessings," he continued. "As Master of Revels, it is my privilege to introduce the evening's entertainment. But before I do, I wish to take a moment to honor one who brought laughter to so many for so long. A great friend of mine, and a friend to all Toulouse, the fool Balthazar left us to entertain for the courts of Heaven this past summer. I wish to propose a toast to his memory. To Balthazar."

Behind the curtain, we had no wine, no goblets. We silently held up our instruments and juggling clubs as the room murmured, "To Balthazar."

"But as he himself used to say, as long as there is laughter, there is life," said Oldric. "I have promised you entertainment, and let no one say that Oldric is not a man of his word. I give you—Jordan and Pelardit!"

Jordan took a deep breath and swept through the curtains.

"Domina, Dominus," he cried. "The season of joy is nigh, and—Pelardit? Where are you, my friend?"

Pelardit, his arms piled high with instruments and props, tripped through the opening in the curtain. We heard a clattering that lasted for an impressively long time, culminating with a crash of cymbals.

We stood in readiness, and listened to a performance that was mostly physical comedy. There were laughs where we expected them, which was good, and laughs where we didn't, which was very good. The only audience we could see were at the ends of the side tables, but to our right and left, the servants stood in the entryways, quaking with merriment, platters of desserts shaking precipitously in their hands.

Then they reached the climax, and there was applause. I signaled Claudia and Helga, then stepped up to the curtain. Pelardit slipped past me with the instruments, a look of relief mixed with jubilation on his face.

"My friends," said Jordan. "It brings me great pleasure, indeed almost as much pleasure as eating, which should tell you how much pleasure is involved, to introduce to you the newest fools in town. Fresh on their triumphant tour of anywhere that would care to have them, and of anyone naive enough to lend them money, from their performances before such notables as Viscount Roncelin of Marseille, Countess Marie of Montpellier, and King Pedro of Aragon, I give you—the Fool Family!"

And I staggered through the curtain clutching a wineskin, blinking uncertainly until I caught sight of Jordan.

"What country is this?" I demanded.

"Why, you are in Toulouse, good fellow," he said.

"Toulouse, is it?" I squinted at the opulence of the room. "Not bad, not bad at all. Where's my room?"

"Your room, Senhor?" exclaimed Jordan. "Where do you think you are?"

"At the pilgrims' hostel, aren't I?" I said. "I tell you, friend, if the hostels in Toulouse are this fancy, then the Count's place must be truly magnificent."

"My good fellow, I'm afraid . . ." started Jordan, but then Claudia and Helga burst through the curtain in mid-squabble and we were off and running.

The first performance after Advent is always strange for a

jester. The shock of a live audience after cooling our heels for a month gave our performances an energy that would be flagging come summertime. But here in our Toulousan debut, the timing was sharp, the clubs flew high and fast, as did little Helga, and by the time we had finished our new repertoire with Jordan and Pelardit, the room was weak for laughing. We took our bows moving backwards, and took the frame down with us when we collectively stumbled into it.

Desserts were served, and Oldric came up to us.

"Well done," he said, tossing me a small purse. "I'm told there is food waiting for you in the kitchen."

"Our thanks, Senhor," I said as we bowed. "We are at your disposal."

A maid led us to the kitchen, where the servants were scavenging anything not devoured by the Count's guests. There was enough for even Jordan to pronounce himself sated. He slipped a few extra pieces into his pouch for his family, then looked behind me guiltily.

I turned to see Oldric standing there.

"Senhor, what may we do for you?" I asked.

"You and your wife come with me," he said.

I glanced at the others. Jordan looked worried.

"Helga, finish packing our gear," I said. "We will be back shortly."

"I hope," muttered Claudia as we followed Oldric. "What do you think this is about?"

"No idea," I replied.

Oldric took us up a flight of steps to a door with guards on either side, and knocked softly. It opened, and he stood back to let us in, then closed it behind us.

Count Raimon the Sixth sat behind a broad oaken desk.

"I want to talk to you," he said.

CHAPTER 9

He pointed to a pair of chairs in front of the desk.

"Sit," he said.

We sat. Out of the corner of my eye, I saw Bernard, Count of Comminges, take a seat off to the side. No one else was present.

Raimon looked at us thoughtfully. His eyes lingered appreciatively for a moment on my wife, then rested at length on me.

"You've been to Toulouse before," he said.

It wasn't a question.

"Yes, Dominus," I replied.

"But not under the same name."

"No, Dominus. I am flattered that you remember me under any name."

"With a snip of a boy who fancied himself a king," he continued as if I hadn't spoken at all. "Named Denis. Whatever happened to him?"

"He died a year later," I said. "Riding accident."

"May his soul rest in Heaven," he said, crossing himself. "He was on pilgrimage, and you were his entertainment."

"I was one part of his entertainment," I said. "He found many other entertainments while he was here."

"As many do," he agreed. "But he found absolution before his death."

"He did, Dominus," I said. "Twice, if you count the Crusade."

"Twice fortunate soul, then," he said. "Why did you change your name?"

"People are more interested in seeing a new fool than one they have seen before," I said. "I change my name every few years or so to take advantage of that."

"Interesting," he commented. "I suspect it also throws any creditors off your scent."

"I have left some places in haste," I confessed with a grin. "Some people don't appreciate a good joke."

"I think that you will find Toulouse quite tolerant of humor," he said.

"Apart from the Bishop," I said.

"The Bishop?" he said in surprise. "What has my good friend Raimon de Rabastens done to displease you?"

"He's banned the Feast of Fools," I said. "I was hoping to arrive here with a splash, and the Church has taken away my puddle."

"That's Rome's doing, not Raimon's," said the Count. "He's pliable enough when you get to know him. So. Fresh from a tour of Montpellier and Marseille, correct?"

Ah. There it was.

"Correct, Dominus," I said.

"And did you truly perform for a viscount, a countess and a king in that journey?"

"To be precise, Dominus, we both performed before King Pedro and Viscount Roncelin, but only my wife appeared before Countess Marie."

"That figures," muttered Comminges.

"Of course," I said, looking directly at him for the first time. "You were Countess Marie's husband before she married King Pedro. They say she wore you out."

He glowered, and the Count chuckled.

"She would wear any man out," he said. "Beautiful but quite demanding. We were happy to cede her and Montpellier to Pedro."

"More than happy," agreed Comminges, and Raimon chuckled again.

"So, you saw Pedro and Marie in Montpellier . . ." continued Raimon.

"No, Dominus," I interrupted. "We saw King Pedro in Marseille, dining with Viscount Roncelin."

"Now, that is interesting," said Raimon, leaning forward. "Tell me about that."

"The king sailed into the harbor one sunny day in early October with four ships," I said. "The Viscount held a welcoming dinner. We performed."

"And in the course of this performance, did you happen to hear any of the conversation between these two great lords?" asked Raimon.

"A fair amount," I said. "I assume you want the meat, not the appetizers."

"You read my desires correctly, Fool."

"The king sought financing for a pair of ventures he had in mind," I said. "The first was to continue on to Rome to be formally anointed as king."

"Pompous ass," said Raimon. "The second?"

"To raise a fleet to invade the Balearics."

"The Balearics," he repeated, leaning back again. "So he's still on that. Good. Let him have them. They'll keep him occupied for a while."

"My wife was supposed to do that," said Comminges.

"Apparently, she's finally met her match in King Pedro," I said. "He left her pregnant to go off on this expedition."

"We have heard about that," said Raimon, turning to my wife. "The blessed event is about two months away, is it not?"

"As far as she can tell," answered Claudia.

"And her mood?"

"Sour," said Claudia. "She's big with child, abandoned by her handsome new husband, and resentful of the world in general."

"That's my Marie," said Comminges.

"What does she think the child will be?" asked Raimon.

"She thinks a girl," said Claudia. "Though one never can be certain."

"If she bears a daughter, Pedro won't be happy," said Raimon to Bernard. "He'll be open to some arrangement. We should look into betrothing her to my son to strengthen the alliance. Let us send a generous gift to the newborn."

"Your son is eight years old, Dominus?" I asked.

"That is not your concern, Fool," snapped Raimon. "I was nine when my father married me off for the first time. If it benefits Toulouse, it will be done."

"I was not criticizing, Dominus," I said. "Merely voicing my curiosity."

"You might want to put a muzzle on that tongue of yours," he said.

"Then I would be a poor excuse for a jester, Dominus," I said. "May I say something further?"

He looked surprised, but indicated that I should continue.

"I suspect that nothing I have told you is news to you," I said. "No doubt I have merely confirmed what your own spies have already told you, which is part of your reason for asking me here."

"And the other part?"

"To gauge whether or not I am working for Marseille, Montpellier or Aragon."

He looked at me again, his eyes narrowing.

"Not such a fool after all," he said. "Who do you work for?"

"For you today," I said. "Tomorrow, for whoever pays me for that performance."

"Then you can be bought?"

"Lacking a regular patron, I earn my way where I can, Dominus," I said. "We are hoping to stay here, however. It seems like a fine place to raise a family."

"That talented girl is your daughter?"

"Yes, Dominus," I said. "And we have a baby girl as well. It does make the travel wearisome."

"Did you know Balthazar?" he asked.

"I met him during my previous journey here," I said. "A most worthy fool."

"He was at that," he said. "Balthazar used to presume to give my father and me advice. Unorthodox, but usually on target. I once said to him in jest, what will I do if you ever die? He took the question quite seriously. He told me that if it happened, I shouldn't be surprised if a new fool turned up about four or five months later. And that if I valued his advice, I should make this new fool a friend as well."

"Very considerate of him to clear the way for a strange jester," I said.

"And I find it interesting that you arrive, and that the two fools who have been here for years immediately defer to you," he said.

"Respect for my superior abilities," I said. "Excuse my lack of modesty."

"I think that I may begin respecting them as well," he said. "We will have you perform for us again, Senhor and Domina Fool."

We stood and bowed.

"One request, Dominus," I said as I straightened.

"Yes?"

"We live in Saint Cyprien. A pass for the gates would be useful to jesters who frequently entertain at night."

"Oldric has them in hand as we speak," he said.

We bowed again.

"Balthazar said it would take four or five months for the new fool to arrive," he said as we moved toward the door. "It took you six."

"An unexpected obstacle on the journey," I said. "Nothing we couldn't overcome, but not a story to interest a count."

"Then I shall not ask to hear it," he said. "Good evening, Fools."

Comminges let us out. Oldric was waiting in the hall, a pair of scrolls in his hand.

"A count as your doorman, a Master of Revels as your guide," he said. "You have risen far today. Here. One for each of you, with my signature and seal."

"You are most kind, Senhor," I said, bowing as we took them.

"Kind, nothing," he said, leading us back to the Grande Chambre. "You have done me credit today. Here are your companions. Good day, Fools."

We bowed one more time as he left.

"You have returned," said Jordan. "And in one piece, too. What was that all about?"

"Tell you outside," I said. "Everything packed?"

"Yes, Dominus," said Helga, passing us our bags.

"Let's go."

We left, acknowledging the waves of the servants inside and the guards outside. Jordan and Pelardit were whistling happily, their share of the proceeds jingling in their purses.

"So?" inquired Jordan when we entered the city.

"He was pumping me for information," I said.

"And you avoided giving it to him through clever badinage, eh?"

"No, I told him everything I knew," I said.

"What?"

"Oh, it was just gossip from the other courts we came through," I said. "Nothing of value to us, so no harm in singing like a bird."

"If you say so," said Jordan. "He did seem to enjoy our antics."

"Everyone did," said Claudia.

"I was particularly good, I thought," said Jordan, puffing up with pride.

"You were," I said. "Now, we need to line up our next performance."

"Done and done," said Jordan. "I was about to tell you. A servant came up and requested our presence at another dinner tomorrow."

"Excellent," I said. "Where?"

"You're going to like this," he grinned. "The Château Bazacle. A command performance before the Guilaberts."

"Most excellent," I said. "How large a party?"

"Oh, he likes to outdo the Count," said Jordan. "Just to show he has money. The food should be outstanding."

Pelardit kissed the tips of his fingers exquisitely in agreement.

"Good," I said. "Same openings, but we should bring in some different material. Pelardit, we should do 'The Mirror.' We have similar builds."

Pelardit nodded, beaming.

"And can the two of you perform 'The Sailing-Master and the Seasick Crusaders' with us?"

"I have some notes on that somewhere," said Jordan. "It's been a while."

"Then you be the Englishman," I said. "Fewer lines to remember. Pelardit can be the drunken Pisan, my wife the Toulousan, and Helga the first mate. Let's meet midmorning at your place to go over it once."

"Very well," said Jordan.

"Is your wife feeling better?" asked Claudia.

"She is, and thanks for asking," said Jordan. "That tissane of rue helped immensely."

"I am glad of it," said Claudia.

"Shall we celebrate today's triumph?" asked Jordan, looking longingly at a tavern as we passed.

"We have to go retrieve Portia," said Claudia.

"But I might put this pass to the test and come back later," I said. "Time for this jester to start working the taverns."

"Then if our paths cross, I will buy you a drink," said Jordan. "You have kept your word about the Count's dinner, and given me some extra laughs to boot. My thanks for both."

Pelardit thumped his chest.

"Our thanks for both," Jordan corrected himself.

"And ours to you, fellow fools," I said. "See you later."

We went our various ways. The sun was low on the horizon as we crossed the Daurade Bridge.

"Count Raimon looks to you for advice already," said Claudia. "That's convenient."

"I do give good advice," I said.

"It showed remarkable perception on his part to see that," she said. "Of course, you came highly recommended by a dead fool who didn't even know it would be you who would replace him."

"When you put it that way, it is surprising that the Count would have so much faith in me on such short acquaintance," I said.

"What you're both saying is that you think he really doesn't trust you," said Helga.

"Correct, Apprentice," I said. "That story about Balthazar predicting my arrival is nonsense. A Chief Fool would never reveal so much about the Guild's practices."

"Then Raimon must have figured that much out on his own," said Claudia. "The Guild's activities are not completely unknown to the world. And, my goodness, after listening to you in there, I was practically convinced that you were a spy."

"Which is fine," I said. "He'll want me close so he can keep an eye on me, and he'll be trying to figure out a way of using me. I want him to use me, because it puts me in a position to bring my influence to bear."

"Unless he just has you beheaded so you won't be a bother," sighed Claudia.

"He wouldn't do that," protested Helga. "Would he do that? Really?"

"Probably not," I said.

"Then you had better start teaching me faster," said Helga. "I need to know everything that's in your head before you lose it."

"Don't fret, dear," said Claudia. "There really isn't that much in there."

"Right," I agreed. "A couple of afternoons at most should do it. Shall we ditch the man following us, just for fun?"

"You already told the Count that we live in Saint Cyprien," said Claudia. "Let's not make the poor soldier feel bad."

"You are a sweet and generous soul, my dove," I said. "Tell you what—if he has to keep watch on us, we'll send Helga out with a cup of warm wine. It's cold today."

We picked up Portia, who was resentful about being left for so long and let us know it. As we went inside our house, I peeked back out through the doorway. Our follower waited for a while, stepping from side to side and sticking his hands under his armpits for warmth. Finally, he turned and walked back in the direction of the city.

"No need for warm wine," I said when I climbed into our rooms.

"At least not for any soldiers," said Claudia, ladling a cup out for me. "Will you be going out tonight?"

Portia scooted over to my feet, looked up smiling, and said, "Papa! Up!"

I scooped her into my lap and bounced her on my knees. She squealed happily.

"No," I said. "I have all the entertainment I need right here."

"You've played the Château Bazacle before?" I asked Jordan as we walked there the next morning.

Rehearsal had gone well, but the weather was foul and playing havoc with our whiteface. We wore wide-brimmed straw hats to keep the worst of it away, but streaks of floury paste were still running down our necks onto our cloaks in spite of that protection.

"Bazacle, sure," said Jordan. "The Guilaberts, unlike the Count, are there year-round. I suppose that's because all of his holdings are local. They're always good for several engagements each year."

"And Balthazar performed here?"

"Not so much toward the end," said Jordan. "He said something that put Guilabert out of sorts, I never heard what, so Pelardit and I were more likely to be here than he was."

"Children?"

"Three, all grown. Two sons, one daughter. There will be some very small grandchildren. We could put Portia to work."

"Ready to start earning your keep?" Claudia asked our daughter, who was riding contentedly on my shoulders, a tiny cap and bells on her head.

"Ba," she said, and Pelardit gave her a thumbs up.

"What notables will be there?" I asked Jordan.

"Merchants, some of the newer consuls from the last election, some of the wealthy families from those big new houses near Saint Sernin."

"Anyone from Saint Sernin itself?"

"I doubt it. The Benedictines don't go in for parties in my experience. And it's the Feast of Saint Thomas today."

"What about the Count and his coterie?"

"The Count does not deign to dine with millers' sons," he said grandly. "Even if the miller's son is worth half the town. Count Raimon is more likely to be found in a crumbling tower of a destitute, debt-ridden derelict clinging by his teeth to what's left of his gentility than passing through the gates of Bazacle."

"Which we are about to pass through," pointed out Claudia as Helga looked up at the fortifications with her mouth hanging open. "I guess we left our nobility back home."

"We're fools. We go everywhere," I said. "Let's go here now."

Once inside, we saw that the tower with its surrounding outbuildings echoed the octagonal design of the walls. The parapets were patrolled by a few guards rather than manned by many, but there were a pair of barracks, suggesting that the place could become well defended in a hurry.

We were met at the entrance to the tower by Arnaut Guilabert himself, who was taking charge of the arrangements for the dinner.

"Ah, good, the fools are here," he said. "Hello, Jordan and Pelardit, hello, Senhor Pierre and Domina Gile, hello, little girl, and hello, even littler girl. Let's get a look at that one."

I pulled Portia off my shoulders and held her in front of me for inspection. He put his face in front of hers and growled, wiggling his eyebrows. She reached forward and touched his nose.

"She likes noses," I said.

"Who doesn't?" he said, tapping her gently on the nose in response. "Adorable. I love babies. I have three grandchildren now. Grandchildren, Jordan! How could I be old enough to be a grandfather?"

"You're not," said Jordan. "I think it was very silly of you to even try."

"Well, glad you brought her along," said Guilabert. "This means I have six fools at my dinner, and the Count only had five. Come on in, everyone!"

"See, she is earning her keep," I said to the others.

The Bazacle great hall may have been slightly larger than the Grande Chambre of the night before. Certainly it was more richly decorated, The tapestries, interestingly, did not depict scenes from mythology or history, but showed instead millers hard at work, sawyers turning out planks, water-wheels so realistic that you would swear you could see them move, and sacks spilling forth flour and all the other abundant products of the area.

"You like them?" the lord of Bazacle asked as he saw me looking at them.

"I do," I said. "Nice to see working people on a heroic scale."

"Working people are heroes," he said. "I started in my father's mill just like everyone else, performing every task under the sun to keep it going. That's how you learn about the world."

"It certainly is one way," I said.

"I'm putting your curtain and frame over there," he said, pointing to the opposite end of the hall. "I had them build it out of scrap wood, so don't feel bad about knocking it apart. You! That goes on the sideboard, not the main tables." A servant scrambled to make the change. "And Pelardit?"

The fool came up to him.

"I want you to do that Cups and Balls trick right in front of me," ordered Guilabert. "I'm going to figure out how you do it this time."

Pelardit bowed, and several balls came tumbling out of the sleeves of his motley. He looked at them as if he had never seen them before, then strolled nonchalantly away, whistling.

"I know that part," Guilabert called after him. "That's misdirection, isn't it?"

"I will wager you a song that by the time he's done, you will be as befuddled as before," I said.

"Do you know how it's done?" he asked me.

I reached out with an empty hand and produced an apple from behind his ear.

"I know how everything is done," I said, winking.

I tossed him the apple and went to set up.

The guests started arriving shortly thereafter. Portia was passed from fool to fool, depending on who was performing what specialty, but she was cute enough to merit attention for herself, mostly from the wives.

The crowd was much more convivial than the one at the Count's affair, and there was much less ostentation on display. It was by and large a different group, although I saw with interest that Bonet Borsella was there. It made sense, given his sawmill was at the Bazacle dam, but I wondered about the true nature of his relationship with our host.

Guilabert welcomed everyone from the start, and his wife, rather than making a grand entrance, simply walked in from the kitchen, where she had been attending to some last-minute preparations, and began embracing her friends. She did not glitter with jewels as she had the day before, but seemed all the warmer for their absence.

The dinner was announced, not by fanfare, but by the bringing of soup in giant tureens. We moved about the tables, juggling, singing and, in Pelardit's case, performing magic tricks. When he came to Guilabert, he stopped, and the rest of us drummed our hands on the tables to direct everyone's attention to him. He held his hands up to show they were empty, then proceeded to run through the Cups and Balls at a blinding speed, balls of different sizes and colors appearing and disappearing under the three wooden cups while Guilabert's eyes kept darting back and forth.

Finally, Pelardit looked at our host with an evil grin and indicated that he should choose.

"You think you have me, don't you?" said Guilabert. "Well, this time, I have you."

He tapped on the right cup. As he did, it split into two, and a yellow chick stood on the table, peeping in bewilderment.

"But how did you—?" exclaimed Guilabert, then he sat dumbfounded as Pelardit lifted the middle cup to reveal a red ball underneath. He tossed it to a young boy on the right, then gently gathered up the chick and offered it to Guilabert, who roared with exasperated laughter.

"You owe me a song, Senhor," I said.

"But if I sing, I'll drive everyone away," he called.

"I will teach you one, and everybody must join in the chorus," I said.

It was a raunchy little ditty that we sometimes sing to the Cups and Balls routine, with a refrain that ends in, "Because I did not have the balls." Better suited to taverns, of course, but the ladies here were delighted to be scandalized, and sang right along with the men.

We segued into our full repertoire after that, and then there was dessert and more wine.

"Ably done, Fools," applauded Guilabert as we disentangled ourselves from the collapsed curtain frame. "I must say I envy you, living a life of nothing but merriment. So much better than the toil and trouble that most of us have."

"Oh, we have our share, Senhor," I said. "But there are music, magic and mirth to compensate us."

"You forgot the fourth 'm,'" he said. "Money. The

compensation that actually allows you to eat. Laughter is a wonderful thing, but it is worthless."

"On the contrary, laughter is priceless," I said.

"Except that in our case, many of the laughs are cheap," added Claudia.

"All I am saying is that entertainment is a luxury," argued Guilabert. "One that we can afford, but a luxury nonetheless."

"But think of living life without it," I replied. "It would be the most miserable existence imaginable."

"But it would be existence still," he countered. "Imagine living without flour for bread, or mash for beer."

"You certainly have me on the beer," I agreed. "In fact, without it filling our audience, many of our laughs would fall flat."

"I don't mean to belittle your profession, good Fool," he said. "I just see more value in honest labor than in foolery."

"I hope that I may prove an honest and valuable fool, Senhor," I said.

There was a snort from Bonet Borsella, which he covered by some coughing.

"Certainly a hardworking one," I continued, ignoring it.

"Hardworking?" scoffed Guilabert. "When do you ever rise at dawn, Fool?"

"Never, Senhor!" I said, offended. "Dawn is when a hardworking fool goes to sleep!"

"I stand corrected, Fool," laughed Guilabert. "And I beg your forgiveness."

"With all my heart, Senhor," I said, bowing.

"And with that, I think we should let these hardworking fools eat," he said. "Applaud their way to the kitchen, my friends."

And they did as we trooped off to our rewards, Portia waving from atop my shoulders.

"I so love this brief time of the year," Jordan groaned happily when we had finished eating. "If only I could live off it when Lent begins. I could hibernate like a bear and emerge at Easter, thin and ready to repent."

"At least we can jest during Lent," pointed out Claudia.

A maid came in, a pretty little thing with brunette curls. She stepped wide of Pelardit who leered at her.

"If you're done eating, there is dancing now," she said. "They like to have the juggling going on with it."

"We'll be right there, Audrica," said Jordan.

"Oh, are you Evrard's sweetheart?" asked Helga.

"How did you know that?" asked Audrica, blushing.

"I was helping out at the Borsella place," said Helga. "The cook told me. He's a very handsome man."

"I'm lucky to have him," she whispered, looking down at her feet.

"And he's lucky to have you," I said, gathering up my gear. "Let's go, my hardworking colleagues. Let's juggle as many clubs as we can, and first one to drop buys the first round later."

"Portia can't afford that," protested Jordan.

"Portia never drops anything," I said, as I placed her on my shoulders.

She promptly removed her cap and bells and let them fall to the floor, then giggled.

"That's going to cost you," I said, kicking it up to my hand and placing it back on her head.

The dancing had already begun by the time we came out, the musicians pounding out a raucous jig. We sailed through, clubs and balls passing over us. Portia hung on to my head and bounced happily with the beat.

The guests milled about, the wine propelling them into increasingly wild displays of terpsichorean endeavor. Guilabert was at the center of it all, capering wildly, stomping with his thick legs as loudly as any drum. He had one of his grandchildren in his arms and swung the poor boy this way and that, tossing him up into the air and catching him.

Off to the side, I noticed that Bonet Borsella was watching rather than dancing. Audrica, the maid, came over to him with a tray of pastries. He leaned over and whispered something into her ear. She turned nearly crimson with anger. He smirked and swatted her on the rear, and she stormed away.

Pelardit ended up being the first to drop a club, and the rest of us hooted at him, startling the people nearby who were unaware of our game. Then the music came to an end, people applauded, and it was time to leave.

Guilabert came up to thank us, staggering from the drink.

"Most excellent foolery, all of you," he said, clapping Pelardit, Jordan and me on the shoulders. When he came to Claudia, he seized her and kissed her hard, then did the same with Helga who was openmouthed with shock.

"There's for all of you," he said, tossing me a purse that felt heavier by half than the one we had received from Oldric. "I must say, friend Pierre, you far surpass that old fraud Balthazar, God rest his soul."

"God rest his soul," I repeated, suppressing my anger.

"Come by any day at dinner time," he said, patting Portia's cheek. "You are always welcome at Bazacle."

"My thanks, Senhor," I said, nodding politely.

We packed our gear as he went to pay the musicians.

"Let's get out of here," I said, and we filed out of the tower, subdued.

"Of all the rude behaviors," sputtered Jordan when we were out of the château. "Yes, he was drunk, and yes, he's obscenely wealthy, but that gives him no right."

"Leave it be," said Claudia. "Helga and I are the offended parties. I saw his wife looking daggers when he did it. She will be our champion this evening, I'll warrant."

"I hope that wasn't your first kiss," I said to Helga.

"There was a boy back at the Guildhall," she said sadly. "He was very sweet. I will probably never see him again."

"Ah, but the paths of fools often cross," I said, patting her shoulder. "Why, I myself . . ."

"Fool!" called a voice to my right.

Bonet Borsella was standing in front of his sawmill.

"Another job?" asked Claudia.

"Somehow, I doubt it," I said, handing Portia to her.

He motioned me inside when I came up to him. The sawmill was busy, the shrieking of the blades more than able to keep our conversation from being overheard.

"Have you enjoyed our performances, Senhor?" I asked him.

"I find it difficult to warm to your humor, Fool," he replied.

"Understandable," I said. "We got off on the wrong foot the other day. Have you reconsidered improving our relationship since then?"

"Why should I?" he asked. "If anything, my position has improved since then."

"Yes, the man who posed a threat to you was stabbed in the back," I said cheerfully. "One might almost see our conversation and his death as connected."

"Which makes me wonder why you killed him," he said.

"Me?" I laughed. "I had no reason for wanting Armand dead. Quite the contrary."

"How so?"

"For reasons you know too well, Senhor," I said.

"You're bluffing," he said carefully. "He's been dead four days, and you haven't gone to the baile with anything. Nor have you come to me seeking payment."

"My busy season is upon me," I said. "When things get slack, I will—"

"You have nothing, you know nothing," he pronounced. "Get out of here."

"We still have open dates available, if you're interested," I said as I left.

"Well?" asked Claudia.

"He thinks I know nothing," I said.

"Then he and I are of the same mind," she said.

"Of course, that he is so concerned with establishing that I know nothing means there must be something," I said.

"Poke, poke, poke," she sighed. "Let's go. There's little daylight left."

"It's the Feast of Saint Thomas," said Jordan. "Shortest day of the year."

We passed by the communal ovens of Saint Pierre des Cuisines. Women were lined up, waiting for their Christmas loaves to be finished.

"It's been a profitable two days," said Jordan. "We should probably split up tomorrow. There are no dinners comparable to these two."

"Fine," I said. "We'll be hitting the markets tomorrow if you need to find us."

He waved and headed home.

"Know a pilgrim's tavern that's likely to be lively tonight?" I asked Pelardit.

He grinned.

Most of the pilgrim's taverns were situated where the road from the Daurade Bridge crossed the Grande Rue. Pelardit led us to one called Balaam's Ass, where he was greeted with a welcoming roar that quickly extended to the rest of us.

We sang, we juggled, we did our tavern routines, and when Helga flitted about with her tambourine held up, enough pennies dropped to make the evening more than worthwhile. But when she came back with her collection, she slipped something into my hand.

"From that man going up the stairs," she said.

I looked to see a grey-cloaked figure leaving the room. There was a small scrap of paper with a message scrawled on it.

"Third room on the right," I read.

"Be careful," said Claudia.

"You're in more jeopardy down here than I will be up there," I said. "Back in a few minutes. Entertain them, will you?"

I left as Pelardit commenced a juggling routine where the balls occasionally bounced off Claudia and Helga's heads, to their increasing chagrin. I went up the steps, paused at the top to take my knife out of my boot, counted three doors, and knocked.

"Come in," said a man.

I opened the door and made sure no one was waiting on either side of it, then went in. He was alone, seated on the bed, a man in his late fifties wearing a merchant's garb, yet not somehow seeming anything like a merchant. Not a soldier, either. He lacked the hardness of a man who had been in the military. But there was nonetheless a sternness in his demeanor.

"All right, I'm a fool," I said. "What are you?"

He held out a scroll. I took it and read it, noting the seal at the bottom with surprise.

"Satisfied?" he asked me, smiling slightly.

"For now," I said. "So, how is the Pope?"

CHAPTER 10

The Pope was in good health when I saw him last," said the man.

"He didn't ask about me, by any chance, did he?" I asked.

"Sorry, no," he said. "I was unaware that you were acquainted."

"We're not," I said. "I was just wondering if he knew anything about me."

"He doesn't know that I'm meeting anyone from your little organization," he said.

"What organization is that?"

"You know what I'm talking about," he said. "You've seen my credentials."

"I have seen a piece of parchment that says you are one Peire of Castelnau, and that you are a papal legate," I said. "Very impressive, if it's real, and if it's true, and if you're him, but what does any of that have to do with me?"

"Didn't Father Gerald . . ."

"Who's he?"

"The leader of your organization," he said impatiently.

"What organization is that?"

"God give me patience," he sighed. "Of course. 'Unexpected source.' That's what I was supposed to say, wasn't it?"

"And about time, Brother Peire," I said. "Is that the correct way to address you?"

"It is," he said. "I am a monk of the Cistercian order."

"Interesting," I said. "I don't see a white robe on you."

"When one wears a white robe, people mostly notice the white robe," he said. "Dress as others do, and you are unrecognizable. I imagine what works with a white robe works even better with whiteface."

"It does," I said. "Welcome to Toulouse."

"Oh, I've been here before," he said. "In my official capacity, about a year ago. I ended up excommunicating the Count for a while, but he made amends and has been admitted back to the fold. I must say, it's quite exciting to be sneaking around here in disguise, using secret passwords and having covert meetings. Nothing like my normal existence. I imagine you do this sort of thing all the time."

"Hate to disappoint you, but what I usually do is juggle and tell jokes," I said. "How is it that you know Father Gerald?"

"I don't," he said. "But I owe my life to another member of your Guild, so I am here to help you if I can."

"Thanks. Do you know what you will be helping me to do?"

"Not exactly," he confessed. "My instructions were only to find you and assist you. I assumed it would be in a task that I could support."

"Maybe. My mission is to depose Bishop Raimon and replace him with someone we favor."

He smiled and cracked his knuckles.

"The first I support wholeheartedly," he said. "He's a pathetic excuse for a priest, a whining, fawning hypocrite. None of which is sufficient reason for deposition by Rome. That's the problem with bishops. Once they're elected, they are almost impossible to dislodge. Who do you have in mind for his successor?"

"Abbot Folc, from Le Thoronet."

"A Cistercian," said Brother Peire. "I've never met him, but he's one of ours. And, I suppose, one of yours as well. He was a troubadour at one time, wasn't he?"

"One of the best," I said. "So, help me. How do I trip up Raimon de Rabastens?"

"Tell me what's been happening here," he said. "I've heard about the murders."

I gave him a truncated account of what I knew and what I didn't know. The latter part was longer. When I was done, he leaned back on the bed and put his feet up, his hands clasped on top of his chest as if posing for his sarcophagus.

"I don't know this city well enough to see how these deaths are connected to the Bishop," he said. "But I sense that they are. This story of Mascaron's about the secret book of debts is clearly meant to cover something more serious. Perhaps some threat to the Bishop's position."

"My thinking as well."

"What puzzles me is that the Bishop of Toulouse has almost no power to speak of," he said. "Why would he fear losing such a tiny thing?"

"You can't say he's in it for the money," I said. "The cathedral is falling apart, and his rents are all pledged to creditors. I don't even know why anyone would want to be Bishop here in the first place. He probably wishes he was back in Rabastens, doing whatever he was doing before. What was he doing before?"

"He was a deacon or something low-level in Agens," he said. "Came from a well-connected family in Rabastens, but no one ever thought much of him."

"How did he get the post here?"

"Like I said, well-connected, although I heard it was a close vote among the canons. Everyone thought the Bishop of Comminges would get the nod. Much better man than Raimon de Rabastens, from all reports."

"So, they made Raimon de Rabastens bishop, and he's been impoverished and whiny ever since," I said. "That was three years ago?"

"About that," said Brother Peire. "I wasn't here then."

"What about his family in Rabastens?"

"Rumors of heretics among them," said Brother Peire. "Nothing we could substantiate."

"The Bishop of Toulouse has Cathars in the family?" I laughed. "No wonder he's preaching against them so much."

"Is he? Interesting. He never took a strong position on them before," said Brother Peire. "Frankly, I am glad to hear of it. If we do not bring them back to the Church, their souls will burn in eternal Hellfire."

"To be sure," I said. "But that's your mission, and I'll leave you to it. I don't think having Cathars in the family is the threat facing the Bishop. It's already known."

"I know nothing else useful about him," said Brother Peire. "But bring anything incriminating you find to me, and I will bring the full force of Rome down upon him."

"As you did with the Archbishop of Narbonne?"

"The Archbishop of Narbonne is a member of the royal family of Aragon," he said, frowning at me. "Raimon de Rabastens, on the other hand, is not that substantial a man."

"It's who you know," I said.

"And now you know me," he said, getting to his feet. "I am returning to my abbey at Fontfroide for Christmas. After that, I shall return. You'll find me at this inn."

He held out his hand. I took it.

"I've never shaken the hand of a papal legate before," I said.

"I have shaken the hand of many a fool," he said. "You'll get used to it. Good hunting."

I left, and rejoined my fellow fools. A ball bounced off my forehead, courtesy of Pelardit, and I staggered around in a mock daze as the patrons laughed.

"Don't know what was in that last drink, but it kicked like a mule," I bellowed. "Time to sleep this one off. I bid you good night and safe journey, good pilgrims."

I plucked Portia from her mother's arms and put her on her accustomed perch. She waved to the crowd as we exited to their cheers and good wishes.

"How'd we do?" I asked.

"Not bad at all," said Claudia, patting her purse. "How did you do?"

"Reinforcements from an unexpected source," I said. "All we need to do is all the work."

" 'Twas ever thus," she said. "Good night, Pelardit."

"Good night, Pelardit, it was fun," said Helga.

He bowed to us, and two balls slid from his sleeves. This time, he snatched them just before they hit the ground. He held them up for us to see, turned his palms toward him, then turned them back to us. The balls were gone.

"I do know how it's done," I said.

His face fell.

"But you do it better than anyone I've ever seen," I added.

He smiled, and we parted for the evening.

"We have a papal legate helping us?" Claudia exclaimed in disbelief when we were alone in our bed.

"Apparently so," I replied.

"Does this mean that the Pope is on our side?"

"Not at all," I said. "But this monk seems to favor the Guild no matter what the Pope thinks."

"So you trust him."

"Not entirely," I said.

"Why not entirely?"

"Because if Father Gerald wanted me to trust him entirely, he would have given him one of the Guild passwords. 'Unexpected source' was one he arranged just for me."

"What a sneaky man we work for," she murmured, nestling into me. "How delightful."

I felt warm and comfortable, and was starting to drift off when she said, "Theo?"

"Yes?"

"Do you think the Church will really come after the Cathars?"

"They came after the Fools' Guild, and all we did was make fun of them," I said. "When it comes to the competition . . ."

"How bad will it be?" she asked. "What did Father Gerald think?"

"He thinks it will be persecution," I said. "I think it's going to be war."

I woke to hear someone pounding on our trapdoor. I glanced out the window. It was midmorning, and a light snow had fallen during the night. I like snow. It muffles my footsteps.

I opened the trapdoor to see a soldier looking up at me. I recognized him immediately as the one who followed us from the Château Narbonnais the other day.

"From the Count," I said.

"Yes," he said. "He wants you to attend him this morning."

"All of us, or just me?"

"Just you," he said. "I am to escort you."

"Come up and take a bench while I prepare," I said, holding out my hand.

He took it, and I hauled him up.

"I owe you a cup of hot wine," I said.

"You do?" he replied in surprise.

"But we have none at the moment. Have some bread and ale while you wait."

"My thanks, Senhor Fool," he said, pouring himself a cup.

"The name's Pierre, friend soldier," I called over my shoulder as I went to fetch my gear.

"Sancho," he said, watching in fascination as I came back to apply my makeup.

"You're a long way from home," I observed.

"From Alarco," he said. "I left during the famine in '95. Joined up with the Knights of the Holy Sepulcher for a while, but heard that the Count of Toulouse paid better."

"That's why I came to Toulouse," I said, grinning, my makeup complete. "Let's go get paid."

We chatted as we walked through the snowy streets. A trio of cormorants were perched on the base of one of the mills under the Daurade Bridge, their wings spread, drying in the breeze generated by the slowly turning waterwheel.

"We'll be getting ice on the river soon," said Sancho. "A sight that never ceases to amaze me. I didn't even know a river could freeze over until I came here. But some of my fellows come from places where it gets two feet thick and lasts for months."

An image of a body trapped under the ice arose in my mind, hands bloodied, a look of reproach . . .

"I've seen it myself in my travels," I said, driving it back down. "The novelty wears off quickly. I'd rather be somewhere warm."

We came to the Château Narbonnais. Sancho led me to the door to the Grande Chambre, which stood open.

"My orders end here," he said. "See you around, friend Pierre. Next round is on me."

"Until then, friend Sancho," I said, and I went in.

A servant was setting up a group of chairs, one of which dominated the others by its height and the richness of its carvings and cushions. He saw me and waved me over.

"You are to play while the meetings go on," he said to me. "You are to otherwise remain silent unless spoken to."

"Who bids the fool stand mute?" I asked.

"The Count's precise words were, 'Make sure he keeps that damn yap of his closed, or I'll have his tongue ripped out.' "

"I am persuaded," I said, unslinging my lute and tuning it.

I strolled about the room, playing as I looked at the various tapestries and weaponry hanging on the walls. I came back to the group of chairs, and bowed to the largest. Then I took out my flute and started playing. Quite a lovely echo in that large, stone room.

There were footsteps. I turned to see Bernard, Count of Comminges, enter the room. He did not look pleased to see me. I bowed anyway.

"You've had your instructions," he said.

I nodded.

"Good," he said. "And if you ever bring my former wife up in front of the Count like that again, you will have me to deal with, do you understand?"

"I understand," I said. "But I do not obey."

"Do you dare flout me thus?" he thundered.

I trilled a few notes in his direction.

"As you can hear, Senhor, I am a skilled floutist," I said. "I am here at your master's invitation. I follow his orders, not yours."

"I speak for him," said Comminges.

"No, you don't," said Count Raimon, entering the room. "Leave off the jabbering, Bernard. It ill becomes you to wage a war of words with a fool. Especially when he is winning."

We both bowed.

"And you, Fool," he said, taking his seat. "I ordered you here to watch, not to speak. Be like your friend Pelardit. He knows how to keep quiet."

"Actually, Dominus, he doesn't know how to speak," I said. "It's a different thing entirely."

"That's the last word out of you," he said. "Keep the music soft and lulling. I am expecting some people who need to be lulled this morning. Good morning, friends."

Raimon Roger, Count of Foix, and Rostaing, Baron of Sabran, entered the room and bowed. Peire Roger, the viguier, followed them in. I threw in a little fanfare on the lute for each.

"Good, you're all here," said Count Raimon. "We will be hearing official business today. A number of people whom I supposedly rule will be coming in to tell me what to do."

"Always amusing," said Foix.

"Is it going to take very long?" asked Sabran.

"You have something more important to do than attend your lord?" asked Count Raimon sternly.

"Or is it someone to do?" jibed Comminges.

"Let's just say I would like to be out of here by noon and out of there before sunset," said Sabran.

"Sunset being when an honest working husband returns home to his beloved wife," said Foix.

"What do you know of honest working hours?" retorted Sabran.

"Enough," said the Count wearily. "Who is first before us?"

"The Bishop," said Peire Roger.

"Who will give us his blessings and ask us for money in exchange," said the Count. "Show him in."

The viguier bowed and left the room. I sauntered over to a position behind one of the pillars supporting the balcony and stopped playing. The Count watched me, amused.

The Bishop entered, Father Mascaron close behind. They nodded rather than bowing, and the Count returned the nod.

"Thank you for coming, Your Holiness," he said. "Father."

"God's blessings upon your head," intoned the Bishop. "May His mercy rain upon you."

"His blessings and mercy are both welcome," said the Count. "Now, tell me what you really want."

"Why, Dominus, merely to pay the respects of the Church," said the Bishop unctuously.

I started strumming my lute softly. At the first note, the Bishop jumped slightly and the two holy men turned toward me. The Bishop looked surprised and displeased to see me there. Father Mascaron was expressionless.

"Thought I would have a little music today," said the Count, smiling. "I hope you don't mind. It soothes me."

"Not at all, not at all, Dominus," said the Bishop. "I was merely startled, having not remarked him when—"

"Well, now that you have paid me the respects of the Church, you may attend to those parishioners who have greater need of your ministrations," said the Count.

There was a subtle prompt by Father Mascaron as the Bishop looked to him for help. The Bishop took a deep breath.

"Actually, Dominus, there is a matter that I wish to discuss with you," he said.

"Then by all means," said the Count grandly. "Let no man come to the Count of Toulouse during Christmas season and walk away empty-handed. How much do you want?"

"Well, that isn't it," stammered the Bishop. "I mean, yes, of course, anything you care to give would be most—it's just that, I'm not here to talk to you about money."

"Forgive my astonishment," said the Count. "Why, then, are you here?"

"To warn you, Dominus," said the Bishop. "To have you look to your soul if you seek salvation."

"Is my soul in danger?"

"Well, there are the Jews," said the Bishop. "You have Jews working for you, many in positions of great responsibility."

"And you object to that?"

"The Church objects," said the Bishop.

"They do my bidding and are a threat to none," said the Count. "You don't like them because they have no obligation to tithe."

"You also employ mercenaries," continued the Bishop.

"As do the Kings of France and England," said the Count. "I am forced to pay foreigners to protect us from other foreigners working for still more foreigners because I have so few soldiers of my own."

"And you permit heresy to be practiced openly in the city, even after taking an oath to end it," concluded the Bishop.

"I have honored that oath," said the Count. "You are confusing efforts with results. I could just as easily take you to task for not filling your cathedral every Sunday."

"But the heretics—"

"Will be quashed," promised the Count. "But these things take time. As for the rest—it is not up to the Pope to tell me how to conduct the business of running my holdings. Let him look to people's souls, and leave the governing to those who govern."

"I only seek to guide you toward God's grace," said the Bishop.

"And you have conducted your master's warning with the utmost respect and sympathy to our office," replied the Count. "So, Raimon, now that the preliminaries are over, what may I truly do for you? The cathedral is in deplorable shape. May I at least get something done about the walls? That plaster will come down with the next stiff breeze."

"That—that would be most generous of you," gulped the Bishop.

"Consider it done," said the Count. "And I'll make sure that there are no Jews among the workmen. There may be a few Cathars among them, because you really can't tell them apart from the Christians when it comes right down to it, but I expect that a holy man like you will be able to sniff them out and convert them. That will be all, thanks for dropping by."

The Bishop was slow to appreciate that his audience was over, but Father Mascaron plucked at his sleeve. They stood quickly and left.

"Let's make sure there are a few Cathars among the workmen," said the Count. "It will be good practice for him. Who's next?"

"A delegation from the consulate," said Peire Roger.

"Let's get this over with quickly," said the Count. "Bring them in."

A dozen men entered, each trying to look more important than his fellows. I saw Bonet Borsella, and recognized most of the others from Guilabert's dinner. I noticed that the Count was frowning slightly as he looked at them. I ran my fingers down the strings of my lute, playing an intricate instrumental that held my attention, if no one else's.

"Well?" said the Count.

"You've raised the tolls on the Narbonne road," said one who was acting as their leader. "Again."

"It's a well-traveled road," said the Count. "It needs maintenance and security. Those things cost money."

"It won't be so well-traveled if no one can afford to make the journey," said the consul. "We ship goods through Narbonne. We receive goods through Narbonne. And you've made all of that more expensive, just so you can pay for this army that sits around and eats every scrap of food in the Toulousain."

"You liked my army just fine when you used it to conquer the competition," said the Count.

"We had to expand," said the consul. "Our markets were threatened."

"And thanks to your little wars I have to spend half my year riding around and putting out all of these little insurrections just because your markets were threatened," said the Count. "With precious little help from the consulate, I might add. I've cut your taxes over and over. You're richer than you ever were, and you complain about the tolls? You couldn't afford to buy anything outside the Toulousain ten years ago, do you remember?"

"You didn't cut the taxes," said the consul. "We did."

"With my consent," said the Count. "Freely given, mind you. And I have been doing everything in my power to keep the peace with our neighbors. We are at peace with Aragon, which means the Trencavels can't stir up any mischief; with France, and with England, which means they are free to go at each other without our needing to get involved; and Rome— well, I'm holding them off as best I can. But the last thing I need is trouble from my own city."

"Yet you permit your own baile to send his men into the bourg to harass ordinary citizens," said another consul. "People who live peaceably, indeed more peaceably than most."

"You mean the Cathars," said the Count.

"I do," said the consul.

"Tell your Cathar friends it would go easier if they would simply turn over whoever did these murders," said the Count. "Until they are brought to justice, my baile will continue his investigation in whatever manner he deems fit."

"What makes you think a Cathar did this?" shouted the consul.

"Raise your voice in here again, and I'll have you thrown in a dungeon," said the Count softly. "I can still do that, despite what you think. Now, get out, the lot of you."

They looked defiant. But they shuffled out for all that.

"You were supposed to soothe them with that instrument of yours," the Count said to me.

"If they had been savage beasts, I would have," I said. "Alas, they were merely men."

"They've been savage enough since the last election," grumbled Comminges. "We should throw them all into a single dungeon. A small one."

"You see, Fool, I am the master of everywhere in the Toulousain except for my own city," explained the Count. "My father ceded local rule to the consulate to keep from being overthrown. Now, I suffer the consequences of that ill-fated decision. Is Calvet here?"

"He is, Dominus," said the viguier.

"Send him in," ordered the Count.

The baile strode forward and knelt before the Count.

"Thank you for being the first person this morning to show me the proper respect," said the Count. "Rise, my friend, and tell me if you're any closer to catching any murderers."

"We have no solid information, Dominus," said the baile. "No witnesses, but many rumors, and each one is being investigated."

"Good," said the Count. "Do you believe that these deaths were the work of Cathars?"

"Based on Armand's testimony, and more upon his murder, I do."

"In death, he gains credibility, whereas in life, he had none," said the Count. "Very well. You keep shaking them out of the trees until you find the right one."

"And then?" asked the baile.

"Bring him to justice," directed the Count.

"But should I bring him to you first?" asked the baile.

"I think we should maintain the appearance of integrity in this matter," said the Count. "Hang him in public. Let justice be done so that all may see it."

"Very well, Dominus," said the baile, bowing.

He left, and the Count signaled to his viguier to close the doors to the room.

"If the murderer turns out to be a Cathar, there will be trouble," he said to the others.

"Half this town is either a Cathar or related to one," said Foix. "If this gives the Church more cause to stir up resentment against them, then these two deaths may be a drop in the bucket compared to what will come."

"Do you think Calvet will find his man?" asked Comminges.

"He won't rest until he drags him to the gallows," said the Count. "Let's hope that our murderer turns out to be nothing more than an insanely evil Christian. That would keep the peace for a while. Good, we're done here. Go off to your assignations, my friends. I expect full reports later."

They laughed as they left him, still in his chair.

"Fool, you may stop playing," he said, noticing me. "Your fingers must be numb by now."

"If you wish, Dominus," I said. "But I can play all day if you like."

"What did you think of this morning's business?" he asked.

"I thought, how magnanimous is this count to so entertain a jester."

"You found it entertaining?"

"You put on a show for me, Dominus," I said. "For all the pomp and formality, you can't tell me that this was anything more. The real work will be discussed in your private chamber, hidden from casual observation."

"No one is observing us here," said the Count.

"You have two men hidden in the balcony at this very moment," I said. "No doubt armed with crossbows."

"Apart from them, of course," said the Count. "Alfonse, you're getting careless."

"Sorry, Dominus," called one of the men in the balcony.

"You are a shrewd observer," said the Count, softly so that his elevated guards could not hear. "What have you discovered about these murders?"

"Why would a fool bother about such things?" I replied.

"Try answering a direct question directly," said the Count.

"I have not discovered the identity of the murderer, or murderers," I said. "But I have kept my eyes and ears open. Let's say I do learn something useful—should I bring it to Calvet, or directly to you?"

"Do you think Armand told the truth about seeing a sandal-shod man?"

"Not for an instant," I said.

"Then you might as well bring it to me," he said. "Calvet's a good man, but he's obsessed with the Cathars."

"Very good, Dominus."

"Tell me something, Senhor Fool."

"Yes, Dominus?"

"Why is my friend the Bishop so jumpy around you?"

"I cannot say for certain, Dominus," I said. "But I enjoy seeing it."

"I know that you are disappointed over losing the Feast of Fools," he said. "But the Bishop is an ally of mine. Tread carefully."

"Dominus, I can walk a rope so thin that it could have been made by a spider," I said.

"Ropes can be cut," he said. "And spiders can bite. You may go."

He tossed me a coin. I bowed and left.

It was past noon. It occurred to me that I had spent the morning performing for the Count without being fed. Shameful. I stopped in a tavern for a quick lunch and a slow drink. I wondered about the whereabouts of my colleagues. They wouldn't be likely to be working the taverns this early in the day. More likely at the markets or the squares.

I walked up the Grande Rue until I passed through the

Portaria into the bourg. I glanced at the courtyard of the Borsella place, but saw no Helga amongst the children playing. I kept going until I reached the plaza in front of Saint Sernin, where I saw a small crowd circled around my wife and our apprentice, who were busy juggling clubs back and forth to each other.

The bells rang for None, and monks began filing toward the church from different directions. I had a sudden inspiration. I ducked into a doorway and pulled out Pelardit's Benedictine robe. I threw it on and tied it quickly, then plodded toward the church, my head bowed inside the cowl so the whiteface would not be visible to anyone. I trailed the last monk I could see toward the north entrance, but held back at the last second while the doors closed for services. Then I turned and walked to the dormitorium. I listened for a moment at the door, then went inside.

There was a set of stone steps leading up, and another leading down. I went up. An entrance opened up into a long, narrow room. There were twenty-four beds, a dozen on each side, each with a freestanding wooden closet next to it. All identical. I had no way of knowing which belonged to Vitalis, or Donatus, for that matter. Which meant I had to search them all, and be out before the monks resumed their chores.

I started reciting the service for None as I searched quickly through each bed and closet, making sure to replace everything as I had found it. I had gotten through one side of the room by the time I reached the *Rerum Deus tenax vigor*. I came back down the steps, humming the hymn, and walked toward the cloisters, my hands folded in prayer. No one took any notice. It helped that Claudia by this point was juggling knives instead of clubs, Helga holding Portia a safe distance away. I found some cover, stripped off the robe, and stuffed it inside my pack. I put my cap and bells where they belonged, and was a fool again.

I wandered to the edge of the crowd watching Claudia, and led the applause when she was done. I swooped in on Portia, who was sitting on the ground, playing with some juggling balls, and lifted her high in the air.

"Well met, husband," murmured Claudia as Helga dashed about with her tambourine to collect a few coins. "How was the dormitorium?"

"How did you know?" I asked.

"Should I not know my own husband, even in disguise?" she said, smiling. "Especially when you are taller and leaner than any monk in that abbey. I thought you might show up here."

"There is no surprising you anymore," I sighed. "I must remember to slump next time. I have to take another turn tomorrow. I only got halfway through the beds. And there's a kitchen as well."

"And you're still looking for that book?"

"Or whatever Vitalis is hiding there. Thank you for providing a distraction, by the way."

"I had my own reasons for coming here," she said.

"We have enough for dinner," said Helga, coming up with her tambourine.

"Let's go to one of the taverns by the Bazacle Gate," I suggested. "And you can tell me about why you're here while we walk."

"After you left, I thought I would pay another visit to Béatrix Borsella," said Claudia. "It's been a few days, and I didn't want her to think I had only been there to play mourner for a day. I sent Helga on ahead, because they haven't connected us yet."

"I visited the cook," said Helga. "I told her that I was earning some money helping out at the big Christmas dinners everyone is having, which is why I haven't been by as much."

"You could tell her you're a fool," I said. "She's going to see you performing at the markets sooner or later. How fares the widow?"

"Still in mourning, still being comforted by Brother Vitalis," she said. "She was surprised to see me in makeup and motley, but I explained about Advent. I played for a while, then she asked me to leave because she was planning to visit her husband's grave."

"A proper thing for a widow to do," I said.

"Only she hasn't," said Claudia. "I came there straightaway, and she hasn't been all day."

"But she did leave after Claudia did," said Helga.

"And you followed her."

"I did," declared Helga proudly. "She left with Vitalis and Evrard, but Vitalis took the road to Saint Sernin."

"And where did the widow go?"

"To the Château Bazacle," said Helga. "She was there for an hour, then came home again."

"That place keeps coming up, doesn't it?" I said. "Here's the tavern."

The Tanners' Pit had mutton stew, watery but hot. We secured a table and ate. I took some small pieces of bread and sopped them in the stew for Portia, who sucked on them with a quizzical look before deciding she liked them.

"What's interesting to me about the Château Bazacle is that the defense of the northern part of the city is entrusted to a private citizen rather than the Count," I said. "That makes him tremendously powerful."

"Guilabert is powerful because he's rich," said Claudia.

"He controls Bazacle, which means he controls anyone who makes their living from Bazacle."

"That would include Bonet Borsella," I said. "He built that new sawmill. And Milon had been complaining about him throwing all of his money into that venture. It doesn't sound like he would have lent him any more. I wonder if Bonet had to borrow from Guilabert?"

"But how would that lead to Milon's murder?" asked Helga.

"I don't know," I said. "But with the widow Béatrix choosing to visit Bazacle instead of her husband's grave . . ."

"We know that her husband beat her and cheated on her," said Claudia. "Could she have turned to Guilabert for solace? He wouldn't be my first choice, but that's because I don't like the way he kisses. She might find money and power to be enough to compensate for that failing."

"Or maybe Milon the moneylender owed money to him, and his debt passed to her?" I speculated. "Whatever it is, it's our first real connection between the dead man and Guilabert."

"Second," said Helga. "There's Evrard and Audrica, the Bazacle maidservant."

"True enough," I said. "Then there's Brother Donatus. Let's say he was Guilabert's conduit to Saint Sernin."

"Why would Guilabert want a man in the abbey?" asked Claudia.

"If he wants to control the bourg, then influence in the abbey would be useful," I said. "It's the religious center for all the new money in the bourg, and it controls Saint Pierre, the Taur, Saint Cyprien—everything but the cathedral itself. And even there . . ."

I stopped as a thought hit me. Hard.

"What is it?" asked my wife.

"The Bishop was elected by a council of local canons," I said. "Brother Peire said it was a closely contested election between Raimon de Rabastens and the Bishop of Comminges, and that Rabastens wasn't considered a strong candidate. I wonder if Brother Donatus could have been the deciding vote."

"You mean Guilabert could have bought the bishopric," said Claudia. "If that's true, then he controls the consulate and all of the ecclesiastic power in Toulouse. What does he want to do with all of this?"

"I think we had better find out," I said.

CHAPTER 11

I went through the beds on the other side of the dormitorium as quickly as I could. In one, I felt a small leatherbound book inside the straw stuffing. I pulled it out with a surge of hope, but it turned out to be a set of erotic illustrations. I was tempted to confiscate the source of this poor monk's temptation, strictly as a lesson to him, of course, but reluctantly decided to replace it so as not to call any attention to my handiwork.

It was approaching noon, and the monks were in church for the Office of Sext. I was in the middle of the last bed when a shrill whistle echoed through the windows from the square in front of Saint Sernin. I threw the blanket back and flew down the steps and out the door, reaching the cover of a nearby shed just as the doors to the church opened and the monks poured out to resume their chores.

I slipped off my sacred disguise and took the long way around to the square, coming to it from the northwest. Pelardit was wobbling around on a rickety pair of stilts, whistling in panic whenever he seemed about to topple over, which was frequently. The whistles were answered by shrieks from the children watching him, yet he always regained his balance in the nick of time.

Helga was sitting on the steps by the main entrance to the church, where she had been listening to the monks, Portia on her lap. Since I didn't know the timing of the service for Sext, her job was to signal Pelardit when the final hymn began. Hence the warning whistle.

"You cut it awfully close this time," commented Claudia, materializing by my side.

"What's life without risk?" I asked.

"Longer," she said.

"Any luck?" asked Helga as she came up to us.

"None," I said. "A little earlier on the signal next time."

"It's a short hymn," she said. "Personally, I thought they sang it too quickly."

"We'll have them hire you on as choir mistress," said Claudia. "And what do you mean by 'next time'?"

"There's still the kitchen and a few other rooms to consider."

"Right now, we should consider lunch," said Claudia.

Pelardit hopped down from his stilts and beckoned to us, rubbing his stomach.

"You know a good place?" I asked.

He nodded, and walked his fingers in the air.

"Very far?"

He shrugged.

"Is it worth the walk?"

He lifted an invisible cup to his mouth, drank deep, and staggered, smiling cherubically.

"You make a compelling case," I said. "Lead on."

It was a long walk, all the way across the city to the Porte Montgalhart, which was the first gate east of the Château Narbonnais. A funeral procession was passing through it. Jews, by their dress and their chanting, going to their cemetery outside the city walls.

The tavern was called the Yellow Dwarf, which gave me a momentary pang of longing for the Scarlet Dwarf, our favorite tavern near the Fools' Guildhall before our exile, a rambling, raucous place filled with drunken, competitive jocularity. This tavern, on the other hand, was small and quiet. There was an upper floor with rooms for lodgers, although there was no sign that there currently were any. In fact, there was no one there but the innkeeper when we arrived. Our arrival appeared to wake him from a light nap, but he brightened upon seeing not just customers but fools.

"Pelardit, my old friend!" he exclaimed. "I was hoping to see you here today. And these must be the new fools in town. Welcome, welcome all. I'm Hugo, and this is my tavern."

"I'm Tan Pierre, friend Hugo, and I have never met a tapster I haven't liked," I said. "Pelardit tells us you brew a fine ale here. At least, I hope that's what he meant."

"Oh, you'll find he told you true," said Hugo, filling a pitcher and placing it on our table with a stack of cups. "But confirm it for yourself, Senhor."

Pelardit poured for all, and we raised our cups to our host and drank.

"I now name my friend Pelardit to forever be my guide in all things," I said. "This is excellent ale, Senhor Hugo."

"Now, all I have is bread and cheese for lunch," said Hugo. "Will that satisfy?"

"It will," said Claudia. "But you must join us."

"I will, and thank you, Domina Fool," he said.

He brought in a tray of bread and cheese, straddled a bench, and began slicing.

"It's good to see such a lively crew here again," he said. "Haven't seen this many jesters at my table since Balthazar passed on, God rest his soul."

"Was he a frequent visitor?" I asked, helping him pass the food around.

"He lived here," said Hugo. "Didn't you know?"

"I did not," I said.

"Oh, sure, for years," said Hugo. "He'd be sitting where you are, and Pelardit and Jordan on either side, sometimes a troubadour or two, and they would go on into the evening, one song after another, or stories or tricks or what have you. Those were the days, weren't they, Pelardit?"

Pelardit nodded, looking wistful.

"Well, now that we know that the ale is fine and the host so convivial, we'll make sure to bring those days back again," I said.

"I would enjoy that," he said. "I do miss the old sod. I can still see him, sitting here while I cleaned up after everyone else had gone home, writing notes by a single candle until there was just a stub left."

"And up the next day at the crack of noon," I said.

"Oh, you have the right of it," he laughed. "Wish I could keep a fool's hours."

"This is excellent cheese," said Claudia. "Won't you have some, friend Hugo?"

"Oh, I suppose I will at that," he said, taking a piece. "I'm still not used to eating it after all this time."

"You don't like cheese?" I asked.

"Well, I was a Cathar for a long while," he said. "True believer until I had the darkness pulled from my eyes, so didn't eat cheese, you know."

"Nothing that comes of coition may be eaten," I said. "That's what they believe."

"That's right," he said. "Thankfully, I was shown the error of my ways, and I get the benefit of the better food as a bonus. Forgot how good roast mutton could be."

"I always thought it was a cruel trick to separate the sheep and the goats only to eat the sheep," said Claudia. "So what brought you back to the fold, if you don't mind my asking?"

"Oh, this priest came through back in the spring," he said. "Traveling with that bishop from Osma who was staying with our bishop, only they couldn't handle the entourage, so we got a couple. I always liked picking on the traveling clergy, get them all flustered about theology compared to the Cathar beliefs, 'cause none of 'em were all that good at debating and such. Only this fellow, what was his name? De Guzman?"

He shook his head admiringly.

"I've never met a priest like him. Knew everything, had an answer for every argument I had. And he wasn't just some show-offy type. He really seemed concerned for my soul. He persuaded me, God bless him. I hope he comes back some day. If more priests were like him, I would have come back years ago."

"Where did he go?" I asked.

"They were off to Denmark on some mission," he said. "Who knows when they'll return? Or if? But I'll pray for them in the meanwhile."

"Sounds like you could preach the Word yourself now," I said.

"Naw, I don't have the gift," he said. "And I'm not out to bring the others back. Everyone should find his way without being forced into it."

"I agree with that," I said.

"Of course, if you die a Cathar, like poor Milon, then it's straight to Hellfire with you," he said. "And that's a sad thing. But he had his chance. You never know when life's gonna turn on you."

"Milon? Do you mean Milon Borsella?" I asked.

"Right, the one who got dumped in the tanner's pit last week," he replied.

"I had no idea he was a Cathar," I said.

"Well, it's not like everyone knew it," he said. "But he was, for ages. Not ready to take the final step to being one of the Perfect, you know, and it wouldn't have been good for business if people knew."

"I am amazed," I said, glancing at Pelardit, who listened impassively. "Is his wife Cathar as well?"

"Oh, no," said Hugo. "Just the opposite. Very Christian in her ways. That was kind of a funny thing. He didn't want her knowing he was going to meet with the Cathars, so when he was out nights, she thought he was seeing other women, and would scream at him like nobody's business. And he never would tell her the truth, 'cause he figured that would upset her even more than thinking he was cheating on her, can you imagine?"

"Friend Hugo, you know that Calvet the baile thinks that Cathars killed Milon, don't you?" I asked.

"Well, I doubt anyone in the community would do that," he said. "He was liked among the Cathars."

"Have you told Calvet about this?" I asked.

"Why bother?" he said. "I don't really know what happened to Milon, and even though I'm Christian now, I'm not gonna rat out my friends even if they haven't seen the light. I'm not like that. Oh, let me get you more ale."

He picked up the empty pitcher and went in back.

"This is why you brought us here, isn't it?" I asked Pelardit.

He nodded.

"I wonder if Milon's brothers knew," said Claudia. "Imagine

Vitalis's position, being a Benedictine monk and having a Cathar for a brother."

"Could be embarrassing," I said. "Frustrating."

"Enough to make him want to kill his own brother?" asked Helga.

"I doubt it," I said. "Besides, he allowed them to bury Milon in consecrated ground. Would a Benedictine monk do that knowing he was really a Cathar? Even for his own brother?"

"That might account for his behavior at the grave the other day," said Claudia. "Well, this throws water on a pet theory of mine, I must say."

"What's that?"

"That Milon's wife killed him out of jealousy over some lover. But there was no lover."

"No, he only cheated on her church," I said.

Hugo came back and refilled our cups.

"To Milon," he said, raising his cup. "Too late to save, but a nice fellow for all that."

We drank, and were silent as Pelardit for a while. He was the first to rise, signaling that he was heading out.

"Meet you in time for services," I said.

He nodded, shouldered his stilts, and left.

"Did Balthazar die here?" I asked.

"Naw, he died a good jester death," said Hugo. "He was juggling in Montaygon Square, and his heart just stopped, so they said. Fell on his back, with the clubs landing everywhere. People thought it was part of the act at first, and laughed and laughed."

He chuckled at the memory.

"He got a laugh by dying, just think of that," he said.

"Not a bad death at all," I said. "Could you show me his room?"

"His room?" he said in surprise.

"If it's not currently occupied, of course."

"Well, as it happens, it's available," he said. "Let me take you."

He stood. I tapped Claudia on the knee under the table. She nodded, and I rose to follow Hugo upstairs.

"Here it is," he said, opening a door to an undecorated room, just a bed and a basin inside. "Bigger than a hermit's cell, and I keep it clean. Never had any complaints."

"He lived here alone all those years?" I asked, stepping in.

"Oh, I couldn't say that he never had a woman up here," he said. "Reckless wives, traveling pilgrims on their way to absolution, you know how it goes when there's ale to be had. Why, there was this—"

"Hugo?" called my wife from downstairs. "Have you some rags? I'm afraid the baby has knocked over a cup of ale."

"Oh, no worry," he called to her. "You'd have no idea what I've had to clean up some nights. Be right there. You'll excuse me, Senhor Fool? Take a look. Rates are reasonable if you have a mind to stay over some night. Sing a few songs, draw a crowd, and I'll put you up cheap."

He hurried down. I immediately moved the bed aside and began feeling along the floorboards until I felt one give slightly. I took my knife and slid it along the crack that was revealed and pried it up easily. There was a space underneath, large enough to conceal, say, a coffer or several stacks of gold. But it was empty, only a small scrap of parchment curled at the bottom. I picked it up, but it was blank.

I replaced the floorboard and went back down.

"Here's for lunch and ale," I said, handing him a few coins. "We will certainly be back. Once we get through the Twelve Days, we could arrange a regular evening here, if that suits you."

"It would suit me fine," he said. "A pleasure meeting you, and a happy Christmas to you all."

We took our leave, and walked north.

"What did you find?" asked Claudia when we were out of earshot.

I handed her the scrap of parchment. She turned it over in her hands several times, then held it up to the sun.

"Nothing," she pronounced. "That's unfortunate. I was starting to feel comfortable here. Always a bad sign."

"We'll sort it out," I said. "First, there's the rest of the dormitorium to search. We should be back just in time for Nones."

"The more you go back, the more likely it is someone will see you," said Claudia. "All for a book that may not even be there. For all we know, Vitalis never had it, or moved it if he had."

"If we could only get him to take us to it," I mused.

"Why don't we set the dormitorium on fire?" suggested Helga.

We looked at her sternly, and she flinched.

"You are an evil, despicable child, and you should be ashamed of yourself," I said.

She hung her head.

"I think it's a brilliant idea," said Claudia.

"So do I," I said. "We'll do it tomorrow during Sext."

Back across town and bourg to the square in front of Saint Sernin. Pelardit waved from atop his stilts.

"It's off," I muttered as we came to him. "The wife talked me out of it."

He mopped his brow in exaggerated relief and hopped down to the ground.

"Some eight-handed juggling?" I suggested.

We worked the bourg for the better part of the afternoon, moving from square to square, finishing by the cluster of taverns near the Bazacle Gate.

"What is your schedule like, my dove?" I asked Claudia.

"Why, as it happens, I am free," she said. "I had been asked to be a lookout for an ecclesiastical burglary, but that fell through at the last minute."

"Then may I have the honor of escorting you to dinner?" I said, bowing.

"You may," she said, curtseying back. "Do you have a place in mind?"

"It occurs to me that we have a standing invitation to entertain the Guilaberts at dinnertime."

"Why, so we do," she said. "It would be discourteous not to honor such a courteous invitation."

"And we are the very souls of courtesy," I said, offering her my arm.

She took it with grace. Pelardit looked at us, then offered his arm even more gallantly to Helga, who took it in an exaggerated copy of my wife's movements.

The gates to the Château Bazacle were open when we arrived, and the guards waved us through without challenge.

We paused before the entrance to the tower.

"Instruments out," I said. "And Helga and Claudia? Do not leave each other's sight while you're in here. I don't want Guilabert to catch either of you alone."

Pelardit produced a ram's horn from his bag and stepped through the doors. He blew a loud note, and the three of us barged in after him, Helga cartwheeling in the lead.

"The fools are here!" exclaimed Guilabert from the dinner table. "How marvelous!"

The long tables from the previous Tuesday's dinner had been removed, leaving only the family table. Guilabert and his wife, Gentille, were at the center, the sons and their families flanking them. An enormous roast pig, half carved, was on a large platter in front of them, and they were busy soaking up the drippings with bread.

"Where's the fat man today?" one of the sons called.

"Eating somewhere," I said. "Which means there's not enough food for the rest of the world. That's why we're here."

"There is food to be had," said Guilabert. "But first, my friends, you must earn it."

We bowed, and launched into material we hadn't used here before. We hadn't rehearsed any of it with Pelardit, but he adapted to our style quickly. I called for each routine on the fly, extending them when bits of business or fortunate improvisations got laughs, cutting them short when they fell flat. The Guilabert grandchildren came out from their seats and let us pick them up and throw them into the air. The youngest one, who was two, sat on the stone floor with Portia, and the two of them became absorbed in rolling some colored balls around, completely oblivious to the mayhem we generated nearby.

After about an hour, Guilabert cried, "Enough, Fools! I am becoming too weak with laughter to eat anymore, and there is still dessert to come."

"Senhor, you are taunting the starving," I complained. "The only way to stop a fool's mouth at a banquet is with food."

"Bring them dinner," he ordered. "And dessert for the rest of us."

We pulled a couple of benches away from the walls and sat as servants dashed back and forth from the kitchen. The maid Audrica brought us some of the roast and some bread and vegetables, smiling as Pelardit made a show of leering at her again.

"I saw that, you rascal," called Guilabert, and Perlardit affected a look of innocent surprise that fooled no one.

We were also given wine. It was good wine, and I had rather a lot of it. Finally, I poured myself another cup and rose unsteadily to my feet, ignoring my wife's look of warning.

"A toast!" I shouted. "A toast to our host and hostess, long may they prosper. A toast to their children, and their children's children, and all children everywhere!"

"To the children!" they chorused, raising their cups.

"And, most importantly," I continued, "a toast to what sustains us, what turns the wheels that bring us flour and ale, what soaks the bark that gives us leather, what sinks to reveal our sins, then rises up to cleanse them again, what will never be as thick as blood, but will nevertheless wash it away when it is spilled. A toast, my friends—to water!"

I upended my cup. I heard no echoing of the toast as I did. When I finished, I looked across the room to see Guilabert watching me.

"You toast to that which you do not drink," he said.

"I drink water all the time," I said. "But I prefer it when it's been transmuted to its ideal form."

"Which is?"

"Beer, of course. Water is given to us by God, as is all of the earth and everything in it, to do with as we please. What can be more pleasing than a good beer on a hot day? What greater evidence of Man's supremacy over his world?"

"I must apologize for giving you wine, Fool," laughed Guilabert.

"I like wine, too," I said.

"A little too much," said Claudia in a loud stage whisper.

"What you say, Fool, strikes a chord with me," said Guil-abert.

"A man with no beer strikes a chord with a man with no lute," I said. "Tell me how this came to be."

"You speak of Man's supremacy over the earth, which was first given to him in the Garden of Eden," he said. "And you say beer is the best evidence of that. But I see a work of Man that is greater than beer."

"Then we must have war," I said. "I am beer's champion. Since you have challenged me, I give you the first essay. What is this false pretender to beer's crown?"

"The waterwheel," he said. "The constant genius of Man, who has received the gift of Nature for his plaything, and has taken the very landscape and the course of rivers and altered them, bent them to his will to power this fantastic machine. You speak of beer—think of how much more beer there is in the world because of waterwheels. Everything man uses in life, everything he eats, he wears, he fights with, is improved and multiplied because we take the gifts of God and exploit them as He intended us to."

"No, no, Senhor," I said, shaking my head. "You will never persuade me of the superiority of the waterwheel when I almost got killed by one of the damn things last week."

"How did you manage to do that?" he asked, chuckling in anticipation of whatever story he thought I was going to tell.

"By going in after that poor bastard Armand when he floated into the sluice," I said. "Tried to be a good Christian, and nearly got myself sucked under and sliced up for my pains. Sliced in a sluice—there's a poor epitaph for a jester."

There was a shocked silence from the Guilabert family.

"I had heard that he had ended up there," said Guilabert. "I had no idea you were the one who found him."

"Me and Jordan," I said. "Do you know what I thought when we found him? Here's this poor fellow, who they say has never lived anywhere but Toulouse his entire life. Yet in death, he had one last chance to see the world, for he might have floated all the way to the sea had it not been for that accursed wheel."

Claudia tugged on my sleeve.

"Sorry, Senhor," I said, pulling myself together. "Not a proper topic for the dinner table. It was the twinned heats of the debate and the wine that carried me away. My apologies. But you understand why I regard waterwheels as dangerous things."

"Yet less so than beer, wouldn't you say?" he asked. "I've seen drink slay far more than any waterwheel ever has."

"You have me on that point, Senhor," I said. "Indeed, I have seen drink do in more than armies or plague. But at least, those who march bravely to their deaths by drink did so voluntarily."

"My dear, this is fascinating," said Gentille to her husband. "But you must forgive me. I find myself suddenly weary, and, by your leave, will retire for the evening."

"Of course, my love," he said, rising to help her from her seat.

We bowed as she left.

"I think that we have come to the end of our dinner," announced Guilabert. "Fools, I see that you have not finished your meals. I pray that you take your time, but please remove yourselves to the kitchen. There are some matters I must take up before the night is over."

"We thank you for your generosity, Senhor," I said.

"Nonsense," he replied. "I enjoy a good argument, even if it's with a drunken fool. And may I add that it was very Christian of you to try and save poor Armand."

We bowed, and carried our food and gear to the kitchen.

The servants cleaning up were glad of our company, and we took turns playing for them while we ate. After a suitable interval, I asked one of them to direct me to the privy and left.

I followed the hallway that led to the great hall. It was empty. I went to a door at the rear which I thought might lead to Guilabert's office. I wanted to see if there was anything that might illuminate his dealings with any of the players who had come to see him. I was hoping the display of feigned drunkenness would give me a plausible excuse for wandering into the wrong room.

Except when I listened at the door, I realized the room was occupied. And that the occupants were occupied as well. The hoarse grunting was clearly coming from Guilabert. The woman was just as clearly not his wife, but I didn't recognize her from the guttural moans she was making. I wondered if it was Béatrix. Could an affair with the master of Bazacle have been what led to her husband's murder? It was my wife's pet theory inverted, but certainly a reasonable possibility.

The sounds subsided, and I heard the rustling of clothing being slipped back on. I crept back to the gallery at the far end and concealed myself.

The door opened, and Guilabert strode out, a smirk on his face. Directly behind him, still tying on her apron, was Audrica, the maidservant. He swatted her playfully on the rump as she walked by him, and she giggled and skipped away.

"Same tomorrow," he said.

She blew him a kiss, then vanished into the hallway. He turned and went back into his office.

Well, a tawdry enough matter, but of no interest to me that I could see. I gave her a head start, then left my hiding place and walked back down the hall to the kitchen.

"Did you find everything all right?" asked Claudia when she saw me.

"Yes," I said. "Let's call it a night."

It was past sunset as we left the château, but there was a decent amount of moonlight to keep us from walking into the river. We could hear the water coursing through the sluices of the dam and the wheels turning, their axles and gears creaking continuously, producing nothing at night.

"A mill for everything but justice," said Claudia.

"Justice should still be handmade," I said.

We walked through the bourg, then through the city. Pelardit left us at the bridge. We went home, Portia fast asleep in my arms.

"So, who was she?" asked Claudia when we were safe in our bed.

"How did you know?" I asked.

"I saw Guilabert slip something into his wife's drink," said Claudia. "Then she became sleepy. I thought you had noticed that."

"I didn't," I said.

"Obviously, he wanted his wife to go to bed early," continued Claudia. "And it was easy enough to guess why, considering his character. So, who was the unlucky lady?"

"Audrica, the maid. And she didn't look like she thought she was unlucky. She seemed like a cream-filled cat, and she gets another bowl tomorrow night."

"So, it's like that," sighed Claudia. "Powerful man gets

what he wants. Not that unusual. Why, I personally know a duchess who ended up with a jester."

"Was it a happy match?" I asked her.

"So far," she said, climbing on top of me.

CHAPTER 12

The trick was to start a fire without actually burning the place down.

We needed smoke more than we needed flame, but we still needed flame, enough to sow panic and confusion among two dozen monks. While arson was not a regular part of my arsenal, I have manufactured a conflagration or two in my time, and seen a few more started by others. And on a smaller scale, I've juggled torches more times than I can count. It was that particular expertise that came in handy here. The collective experiments of the Fools' Guild over the centuries had led to the right proportions of oils, resins and pitch to create a flame that would burn steadily but not spread. Ideal for a juggling torch, because you still needed one end that was not on fire if you ever wanted to do that trick again.

We bought some firewood and soaked a piece in a bucket of water. When we applied our preparation to it and stuck one end into the brazier, it caught fire fitfully, spitting and casting off a great deal of smoke.

"Too wet," I said.

I dipped the next piece in the bucket for a shorter time, then shook off the excess water before applying the combustant. This time, the flames seized hold nicely while still producing enough smoke to attract notice. I flipped it once and caught it.

"Do they still have the game at the Guild where a flaming torch gets tossed from novitiate to novitiate until someone gets burned?" I asked Helga.

"Not since we fled the Guildhall," said Helga. "With all the novitiates living in that barn and sleeping in the hayloft now, Brother Timothy decided it wasn't the best idea."

I tossed it to her. She caught it easily and tossed it back. Claudia stepped forward and grabbed it before it reached me.

"At the risk of sounding like a mother," she said, waving it at me. "Not inside!"

"Yes, dear," I said meekly as she doused it in the bucket.

We made up two bags of the treated wood. I slung them over my shoulder along with the bag containing the Benedictine robe. I was in civilian clothes for this little jaunt, with my ordinary face affronting the world without the help of makeup. I went first, knowing that the others would be keeping me in sight. I took a circuitous route to Saint Sernin, coming up to the cemetery just as the bells in the tower in front of me were calling the brethren to Sext. I knew that Claudia was somewhere behind me, and that Helga had moved to the square in front of the church.

I watched the monks pour into Saint Sernin like devoted ants. I waited another few minutes in case there were any late-comers, but they were a punctual group. I squatted between a pair of mausoleums and threw on my robe, then walked, hunched slightly to conceal my height, until I came to the dormitorium entrance.

Once inside, I ran up the steps to the sleeping quarters, dropped one of the bags and untied it so that the wood could breathe. Then I ran down to the kitchen area and dropped the other bag. I took one piece out and lit it at the cooking stove, then touched the flame to the bag. It caught, and began spreading to the treated wood within. I ran back up the steps with the lit piece like I was an emissary from Hell and touched it to the other bag. It caught. I watched it for a minute, and smoke began to fill the room. I ran downstairs, caught my breath, and walked quickly from the dormitorium to the church entrance, trying my best to look like a hurrying late-comer with a guilty conscience. I opened the door silently and slipped inside, standing in the side gallery, watching the backs of the Benedictines, searching among the tonsured heads until I marked Brother Vitalis, deep in a prayer that was about to be interrupted. I hoped he wasn't praying for anything important.

Then I heard shouts from outside. The main entrance to the church opened, and several people barged in. I heard Helga screaming among them in her best little girl voice, "Senhors! Hurry! The dormitorium is on fire!"

Brother Donatus was the first monk to react, rising to his feet and charging the side door so quickly that I barely had time to duck behind a pillar. He ran past me and burst outside as the rest of the brethren followed in his wake. I brought up the rear, taking care to keep my cowl covering my full and untonsured head of hair, making sure I had Brother Vitalis in view at all times.

The monks for the most part stopped short to gape at the smoke which was now pouring out of the upper and lower windows, but Brother Donatus never hesitated, plunging into the building. He emerged a minute later.

"Two fires!" he shouted. "Looks like it started in the kitchen, but somehow got upstairs. Grab every bucket you can find and get a line going to the well."

The monks scattered in several directions as Brother Donatus continued to bark out orders like a sergeant. Some headed toward a well by the cemetery, while others ran back into Saint Sernin in search of buckets. Parishioners were emerging from the church behind us to gawk or run home for more buckets. In the general melee I saw Vitalis staring at the smoke in horror. Then he made a sudden dash toward the entrance.

"Wait!" cried Brother Donatus, but Vitalis brushed him off and ran in.

"I'll get him!" I shouted as I flew by, hoping that he didn't get a clear glimpse of my face.

Next time, less smoke, I thought to myself as I dove through it. It took me a moment to get my bearings, but the footsteps I heard were above me, so I ran up the steps in that direction. The upstairs fire hadn't spread to anything yet, I was relieved to see, but it wouldn't be long before the hardwood floor would start to catch.

Brother Vitalis was not in the sleeping quarters, but I heard coughing from my right. There was a small closet that I had missed in my earlier hasty visits. He was standing on a small stool inside it, reaching for something on the highest shelf.

A book.

Then he turned and saw me and froze.

"Come on!" I shouted. "They need help with the buckets! What are you doing?"

He nodded and put the book into a pouch tucked into the rope around his waist, then headed toward me.

Damn.

I had hoped that I would see his hiding place and then come back later for a spot of surreptitious pilferage. I hadn't counted on his keeping the book with him, but I should have anticipated it. The question was how to get it from him without his realizing. And there was the little matter of the fire around us, which was my responsibility.

I followed Brother Vitalis back down. We were met by Brother Donatus who had two buckets of water in his hands.

"Get the upstairs one first!" he ordered us, and we each grabbed a bucket and ran back.

Like most fools, I am a proficient pickpocket, and God knows I had provided myself with enough to distract my quarry. But I still had to get away once I had taken the book, and there was a line of monks between me and the outside.

We dumped our buckets on the fire, fortunately getting most of it on the first try. As we started back down, I slipped my dagger from my sleeve and held the handle so that the blade pointed up my wrist, concealing it from view. Two other monks were running up the steps with fresh buckets, and I hurled myself to the side to let them pass, stumbling into Brother Vitalis as I did. He caught me to steady me, and with a single swipe I sliced his pouch from his waist. I caught it before it fell and shoved it inside my robe.

"Thanks," I muttered, and I ran downstairs ahead of him.

"Out of my way!" I shouted as I hit the door, and monks scattered like pigeons as I ran with the bucket to the well by the cemetery. One of the monks was cranking the windlass as fast as he could while others stood with buckets waiting to be filled.

"Wait!" cried Brother Vitalis from behind me.

"Here," I said to the monk next to me. I handed him my bucket and took to my heels.

I am certain that anyone watching would have found us a comical sight, one black-robed monk chasing another through the bourg. As the one being chased, however, I was uncharacteristically less concerned with the comedic aspects of my plight, and more with avoiding the beating I anticipated receiving from my pursuer. I had arranged to meet Claudia at an alleyway in the cluster of buildings northeast of the church. As I turned into it, I saw her concealed in a doorway. I took Brother Vitalis's pouch and tossed it to her without breaking stride. She caught it and vanished inside without a word. I kept running.

As I reached the end, I risked a glance behind me. Brother Vitalis was about halfway down the alley, and looking like he could run all day if he had to. I had better things to do. As I made the turn, I saw a water barrel by the side of the building. I vaulted on top of it and jumped, catching the edge of the rooftop, then used my momentum to swing my body up to the top. I rolled away and lay flat, hoping the roof would support my weight. I heard the monk turn the corner and stop. I held my breath as my heart pounded in my body. I heard him walking around, kicking doors open. Finally, he gave a roar of frustration and walked away.

I took a deep breath. Still lying down, I slid out of my robe and rolled it up, then stuffed it inside my bag. I raised up my head a little, and saw the monk trudging disconsolately back to Saint Sernin. There was no more smoke coming out of the dormitorium, I was glad to see.

The neighborhood was quiet. I guessed that everyone had gone to help. Or to gawk, more likely. I slipped down from the roof, shouldered my bag, and walked away, whistling like I had not a care in the world.

I cut down to the Portaria and crossed into the city. I was ravenous from the running. Perversely, the smoke had given me a craving for sausages. I bought some hot off an outdoor brazier that an enterprising pair of young men had set up near the Maison Commune. I don't know if it was the actual sausage, or the relief at getting away with a remarkable number of crimes over a short period of time, but they tasted better than any sausage I had ever eaten.

I swung by Jordan's house. Martine's shop was open, and the boys were kicking a ball back and forth in front of it.

"Your father home?" I asked.

"He's out working," said the older one. "Some party somewhere."

"Good for him," I said. "How about your mother?"

"She's working, which means in there," said the boy, pointing to the shop.

I reached into my purse and handed each of them a penny.

"For Christmas," I said, and they took them gladly and ran off to spend them.

I walked into the shop. Martine was sewing beads onto a gown.

"Stupid ninny decides the day before Christmas she wants beads to wear in Church," she muttered, a needle between her teeth. "And only Martine must do it, and it must be done before sundown."

"It's superb work," I said. "Have you had any time for my little project?"

She reached behind her to a side table and handed me a large cloth bag. I looked inside.

"Perfect," I said, and I handed her some coins. "Have you had a chance to eat? I have some sausages."

"Smells like the ones from those boys by the Maison Commune," she said, wrinkling her nose in disgust. "Don't trust 'em one bit."

"I wish you had told me that before I ate them," I said ruefully.

"Ah, well, most survive, so I expect you will, too," she said. "Any messages for my husband?"

"As a matter of fact, yes," I said. "Tell him we'll meet him after Mass tomorrow at Montaygon Square."

"Are you really going to do the Feast of Fools on your own?" she asked.

"The Pope banned it from the Church," I said. "He never said anything about Montaygon Square."

"The Bishop won't like it," she said.

"That's the basic idea," I said. "A joyous Christmas to you, Na Martine."

"And to you," she said.

Claudia and I had not worked out any secondary meeting place in case the first didn't work. I berated myself for my sloppiness on that point, and decided to head home and stay there until she and Helga returned.

As I approached the house of Honoret, I suddenly felt uneasy. I glanced around the area, but nothing leapt to my eye to justify the feeling. As I neared the door, however, I heard a birdcall that belonged to no bird. I continued past the building and down the street.

A group of children ran by, chasing a hoop down the street, keeping it rolling with sticks. Helga was one of them. As they passed, I saw her point her thumb to the left. The stables were in that direction. A visit to Zeus would provide me with a reason not to go into my house. I knew I was being followed. The question was what motivation did my follower have, information or assassination?

I purchased a bunch of carrots from a stall and continued on. The cemetery was on my left. An ominous sight, but one that left no good cover in that direction. Which left only the right and rear as possible sources of attack. I slid my dagger from my sleeve and held it nestled against the bunch of carrots.

I nodded to a stableboy who was mucking out the stalls when I came in.

"How's my horse?" I asked him.

"He's a holy terror," he said. "We've been having contests to see who can stay on him the longest."

"Who won?"

"The horse did," he grinned.

I went over to his stall. He whinnied.

"A joyous Christmas to you, Your Malevolence," I said.

I held out a carrot, and he snatched it away.

Another birdcall, and my wife was standing by me.

"Where's Portia?" I asked.

"With the woman who watched her the other day," she said.

"What's going on?" I asked. "Were you followed?"

"Don't insult me," she said.

"Sorry. What's going on?"

"I didn't know what happened after you ran by," she said. "I met up with Helga and came back here, but I didn't want to go inside in case they had caught you and were on their way to grab us. We dropped off Portia and then watched for you. And guess who came by?"

"Brother Vitalis?"

"Right church, wrong monk," she said.

"Brother Donatus?"

"Muscles and all. He set himself up where he could keep an eye on Honoret's house. Luckily, it was in a place where I could see him. And then I saw you coming and became a bird."

"Good thinking."

"Thank you. Fortunately, he didn't follow you."

"So that was you I sensed breathing down my neck on the way here."

"I thought you liked it when I did that."

"I do when I know it's you," I said. "He didn't follow me. We've never been face to face, so he doesn't know me."

"At least, not without makeup and motley," she said. "I think he came looking for a jester."

"I wonder what put him onto us," I said. "Or who?"

"Could Vitalis have told him about losing the book?"

"My sense was that Donatus is the last person Vitalis would want knowing about that," I said. "Maybe Donatus figured out that something was up after seeing him chase me away from the fire."

"Which still leaves the question, why us?"

"Guilabert? Bonet? Maybe even Father Mascaron," I said. "We better make sure we bar the trapdoor securely tonight."

"Nothing says Christmas Eve like a menacing monk," she sighed.

Helga appeared at the stable entrance.

"He's gone," she reported. "I made sure he crossed the bridge, then I came back to find you. Hello, Zeus. May I feed him some carrots?"

I tossed her the rest of the bunch. She raised an eyebrow as she noticed my dagger still in my hand.

"Have you looked at the book yet?" I asked Claudia.

"I have," she said. "See what you make of it."

She tossed me Vitalis's pouch. I pulled out the book. It was much as Father Mascaron had described it—bound in black leather, secured with a golden clasp, gold crosses in each corner. Only . . .

"Borsella's name," I said. "It isn't there."

"No," she said. "Nor has it been scraped off the cover, as far as I can tell."

"Father Mascaron lied to me," I said sadly. "And who will save the soul of our ghostly confessor?"

"That's only the beginning," she said. "You've only judged it by the cover. Take a look inside."

On the first page, written in Latin in a businesslike hand: "By my signature on these pages, I bind myself by oath and all that is holy to the service of A.G.; my lands and my income to be forfeit should I fail in this service; my life to be forfeit if I reveal it."

"Nothing like Latin for an oath," I said. "Was your first guess Arnaut Guilabert?"

"Of course," she said. "He's the only 'A.G.' we've encountered."

I turned the pages. There were about two dozen signatures.

"Peirede Capitedenario, Arnald Ascii," I read. "They're both consuls from the bourg. So is Guilhem Cascavelerius, I think. So are a lot of these. New money types—De Las Tors, Del Claustre, Roaix. They all have those big houses near Saint Sernin. Speaking of which, here's Brother Donatus, surprise, surprise. These names I don't know, but they don't sound Toulousan."

"Mercenaries, I'll wager," she said. "Castilians from the sound of them."

"There are some pages torn out," I said, holding it open for her to see.

"If Milon had this book, then he might have removed his own name," she said. "Or Vitalis could have done the same."

"Why would Guilabert have entrusted this book to

Milon?" I wondered. "Why not keep it inside that fortress of his? Unless . . ."

"Unless Milon stole it," finished Claudia.

"And his life became forfeit," I said.

"But why?" asked Helga. "I mean, fine, a bunch of powerful people are working for Guilabert, but what are they doing?"

"If wealthy men conspire, it's usually about gaining more wealth," I said. "Everyone involved is from the bourg, and the bourg has been increasing its power in the consulate over the past five years."

"And the consulate has been waging war on the surrounding towns," said Claudia. "Conquer the area, conquer the markets, and the rich get richer."

"But everyone knows they are doing that," said Helga. "So what's the big secret of the book? Why was it worth killing for?"

"Oh, you didn't read the last page," said Claudia.

"I was getting there," I said defensively. "I don't like just jumping to the end without reading everything else."

I flipped through to the last page.

Raimon de Rabastens. Bishop of Toulouse.

"I don't think this is just about money," I said. "We were looking for something that would show the Bishop owes Guilabert. Here it is."

"But Helga's right," objected Claudia. "We don't know what it means. And why was Vitalis hiding it?"

"Maybe we should ask him," I said.

"Oh, I don't like the sound of that at all," she said. "Theo, if Donatus thinks we have it, then Guilabert will think that as well. Someone will come looking for it. Maybe a whole lot of armed someones. We can't keep it at our place."

"I'm thinking we can't keep us at our place right now," I said. "Scrub your makeup off, get into civilian garb, pick up Portia and go to the Yellow Dwarf. Tell Hugo we're taking Balthazar's old room for the Twelve Days, but we don't want people knowing about it. By the way, how did your other little errand go?"

"I searched, found nothing," she said.

"That's what I was afraid of," I said. "All right, better be on your way."

"What will you be doing?"

"I need to pick up my gear, then make a few stops," I said, slipping the book into my pouch. "I'll meet you there."

"Remember," she said, patting the book. "That's worth killing for."

I kissed her.

"And that's worth dying for," I said. "See you soon."

I was fairly sure that no one was following me this time, and didn't spot anyone watching Honoret's place, which only ruled out the less skilled. I climbed the steps, checked the padlock to make sure it hadn't been tampered with, and went inside our rooms. I quickly gathered my working gear together, and was about to leave when there was pounding on the bottom of the trapdoor.

I pulled my knife out.

"Who is it?" I asked.

A birdcall was the reply. I put the knife away, and knelt to remove the bar.

"What happened?" I asked as I opened the trapdoor. "We were supposed . . ."

Careless.

The door swung up hard into my jaw, knocking me back onto my rear, and in the instant it took for the stars to stop cascading, Pelardit unfolded his lanky frame into the room with a look of fury. I thought in my stupor that was the first unfeigned expression I had ever seen on him. I tried to regain my balance, but he stepped forward and kicked me in the stomach, knocking the wind out of me. Then he sat down cross-legged in front of me and closed the trapdoor, sliding the bar into place.

"What on earth . . . ?" I managed to croak as he sat and watched me clutch my stomach.

He fanned his fingers in front of him, and they shimmered and quivered like flames.

"The fire?" I asked hoarsely.

He nodded.

"Nothing to do with me," I said.

He snatched my bag from the floor, opened it and pulled out the Benedictine robe that I had borrowed from him. He sniffed it, wrinkled his nose, then shoved it into my face.

"I told you I was going to have it cleaned," I said, my voice muffled by the robe. He pulled it away. "All right, it does smell a bit smoky at that."

He threw it down, then pounded his fists against his chest. He shaded his eyes with one hand and swept his gaze back and forth across the room, then pounded his chest again, looking at me angrily.

"The reason I didn't use you as a lookout this morning was because I didn't trust you this morning," I said. "I'm sorry."

He looked at me questioningly, holding his arms out to both sides.

"Because of this," I said, pulling from my pouch the scrap of parchment that I had taken from Balthazar's room. I handed it to him, and he turned it over and over again, bewildered. Then he looked at me.

"It was in Balthazar's hiding place in his room," I said. "There was nothing else there."

He drew his knees up and rested his arms and chin on them, deep in thought. Then he sat up and looked at me in alarm.

"Claudia searched your place this afternoon," I said. "Sorry. But we had to know."

His jaw dropped. Then he pushed it back up with his left hand and held the right one out to me. I took it.

"It's Christmas Eve," I said. "Have we sufficiently forgiven each other?"

He nodded, then stood and hauled me to my feet. I was finally able to straighten up. I rubbed my jaw.

"Nice move there," I said. "You're lucky I didn't take your head off."

He snorted in derision.

"Fine," I said. "You can make yourself useful. Be a one-man parade back over the bridge. I'll follow your distraction. Peel off to the north once you get to town. I don't want anyone connecting us."

He nodded, then opened the trapdoor and dropped out of sight. I gathered my gear, climbed down, and padlocked the place. I opened the front door cautiously and glanced up the road to where the children were clustering around my colleague. I slipped out and followed from a safe distance.

Everyone waved to the gaily prancing motley character as he capered across the Daurade Bridge. No one paid any attention to the ordinary fellow who trudged along thirty paces behind with a couple of bags slung over his shoulder.

Once through the gates, I turned south. I made one stop along the way, then got to the Yellow Dwarf as the sun was starting to set. The few patrons drifting in for supper were concentrating on their beer. Hugo nodded as I entered, and jerked his head toward the steps. I nodded back and climbed wearily up.

Claudia had her arms wrapped around me before I reached the top step. One more burden didn't matter—I picked her up and carried her into our room.

Portia was asleep in her cradle. Helga was rocking it and looking unusually cross.

"We're all going to be in here together?" she asked.

"Safety in numbers," I said. "We'll take turns standing watch."

"I had twelve—no, thirteen nights in my own room," she said. "That's thirteen nights of solitary sleep in almost thirteen years. I was just getting used to it."

"You could sleep in the hall if you like," offered Claudia. "Guard the threshold like a faithful dog."

"When do I get to be my own fool?" Helga moaned.

"When the Chief Fool of Toulouse decides that you're ready," I said.

I dumped the bags and my wife on the bed.

"Save me some dinner," I said.

"Where are you going now?" asked Claudia.

"To church," I said. "It's Christmas Eve, after all."

"Without your family?" asked Claudia.

"Don't want your foolish minds polluted by that drivel," I said. "I'll be back soon."

The evening services were actually ending when I entered the cathedral. I stepped into the side chapel as the Bishop and the attendant priests bid the scattered congregants a good night. Then a deacon went around the cathedral, snuffing out the torches and candles.

I waited until he left, then walked silently through the darkness toward the apse. Off to the left, light flickered from beneath the door to Father Mascaron's office.

I drew my knife, took a deep breath, then rushed through the door. He looked up in surprise and started to cry out, but I dove across the desk and drove him back against the wall, my hand clamping down on his mouth and the tip of my blade just below his ear.

"Forgive me, Father," I said. "For you have sinned."

CHAPTER 13

I dragged him over to the door, kicked it closed, then patted him down. Sure enough, there was a dagger in his sleeve. I removed it.

"Any good with this?" I asked him.

He glared at me.

"Down on the floor," I said. "Cross your legs and keep them that way. I see a foot move, I'll trim your tonsure closer than you've ever had it before."

"You wouldn't actually kill me," he said softly.

"What's one more body the way things have been going around here lately?" I scoffed. "It will give your master a new topic for his sermon. What greater sacrifice may a priest make for his bishop?"

"You have come to kill me, then," he said.

"I'll hear your confession first," I said. "Start with the lies you've told me, and work your way from there. Any murders you feel like getting off your chest will be held in the strictest confidence until I figure out how to make some money off them."

"You won't make money if I'm dead."

"I may not live to spend it if you're alive," I said. "You're a snake in a cassock, my friend. You used me, and I want to know why."

"To find Milon's book—"

I hit him in the jaw with the haft of my knife. He rocked backwards. I grabbed him by the collar of his cassock to keep him from falling.

"That's going to be nasty if you live long enough to bruise," I said. "I found the book. You described it fairly well. At least the outside. What was inside was quite different."

"It was a book of debts owed—" he began.

I hit him again. Harder this time. I was starting to enjoy this.

"Next lie, I turn the knife around," I said. "There were no accounts, no debts. Not monetary ones, anyway. And the master of the book wasn't Milon Borsella, was it?"

"You know so much, why bother with me?" he asked, then he flinched as I touched the point of my knife to his tender jaw.

"Why did you want me to go after it?" I asked him.

"Because I wanted to know if the Bishop was in it," he said slowly. "And if so, why."

"Didn't you know?"

"I knew nothing about it at all until it went missing," he said. "That accusation by the Borsella brothers in Milon's office was the first I ever heard of it."

"Then what were you looking for in his office?" I asked.

"A will," he said. "Milon Borsella's will."

"His will? Why?"

"Because in this last will, he had left the bulk of his estate to the cathedral," he said.

"You're lying," I said. "Milon Borsella was a Cathar. He would never do anything to help the Church."

"He had been a Cathar," said Father Mascaron. "But I had convinced him to come back to the Church. Or at least, I thought I had."

"When was this?"

"Six weeks ago. It was part of my ministry."

"But he didn't live in your parish," I said. "Why would he be part of your duties?"

"Because my principal duty was helping the cathedral stave off financial ruin," he said. "It's become desperate here. Bringing in Milon would have been an enormous help."

"But why did he want to come here instead of Saint Sernin? His brother was there."

"That was why," said Father Mascaron, a hint of a smile on his face.

"Explain."

"I won't, and there is nothing you can threaten me with that will make me," he said calmly.

"Brave words," I said. "Or . . . is it something you learned from a confession?"

"I couldn't answer you if that was the case," he said.

"So Milon made a will leaving his estate to the cathedral," I mused. "And now it's missing. But that's not what he and the Bishop were arguing about when we first saw them."

"No," he said.

"And he wasn't coming after him for a debt," I said. "That whole conversation was about something else. Was it the book?"

"That's what I have been trying to find out, Fool," said Father Mascaron. "The Bishop was in that book, wasn't he?"

"Yes," I said, a suspicion growing within me. "The Bishop didn't know that you were looking for it, did he? That's why he looked so confused when I said I was still on the hunt. He didn't know you had hired me to find it."

"No," said Father Mascaron. "He didn't."

I slid my knife back into my sleeve.

"Get up," I said. "Stretch your legs if you need to, then sit in your chair. Bear in mind that I will kill you if you take so much as a deep breath."

"Thank you," he said. He stood up slowly, keeping his breathing shallow, then moved behind his desk and sat.

"What side are you on in all this?" I asked.

"I am not sure how many sides there are nowadays," he said. "But I stand for the Church."

"And the Bishop?"

"As long as he stands for the Church, I stand for him," he said. "But I don't know where he stands anymore."

"What made you think this book had anything to do with him?" I asked him.

"When we were walking back after our confrontation with the Borsellas, he asked me what had happened. He knew that I had gone to look for the will, but he came in after the brothers accused me of stealing this book I had never heard of before."

He grimaced.

"When I told him about it, he turned paler than I had ever seen him before, and said, 'The Book of Names stolen! Then we are doomed.' I asked him what he meant by that, but he refused to speak further on the subject. I have endeavored to learn what I could since then. I think that Milon Borsella stole that book from someone. Someone powerful. And it was his discovery of my master's name in it that turned him against the church again."

"That would certainly do it," I agreed. "It's a pity that you did all that good work converting him, only to have it destroyed by the man you did it for. To think I was helping you protect the good name of your church all this time. I feel much more virtuous now. I even feel mildly remorseful about hitting you so hard. Forgive me."

"Forgiveness comes easily to me," he said. "I have a feeling that you are not quite the ruffian that you first appeared to be, either."

"Oh, I am quite the vicious fellow," I said. "Nor do I feel so warmly toward you that I am ready to trust you entirely. But I think that we may part without killing each other for now."

"That's a start," he said. "What next?"

"Depends on what I find out," I said.

"Where did you find the book?" he asked.

"Not yet," I said, shaking my head. "How did you know what it looked like if you had never seen it before?"

"I had seen it. I just didn't know what it was," he said. "When I was in Milon's office once before, I saw him put it in that drawer and lock it. I didn't know it was anything significant at the time, but I remembered enough about its appearance to give you a description."

"I'll accept that for now," I said. "Well, I have abused you enough for one evening. See you at Mass tomorrow. Oh, and a happy Christmas to you."

"May we all live peacefully until the next one," he said.

"Speaking of which, this is yours," I said, tossing his dagger onto the desk.

"Out of curiosity, what would you do if I made a sudden move toward it before you got out that door?" he asked.

"Normally, I would kill you," I said. "But now that we're such good friends, I'd only pin your hand to your desk with my knife."

"Good night, then," he said, putting his hands together in prayer.

I left the cathedral, trying to sort my thoughts into useful little piles, but they kept toppling over into an incoherent muddle. My instincts were to believe Father Mascaron as far as what he said. But he hadn't told me everything. He specifically refused to tell me one thing. Something that came between Milon and Vitalis. Yet Vitalis was the one who ended up with the book. Had he stolen it from Milon after Milon stole it from Guilabert? Or had Milon entrusted him with it?

I thought back to the confrontation in Milon's office between the surviving Borsella brothers and Father Mascaron. Bonet was the one who accused him of stealing the book. Which meant that Bonet knew about it before then. Was his signature on one of the missing pages?

And Vitalis had let his brother's accusation go unchallenged. Indeed, he had encouraged it, helping his brother upend the priest, all the while knowing that the book was safely hidden in his closet. Which meant that Vitalis didn't trust Bonet.

Nice family.

Hugo was cleaning up when I returned to the Yellow Dwarf.

"You're out late," he said. "And without your getup on."

I shrugged.

"Your own business, of course," he said. "Will you be requiring a drink before bed?"

"A pint of something to clear my thoughts," I said.

"You want them cleared or erased?" he asked.

"Just cleared," I said.

He dipped a cup into a barrel and handed it to me. It went down nicely.

"Good night, good Hugo," I said.

"Good night, Senhor."

Claudia was up, nursing the baby, while Helga slept, curled up on a pallet in the corner.

"You look befuddled," she said.

"Then unfuddle me," I said.

I recounted my conversation with Father Mascaron, and she shook her head in disbelief.

"I don't like it," she said. "He still has some game we don't know about."

"Agreed. But assuming what he did say was true, what confessed secret do you think could be of such enormity that it caused a rift between Milon and Vitalis? And was it healed before Milon was killed?"

"The confession had to have come from Vitalis," she said. "Milon hadn't fully returned to the church, from what you described, so he wouldn't have been up to confession yet. And it makes sense that a Saint Sernin monk would go to confession at the cathedral instead of his own abbey to keep things truly private. It must have been an old sin, for him to . . . I wonder."

I waited while she thought.

"An affair," she pronounced. "That must be it."

"Who are you talking about?"

"Vitalis and Béatrix," she said. "It was right in front of me all the time. He was so solicitous toward her. The intimacy between them, it was more than just him comforting a grieving widow. They must have been lovers once."

"That would explain his behavior at his brother's grave," I said. "Interesting. I wonder if you could winnow it out of the widow."

"Theo," she said, looking unhappy.

"What?"

"This makes her more of a suspect in her husband's death."

"To conceal her affair? I suppose it's possible."

"I was thinking about the will," she said. "If it meant she would be disinherited in favour of the cathedral, she could have done it to protect herself. And her children."

"Got rid of her husband, got rid of the new will, and inherited under the old one. Very plausible. But what about Armand? Did she kill him as well?"

"Maybe he really did see Milon's murder, and was trying to get her to pay him to be silent," she said. "Except he was killed the day of Milon's funeral, wasn't he? That means she couldn't have done it. She was surrounded by comforting witnesses the entire time. I give up."

"Let's sleep on it," I suggested. "Big day tomorrow. Our very own Feast of Fools. Oh, and Christmas. We'll stir this town up proper."

"And when the dust settles?"

"We shall see."

I roused Helga for her turn at watch and nestled beside my wife. My thoughts continued to swirl around my poor beleaguered mind, but eventually, I fell asleep.

"Christmas!" hollered Helga, louder than any rooster. "Time to celebrate the First Fool in all His glory. Up, up, up!"

"Up, up, up!" cried Portia, and Helga put her on her shoulders and whirled around the tiny room.

I rolled out of bed and opened the shutters. The sun was just above the horizon.

"What happened to my turn at watch?" I asked Helga.

"That was my Christmas present to you," she said. "You looked exhausted last night, so I let you sleep."

"Very kind of you, Apprentice," I said. "Thank you. Hey, wife!"

I shook Claudia awake.

"What is it?" she asked, yawning.

"Time for your present," I said, handing her a small bag.

She opened it to find a jar of hand cream. She opened it ·and smelled it.

"Lavender," she said, sighing. "How lovely!"

"And for you, my girl, I have this," I said to Portia.

I reached into the bag I had carried back from Martine's shop and pulled out a doll that was nearly as big as my daughter, with buttons for eyes and yarn for hair. Portia gabbled excitedly and clutched it to her.

"Where did you get that?" asked Claudia.

"I had it made," I said. "Stuffed with sawdust fresh from the Borsella mill."

"Lucky girl," sighed Helga. "I wish I had a doll like that when I was little."

"If you're too big for them now, then I have misjudged you," I said, pulling a larger one out and giving it to her.

She looked at it, then at me.

"I am twelve, you know," she said. "Almost thirteen."

"Shall I take it back?" I asked.

"Oh, no," she said, hugging it like Portia was hugging hers.

"I remember you telling me how your only doll was destroyed when you were little," I said. "You shouldn't go through life thinking that will be the last doll you'll ever have."

"Thank you, Theo," she whispered. "I love it."

"And now for you, my husband," said my wife, reaching under the bed.

She pulled out a thin wooden box and handed to me. I opened it to find a knife, with a steel blade honed to a sharpness that could have sliced through sin. I took it out and balanced it on the tip of my finger, then flipped it and caught it.

"It's beautiful," I said.

"Toledan steel," she said. "I thought you could use a new one after you lost your favorite back in Le Thoronet. I bought it off a mercenary who had several. He claimed he could take an ear off from thirty paces with it. He offered to show me his ear collection, but I declined. Oh, and here's the sheath."

It was made from a soft, thin leather that wrapped around my ankle and fit nicely inside my boot. I slid the knife in and out a few times for practice.

"Thank you, my love," I said, kissing her. "I hope that I never have to use it, but I'm glad that I have it."

"I'm glad you have it, too," she said.

"Right," I said, clapping my hands. "Downstairs for exercises. Then on with our makeup and motley and off to Mass."

"You want to wear motley and makeup to Mass with the Feast of Fools banned?" asked Helga.

"Now more than ever," I said. "The Feast may be banned from the cathedral, but fools aren't yet. And let's sing loud enough to drown out that wretched choir. The First Fool ought to have some decent music for His birthday, don't you think?"

Oh, the stares as we took our bench inside the cathedral. Stares of rage from the Bishop and his priests and deacons. Stares of amusement from the Count and his retinue. And stares of what I thought was hope from the rest of the assembly. Did they expect us to start the Feast right then and there? Parade a boy bishop in on an ass and sing parodies of the service? Truly, we could have not made the service any worse had we done so. The Bishop stammered through one inconclusive homily after another, interspersed with more incoherent denunciations of the Cathars; the choir sang half heartedly despite our best efforts to help them. Oddly enough, we caused more distraction by simply showing up and participating enthusiastically in the service than we would have by bringing in the once-usual mayhem.

But the Feast still lived within me, within my wife, within our apprentice, and no doubt within our child. The moment the mass had ended and my feet hit the first step leading out, I seized a trumpet that had been hanging inside my cloak, put it to my lips, and sounded a clarion call that could have wakened the dead in the cemetery before us. Claudia joined in with one of her own, and I continued playing the horn with one hand while pounding on a side drum with the other. Helga danced in front of us, occasionally turning cartwheels or soaring into flips, while Portia rode my shoulders and clapped her hands.

We started marching from the cathedral, the congregation pouring out behind us. I glanced back to see the Bishop standing on the top step, turning nearly apoplectic. I waved and sent one particularly wet blat in his direction, then continued on.

From off to the left, another trumpet sounded, and we turned to see Pelardit on his stilts, a drum at his waist. He started whistling a melody that danced around our trumpet calls. A few streets later, we came up against a raucous crowd that surrounded Jordan, who rode with immense dignity on a small, sullen ass. He hailed us in a pure tenor voice that echoed through the streets, singing something that somehow sounded like Latin while being absolute gibberish.

"To Montaygon Square!" I shouted, and we turned east and headed that way.

There was no market on Christmas Day, of course, so the square was ours. Martine and the boys had wheeled a cart with all of our props there in advance of our arrival. We set up quickly as the crowd surrounded us. Then I stood in the center and swept my arms around grandly.

"The Feast of Fools has been banned from the Church!" I shouted. There was booing, and I held up a hand in admonition. "No, my friends. If the Pope decrees it, then it must be so. But there is no ban on folly, either within the Church or without. Folly cannot be banned. It is everywhere, in all of us. When the Church allowed the Feast of Fools, it kept the folly contained in one place where the Pope could keep an eye on it. But now, he has loosed it upon the world!"

There were cheers.

"Hear me, good citizens of Toulouse!" I cried. "I am Tan Pierre, and for the next twelve days, I am the Lord of Misrule!"

I stripped off my cloak and flung it onto the cart, revealing my full motleyed glory. Then I bowed to the crowd and did a back flip.

And we were off.

They knew the songs, and sang them with us, sending them up to God with more power and devotion than they had any paltry psaltery. They knew the routines and rituals as well as they knew their liturgy. They welcomed the hoariest of gags as if they had never heard them before, and roared at the new ones as if they were revelations of Paradise.

We went on for what seemed like hours, exhausting our repertory and ourselves. I saw people reaching for coins at its close, and held up my hands.

"Today is Christmas!" I shouted. "We accept no money. This is the gift of fools to their fellows! Now, a final hymn."

But as we began it, a martial rhythm interfered. A tramping of heavy boots on stones, growing ever nearer. The song faded without concluding, and uneasy looks passed among the crowd. In the center of the square, the five of us instinctively drew together.

"Soldiers!" cried Helga, spotting them.

"I said this was madness," moaned Jordan. "You knew that throwing the Feast in the Bishop's face would have consequences. You have doomed us all."

"The Bishop has no soldiers," I said. "Let's see what this is all about."

Claudia ran and gathered Portia from Martine's arms, then ran back to me and took my hand.

"Is that Calvet at their head?" she asked.

"Looks like it," I said. Pelardit was on my right. I leaned over to him and whispered, "Do you see her?"

He nodded.

"Good," I said. "You know what to do."

Calvet in full regalia marched through the parted crowd, a squad of twenty soldiers wearing the Count's colors in tight formation behind him. They stopped ten feet in front of us, and the baile looked at us with contempt.

"A happy Christmas to you, Senhor Baile," I said, bowing. "We missed you at services this morning."

"The next word I hear from you will be your last," he sneered. "Take that one. And the woman."

"No!" screamed Jordan as four soldiers stepped forward to seize him.

"What are you doing?" screamed Martine as two more put her in chains. "Jordan? What did you do?"

"By the authority of Count Raimon the Sixth, I arrest the fool Jordan and his wife, Martine, on the charges of murdering

Milon Borsella and Armand de Quinto!" shouted Calvet. "They are to be taken to assizes and held for judgment."

"But I was with him!" shouted Jordan, pointing to me. "Both times, I was with him! Tell him, Fool!"

"Senhor Baile, he speaks the truth," I said, stepping forward. "I will stand witness for him."

He gave me a backhanded blow to the jaw that knocked me down.

"I told you to be quiet, Fool!" he shouted. "Anyone else who interferes will join these two."

He turned and strode away.

"My children!" wailed Martine as they dragged them away. "My boys."

"I'll watch them, Martine!" Claudia cried after her. "It will be all right, I promise."

The boys were huddled together and crying by the cart with the props. Helga ran over to comfort them. Claudia turned to me, a look of horror on her face. I got to my feet, rubbing my jaw. God's payback for hitting a priest, I suppose. I was lucky that the baile had chosen not to wear mailed gauntlets today. Another Christmas gift for Theo. Hooray.

"What now?" asked Claudia.

I looked around the square. Pelardit had vanished.

"You and Helga take the boys back to our place," I said. "I'm going to see what I can do."

"Which place?"

"Might as well go to Honoret's," I said. "There's no hiding us now."

The crowd was chattering excitedly and looking in our direction. We loaded up the cart and put the children in it, then harnessed it to the ass.

"Be careful," I said.

She nodded, and took the ass's reins. Helga trailed them, glancing over her shoulder at me.

A fool and a novitiate guarding three children against the world. My money was on the women. I looked around the square at our remaining audience.

"Ladies and gentlemen, that concludes our entertainment for today," I said. "But we will be back. You may count on it."

I bowed and walked quickly toward the Grande Rue, ignoring all questions. Some people straggled after me, but eventually gave up.

It was late afternoon, and people were hurrying home for Christmas dinners with their families. The taverns were closed to outside business, but I knew a place where there would be wine aplenty, and I was prepared to deplete the supply in my quest.

I pulled a half-emptied wineskin from my pack and swished enough around my mouth to bring my breath to its normal stench, then staggered up a flight of steps to a familiar door and pounded on it repeatedly.

"Open up, you old sod!" I shouted. "It's Christmas, and I've brought a full wineskin. Well, it was full when I bought it, but there's plenty left. Come on, you bastard, let me in!"

Pelardit opened the door, looking perturbed as I fell through it into his arms.

"Happy Christmas, you old fool!" I roared, grappling him in a bear hug. "Were we not magnificent today? Toulouse will never forget what we accom, accom, what we did in that square. Why—good God, there's a lady present!"

He shrugged apologetically as I saw Audrica sitting on the edge of his bed, giggling at my display.

"Why, 'tis the Lady Audrica," I said, bowing low and nearly toppling in the effort, which served to increase the giggling. "Delighted to see you. Pelardit, what debauchery have I stumbled into?"

He waved his hands frenetically in denial.

"Come, come, you rascal," I said, elbowing him in the ribs. "What better way to celebrate Our Savior's birth than with a lovely maid? Why, were I not married, I would be honored, nay, exalted to be at the side of such a one. Lady Audrica, I must salute you properly."

I knelt before her, took her head between my hands and kissed her. I tasted the wine she had been drinking. Good.

"Nectar of the gods!" I sighed.

"And why are you not with your wife?" she said teasingly, pushing me away but not protesting.

"Kicked me out!" I bellowed. "Kicked me out for demanding what any husband is due from his wife on Christmas. And on any day that's not Christmas, when it comes right down to it. Said I was drunk! Me, drunk!"

I took another swallow from the wineskin and passed it to her. She upended it like she had seen one before.

"She has no sense then, Senhor," she pronounced, belching prettily. "Why, if only wives would perform their wifely duties, then sin would be no more."

"Spoken like one who understands marriage from without," I said. "Well, maybe this fool will be the man for you, eh? How came this to pass? Why aren't you at Bazacle?"

"Arnaut lets us have the day off every Christmas," she said, taking another swig from the wineskin. She made as if to pass it on, but we indicated for her to keep on drinking. She obliged us.

"A most generous master," I said. "A strange man, but a jolly one. I liked him tremendously."

"Oh, his generosity of spirit knows no bounds," she said. "Why, I could tell you things."

"Really?" I exclaimed as Pelardit nuzzled her neck and ran his fingers up and down her thigh. "Has the Master of Bazacle been especially generous to pretty little Audrica? Have there been delightful little gifts?"

"Oh, you are a naughty pair, aren't you?" she said. "Just what I wanted for Christmas. I was so surprised when Pelardit accosted me, but he has always been such a dear fool, and I thought, why not?"

"It's always the quiet ones, isn't it?" I said, winking at Pelardit. "I hope your fiancé doesn't mind his borrowing you."

"Oh, him," she laughed. "He's a bigger fool than any of you. Thinks I'm an angel from Heaven. He forgets what happens to angels when they fall."

"Is your master a devil, then?" I asked. "I knew he was no angel, but I thought him merely a man."

"Oh, he's more than a man," she confided. "Like a bull. Why, whenever he has one of his little meetings he—oh, but I'm not supposed to tell."

"Drink up, milady," I said. "And don't worry about us. Confessing to a fool is like confessing to a priest, only safer."

"Ah, priests," she said, dismissing the entire clergy with a wave of her hand. "They might as well be celibate. I've never had one who was any good."

"So you've entertained the clergy at Bazacle, have you?" I asked.

"Not supposed to tell," she sang, waving a finger at me.

"And a consul or two, I'll warrant."

"Oh, that was a night, let me tell you," she said. "There was, let me see, Pons and Guilliem and, whatshisname, Bonet."

"Milon's brother?"

"Right," she said, suddenly sad. "Milon. Poor, poor Milon."

"Tell me about Milon," I said. "What was he like?"

"Never knew," she said. "Would have liked him. He seemed nice. Came to the château a lot, but always about money, money, money."

"Did he and Arnaut argue about money?"

She nodded, almost falling with the motion.

"What happened to Milon?" I asked.

She was drifting off. I shook her a little, and she looked up at me like a child and smiled.

"What happened to Milon?" I asked her.

"Told Evrard about him," she said dreamily. "Wasn't, wasn't true, but he'd believe anything I'd tell him, stupid boy."

"What did you tell Evrard about Milon?" I asked.

"Told him he took me by force," she said. "Wish he had for real. He was a handsome man."

"Who told you to tell him that, Audrica?" I asked her softly.

"My master," she said. Then she leaned back into Pelardit's arms and started to snore.

CHAPTER 14

Pelardit eased the sleeping maid onto his bed, then pulled her legs up so that she was lying comfortably. We looked at her for a moment.

"How much did you give her?" I asked.

He held his thumb and forefinger apart an inch.

"That should keep her out until morning," I said. "Are you ready for the next part?"

He nodded, looking at her regretfully, then pulled off her shoes and began to undress her. I poured some water into a basin and scrubbed my makeup off. I patted my face dry, then stripped off my motley and pulled on some normal work-man's clothing. I selected a brown wig with hair much longer than my own from the collection on Pelardit's shelves, then glued on a matching mustache.

"How do I look?" I asked, turning back to Pelardit.

He was staring down at the now nude form of Audrica, a look of reverence on his face.

"Come on, it hasn't been that long," I said.

He puffed out his cheeks, deflated them in a long, dying whistle, then threw a blanket over her and began taking his motley off.

"I should be less than half an hour, there and back," I said. "Don't fall asleep. And don't do anything you'll regret."

He nodded. I went out the door and closed it softly behind me.

The sun was beginning to set as I reached the entrance to the courtyard of the Borsella place. The children were being summoned inside. I waited and watched. Evrard came out, his keys in his hand, and came to lock the gate. He hesitated as he saw me.

"May I help you?" he asked. "We distributed alms earlier, but I might be able to find something in the kitchen."

"Thought I might help you," I said in a low voice. "You're that Evrard, aren't you?"

"Who are you?" he asked.

"One who would be your friend," I said. "Closing up shop for the night, I see."

"This is no shop," he snapped. "And I will trouble you to—"

"You're the one with the troubles," I said. "World of troubles rolled into one lovely lass."

He went very still.

"What do you want?" he asked.

"I'm the messenger of misery, the bad news bearer," I said. "She's been pulling the wool over your eyes, boy, and I'm here to cure your blindness. Just like Our Savior did, only I do it with the laying on of words, not hands."

"Where is she? Is she safe?"

"As to the second question, do you mean is she safe from danger or is she something other than dangerous in her own right?" I asked. "Yes to the first, depending on what you call danger. No to the second, as are all of Eve's rotten daughters. As to the where, I'm willing to show you, but the information grows stale fast, 'cause she'll be moving on to the next one soon if I'm any judge of drabs."

"You lie!" he shouted, lunging at my throat, and I skipped back a few steps to avoid him.

"Now, that's no way to treat your new best friend," I admonished him. "Do that again, and I won't tell you who her lover is."

"You know this for a fact," he said.

"Any man can say a thing and call it a fact," I said. "I can show you the thing and let you decide for yourself. You coming?"

He pulled the gate shut behind him and locked it.

"Take me to her," he growled.

"I am your servant," I said, bowing. "Follow me."

I led him through the Portaria as the bells for Vespers rang through the city. The gates closed behind us, sealing the town from the bourg. I led Evrard to Pelardit's place.

"You know, the first time I came to Toulouse, I was on a pilgrimage to Compostela," I said conversationally. "Just a kid. We'd been walking all day, and I was thirsty as hell. Saw a pond right after we came through the gate, so I ran down and plunged my hands into the water and drank like there was no tomorrow. Worst water I ever had. Tasted like a cow had died in it. Looked up to see a bunch of fellows laughing their asses off at my expression. It was a tanner's pit. I spent the rest of the day heaving my guts out. Damn near died. That was my welcome to Toulouse."

"What's the point of all this?" he asked me.

"No point," I said. "Just talking. I mean, it's like that girl of yours. You think she's a long, cool drink of spring water waiting for you at the end of a hot day, but she's poison below the surface, boy. I saw her drinking with that fool, the one who doesn't talk. Had her hands all over him. He took her up here, not an hour ago, and she looked like she had more than an hour's worth of fun to give him. She's played you for a fool, and with a fool to boot. Here's the door. Shall we knock first?"

He charged and hit it with his shoulder. Pelardit had thoughtfully left it unlatched, so it swung open easily. Audrica and the fool were entwined on the bed in apparent post-coital bliss. He had draped her right arm and leg artfully over his body.

And there was now a knife in Evrard's hand.

"I'll kill you!" he roared.

I dove at his knees from behind as he rushed toward the bed. He went down in a heap. Pelardit shoved Audrica aside and leapt into the air, gathering himself into a ball as he did. He landed with all of his weight on our jealous keykeeper, knocking the wind out of him momentarily. I grabbed Evrard's wrist and twisted it until he let the knife go.

"I'll kill you! Kill you!" he kept roaring, spittle running down his chin.

"Like you did your master?" I shouted.

"He deserved it!" he shouted. "He defiled her. I avenged her honor!"

"Then you avenged nothing," I said. "She has no honor, and your master never touched her."

"She told me everything!" he shouted.

"She lied to you, Evrard," I said. "And you believed her like the lovestruck dupe that you are. Trust me, friend, your beloved is the whore of Bazacle, and Guilabert her procurer and chief customer."

"No," he moaned, but there was doubt on his face.

"You have any rope in this place?" I asked Pelardit.

He pointed to the second shelf, where it was neatly coiled and stowed. I grabbed it and tied Evrard's hands behind his back. Then I did the same for his ankles, and trussed everything together so there was no chance of him getting out of it.

Pelardit got up and started putting his motley back on. Evrard rolled onto his side and looked at the two of us.

"I know him," he said. "Who are you?"

"Another fool," I said, taking off the wig and mustache. "We haven't met, but I've seen you around. Lovely bit of testimony before the baile at your late master's inquest. Moved me almost to tears. Almost. But now our colleague and his wife are set to swing for a man you killed. We aren't about to let that happen."

"I heard about Jordan and Martine," he said.

"Heard and did nothing," I said, sitting by him. "That would have been another pair of deaths on your hands. Two nice boys orphaned by your cowardice. Don't tell me you did this out of heartsickness. You have no heart."

"I would not have let them hang!" he shouted. "I only found out tonight. I was praying for guidance."

"Your prayers have been answered," I said. "I am your guide. Tell me how your master got the Book of Names from Guilabert."

"How did you know?" he said, gaping at me.

"Answer questions. Don't ask them," I said, resting the tip of my boot on his throat for a second.

"Master was a Cathar," he gasped quickly.

I removed the boot.

"There had been rumors," he continued. "Some kind of plot against the Cathars. They always feared Rome, but this time the danger seemed to be somehow connected to the Château Bazacle. My master had constant dealings with Guilabert, sometimes lending money for his projects, sometimes borrowing when his own coffers were short. He started spying on him. He had me get what information I could out of Audrica, but that never sat right with me."

"Spare me," I said. "When did he get the book?"

"It was a few days before he died," he said. "Master was laughing like a madman when he got it. He sat in his office and started thumbing through it. I didn't know what it was or what it meant, but I knew it came from Guilabert. He wouldn't show it to me. Then he got to one page and stopped laughing. He said, 'No, not him,' and he tore it out and burned it with a candle until it was gone. Then he locked it in that little drawer in his desk and made me give him my key for it. 'No one in here when I am not,' he told me. 'Not you, not a maid. No one.'"

"Did you see the book again?"

"No," he said. "I swear it."

"Tell about the night he died."

He closed his eyes, tears streaming from them.

"He came home, changed, then went out," he said. "Just like I testified."

"But there was more."

"She came to me," he whispered. "I was locking up for the night when I heard her call my name. I came out, and she was hiding in the shadows. When she came into the light she—was bleeding, and her clothes torn half off—"

He started sobbing.

"Whatever she was, whatever she looked like, it was all to deceive you," I said. "Tell me what happened."

"She said that she had been the one who helped Milon Borsella steal the book from Guilabert," he said, nearly choking on his sobs. "She said that he had—had violated her, then threatened her with shame and scandal if she did not help him. But that her master suspected her, and was threatening to kill her if she did not get it back. And that she had gone to Milon that night to try and persuade him to return it for her sake, and that he had raped and beaten her and spat upon her bloodied—by God, I was in such a fury that I ran through the bourg toward where I knew the Cathars held their meetings. I encountered him as he was coming back. He thought there was some emergency, he came right up to me, and before I could think anymore I picked up a stone from the ground and struck him with it."

He stopped, shaking his head.

"He trusted me," he said in disbelief. "And I murdered him. All I could think of was her. I took his keys, and took the desk key that he had taken from me back. Then I threw the other keys into the canal and ran back to Audrica, and she cried and said what a hero I was, and we went into the office together and I unlocked the drawer."

"And it wasn't there," I said.

"No," he said. "I didn't know what to do. She said it must have still been on his body. I didn't want to go back there, but she started crying again and there was nothing else but to do it. I went back, and the book wasn't there. I looked around where he had fallen. Then I heard someone coming. I rolled him into the tanner's pit and fled."

"How did Bonet Borsella find out about the book?"

"How did you know about him?"

"I find things out," I said. "It's what I do. Tell me about Bonet."

"After the fight with Father Mascaron, he drew me aside. He said that Milon had confided in him about the book, and that he needed to find it. It was a matter of life or death. I didn't know if he was telling me the truth or not. I didn't care. I was too frightened of being found out, so I did what he asked and started searching for it. But I never found it. I guess you did."

"Ever learn what this was all about?"

"No. That's all that I know. What are you going to do with me?"

"You had best get used to that rope," I said. "You're going to be seeing a lot of it in the not too distant future."

I pulled him up to a sitting position.

"Fellow looks like he could use a drink," I observed. "Pelardit, do you have anything left in that wineskin from earlier?"

He held his thumb and forefinger apart an inch.

"Then in the spirit of what's left of Christmas, let's give it to poor Evrard here," I suggested. "Might be the last decent taste of wine he'll ever get."

Pelardit picked up the wineskin, fiddling with the opening for a moment. Then he held it to Evrard's lips and tilted it. The keykeeper drank greedily. A few minutes later, he was asleep.

"Better put Audrica's clothes back on," I said. "Then tie her up, and gag them both."

I changed back into my motley and reapplied my makeup. By the time I was done, Audrica was dressed and bound, sitting next to her beloved.

"They make a handsome couple," I observed. "They could get married before they hang. I'll see if I can get Father Mascaron to perform a gallows wedding. All right, looks like you're going to have to be a jailer for the night. Keep them quiet. But keep them alive."

He nodded, then looked at me, a question on his face.

"I'm going home to get some sleep," I said. "Some dishes

need to simmer overnight rather than boil immediately. I'll make sure you get some relief in the morning."

He sighed, and hauled the two onto his spare pallet and tossed a blanket over them. I left, and he bolted the door behind me.

Claudia was still up and waiting for me by the time I got back to Honoret's.

"How are the children?" I asked.

She held a finger to her lips and beckoned me over to Helga's room. The two boys were in her bed, nestled into her arms on either side, the smaller one with his thumb in his mouth. Claudia closed the door softly.

"She insisted on staying with them," she said. "Cheered them up, made them laugh, assured them that the great Tan Pierre would have their parents free by tomorrow. Can you do that?"

"Tomorrow may be optimistic," I said. "But Monday may be good."

"Everything go as expected?" she asked.

"Pelardit lured Audrica to his room quite easily," I said. "I had no idea he was such an accomplished seducer."

"Doesn't surprise me in the least," she said. "What did you find out from her?"

I filled her in on what I had learned.

"Evrard," she said. "Betrayed by his love, betrayer of his master. Hanging will be a mercy for him now. What made you think Audrica was the key to the keykeeper?"

"I thought that there had to be some connection between Guilabert's household and that of Milon, both for Milon to be able to get to the book and for Guilabert to suspect him of the theft. Evrard seemed a likely candidate, given his connection to Audrica, and that conversation Helga overheard between him and Bonet Borsella. When I learned about Audrica's true nature, I thought she might have been Guilabert's means of exploiting Evrard's loyalties."

"And if you had been wrong?"

"Then she would have woken up in Pelardit's bed with a nasty hangover," I said. "I figured that would not have been such an unusual thing for her."

"You realize that this won't be enough to bring down Guilabert," she said. "The word of a drunken maid against his will hardly stand up against scrutiny."

"No," I agreed. "But a murder solved on Christmas. I call that a good day's work. Shall we to bed?"

She bowed her head demurely.

"Senhor, I am prepared to do my wifely duty as you require," she said. "It is Christmas, after all."

"Oh, good heavens," I muttered. "I only said that because I was playing a role."

"Are you turning me down?" she asked, shooting me a coy glance.

"I didn't say that," I said. "Husbands have duties, too."

"And we are nothing if not slaves to duty," she murmured, taking my hand and leading me to our room.

We rose at dawn and awakened Helga, but let the boys sleep while we did our exercises.

"Here's a question for you, husband," said Claudia, who had slid to the floor in a split-legged position. "Mascaron said that Milon had come back to the Church, but all this time he was spying on Guilabert for the Cathars. How could he have been doing both?"

"His return to the Church might have been part of the

role he was playing for the Cathars," I said. "Sounds like this moneylender was capable of making anyone believe anything at the time he said it. A man I could have looked up to."

"Except he got found out," said Helga.

"Yes," I said.

"And got killed," she said.

"True."

"And we've been found out," she continued. "Donatus was watching us. Mascaron suspects us. The Count thinks you're more than just a fool. What's to keep us from getting killed?"

"Nothing, Apprentice. Aren't you glad you joined the Guild?"

"Every minute of my day," she said, grinning.

"Good. What's the older boy's name again?"

"Oliver."

"Does he seem reliable? Do you think he could run an errand for me later?"

"Will it help his parents get out of prison?"

"Yes."

"Then he will do it to perfection."

"Good," I said. "I must to the Château Narbonnais to see how Jordan fares. Helga, mind the boys for now. Claudia, meet me at Jordan's house in an hour."

The Palace of Justice also had dungeons underneath. I showed my pass to the captain of the guards, who was not surprised to see me.

"He's been shouting for you ever since they put him in," he said. "He's got good lungs, so he's quite the shouter. Started running down around dawn."

"I've brought some food for the two of them," I said. "Is that all right?"

He looked around carefully, then pocketed the coin I was holding out and nodded.

"Jordan's down that end, his wife's at the other," he said.

"They're married. They can't be kept together?" I asked.

"Orders," he said. "Besides, you put a married couple facing the gallows in a cell together, and they'll be keeping us up all night.

"Everyone needs to sleep sometime," I agreed.

I went to see Martine first. Her cell had a simple wooden door, barred on the outside. A guard opened it. She sat on the floor, her knees drawn to her chest, one leg shackled to a ring on the floor. She looked up blearily at me.

"I brought you cheese and sausage," I said, handing her a parcel. "The sausage comes from a reputable place, not those boys by the Maison Commune."

She took it from me without expression and placed it on the floor by her.

"None of this would have happened if you hadn't come here," she said flatly. "What will become of my boys?"

"Listen to me," I said, kneeling before her and taking her hand. "Your boys are safe, and we are doing everything we can to clear your names. I vow that I will get you out of this."

"Brave words to a condemned woman," she said. "Stop wasting your time with me and go help us."

She didn't look up as I left.

Jordan was in a larger cell that he shared with two other men. He came forward to the bars enclosing it when he saw me and gripped my hand tightly.

"Thank God," he whimpered. "I didn't know when they'd let you see me. The boys?"

"Safe in our care," I said. "I brought cheese and sausages."

"Oh, bless you," he said, grabbing it from me and tearing

into it greedily. "The fare here is, well, below my usual standards. Have you talked to Calvet?"

"You saw what he did," I said. "But we have made some progress. I am hopeful that I will be able to exonerate you. And if Calvet won't listen, I will go to the Count himself."

"Thank you," he said fervently.

"There is only one thing I need," I said.

"What's that?" he asked, tearing off another piece of sausage with his teeth.

"Balthazar's notes," I said.

He nearly choked, finally spitting the half-chewed sausage onto the floor.

"I have no idea what you're talking about," he said finally.

"Oh, that wasn't convincing at all," I said. "Had a chat with Hugo over at the Yellow Dwarf. Excellent fellow. Makes a lovely ale. You know him?"

"Of course," said Jordan weakly.

"He talked quite fondly about his late tenant, Balthazar. Fond memories of seeing him up late, writing his notes down. One of the duties of a Chief Fool is to send reports back to the Guild. I've done it throughout my career. So, I was curious as to what happened to those notes of his. I checked his room, found his hiding place, and all I found was a torn piece of parchment that someone had left behind when they were taken."

"And you suspect me?" he protested. "Why not Pelardit?"

"I suspected both of you," I said. "But we already searched Pelardit's place and found nothing. Which leaves you. I know you didn't murder Milon and Armand, but if I am going to clear this mess up, I'll need every scrap of information I can lay my hands on. I am certain that you have the notes, and no doubt failed to turn them over because you still have ambitions to be Chief Fool here."

"But—"

"I could take the time to find out what I need to know on my own," I said. "It might be better for you if I'm thorough rather than quick. I don't think they'll get around to trying the two of you until after Twelfth Night, so there's some leeway. Of course, you'll be sitting here. You might want to pace yourself on the cheese and sausage—it's all I'm bringing you."

"Please, you can't leave me here." he begged me. "I'm sorry. It was a stupid, selfish thing to do, I see that now."

"The notes," I said. "I will tear your place apart until I find them, but it would be quicker if you told me the exact location."

"In my wife's shop," he said. "In the back, there are several bolts of cloth. The notes are rolled up inside the dark green one at the bottom. Pelardit has an extra set of keys."

"By this time tomorrow, either you will be walking out of here, or I will be joining you," I said. "Pray for all of us."

He went down to his knees immediately. I turned and left him, but as I glanced back, he wasn't praying. He was scrabbling through the straw on the floor for the piece of sausage he had spat out.

It was Sunday. Saint Stephen's Day, in fact, and I remembered that with a pang of regret for poor Zeus, languishing in his stable instead of going to the cathedral for the blessing of the animals. The petty betrayals of those you care for while pursuing the greater good add up over time. I decided to get him a few bushels of dried apples as a belated present.

Assuming I didn't get killed over the course of the day, which seemed like a real possibility.

I made some arrangements, then went to visit Pelardit. I knocked, using the pattern we had set up beforehand. He opened the door a crack, one hand concealed behind it, then opened it wider when he saw that I was alone. I entered. He sheathed the knife that he was hiding.

"Sleep well?" I asked him.

He shook his head. I looked over at Evrard and Audrica, who stared at me in terror.

"Good morning, lovebirds," I greeted them cheerily. "I apologize for the accommodations. I hope to have something a little more appropriate for you shortly."

This didn't seem to improve their spirits much, but I didn't particularly care at this point.

"Have you got Jordan's spare keys?" I asked.

He nodded and took them from a hook on the wall.

"Good," I said. "Your relief should be arriving shortly. When they do, I want you to go to our place. Check in with Helga and make sure she and the children are all right, then keep watch from somewhere outside. We'll be back by noon."

He nodded. I beckoned to him, and he drew closer.

I leaned forward to whisper, "I'm asking you to protect my child. Do you understand the level of faith that I have in you?"

He nodded, a look of resolve on his face.

"Thanks," I said. "See you later."

I walked quickly to Jordan's house, then looked around for Claudia. I didn't see her. I sighed.

"Come out, come out, wherever you are," I sang.

She emerged from a rubbish heap that I swore would not have concealed a mouse.

"Jordan has Balthazar's notes," I said, holding up his keys.

"You are starting to be right a lot lately," she observed, smiling. "Let's hope it continues."

We unlocked the padlock on Martine's shop and went inside, closing the door behind us. In the back were the bolts of cloth, just as Jordan had said. We took the dark green one and unrolled it. At its core were five sheaves of parchment, rolled tightly together and secured with red ribbons. We untied one and separated the leaves. There had to be fifty pages, each covered in cramped, spidery handwriting. The other sheaves looked to contain the same.

"This is going to take a while," said Claudia.

"Good thing you know how to read," I said.

"In almost as many languages as you," she said. "What am I looking for?"

"Anything about the people we've been dealing with," I said. "Especially Guilabert."

The first page I looked at was dated September of 1179. I skimmed through the sheaf as quickly as I could, scanning for names.

"Hey, I found your visit to Toulouse," said Claudia. "You were still calling yourself Droignon then, weren't you?"

"Yes."

" 'He comes across like a drunken idiot,' " she read. " 'I sense that the idiocy is an act, but the drunkenness is all too real. I wonder what he saw in Beyond-the-Sea that drives him to this excess, but his time here was too brief for me to learn what it was.' "

"Sounds like me back then," I said. "This one goes too far back to be useful today, I think. I'm going to try a more recent one."

I pulled out another sheaf and started thumbing through it.

"Here's something about Donatus," she said. " 'Captain Donat showed up with returning contingent from Acre. While others boasted of battles and slaughter, he was reticent, yet I sensed that he had seen more than any of them. One particularly rowdy soldier drew his knife in anger over nothing, and Donatus moved with frightening speed and strength to disarm him before anyone else could react. Upon seeing who did it, soldier quailed noticeably.' "

"Keep looking for him," I said.

I worked my way backwards from the most recent entries.

"Balthazar mentions the rumors of the conspiracy against the Cathars here," I said. "He was friendly with their leaders. He was looking into it, but didn't come up with anything solid."

"Donatus next shows up supervising the construction of the Bazacle dam," she said. " 'He is quite the brutal taskmaster. Rumor he nearly beat man to death for not keeping pace as example for the rest. I have seen him talking many times with Arnaut Guilabert, one of the millers behind project.' "

"Interesting. Follow that up."

She flipped through the pages rapidly.

" 'Spoke with Clermont about why he's leaving,' " she read. " 'He sold his shares to Guilabert at low price. Frightened, but won't say why.' Here's something else. 'Two more millers sold shares to Guilabert. Someone getting to them. On a hunch, mentioned Donat's name to one, and he looked around fearfully and told me never to say name again. Guilabert must have lion's share of Bazacle by now. If he guessed right, stands to make a fortune.' "

"Guilabert certainly guessed right."

"Why didn't Balthazar try and stop him?"

"The Fools' Guild has enough on its plate trying to keep the peace," I said. "This is about markets, not something that would concern us. If it turned out that Guilabert was acquiring all of that wealth and using it to foment war, that would be a different matter, but—"

We looked at each other.

"My God, Theo," she breathed. "What if that was it? What if this was about power?"

"But whose power?" I asked. "Certainly not the Count's. It would be madness. He has an army."

"Which is spread out over the Toulousain trying to maintain all of the recent conquests," she pointed out. "And those conquests were made at the behest of the consulate, not the Count. He was fine with the way things were before."

"And the consulate started those campaigns only after the recent elections tilted the balance toward the bourg," I mused. "And all of the bourg consuls derive their wealth in some manner from the Bazacle mills, so are beholden to Guilabert. We saw many of their names in the book. But why Donatus and the Bishop? There must be something about them in particular."

I went to the beginning of the sheaf in my hand. The entries were about four years old.

" 'Donat has become a Benedictine,' " I read. " 'Puzzles me. Never saw man more unsuited to life of peaceful contemplation. Yet there he kneels, bull with tonsure amidst flock of timid sheep. Of them, Vitalis Borsella might have balls to stand up to him, but only if saw him as threat. But why would he? Why should I? Yet I do, though cannot fathom it.' " I flipped through more pages. "Here's something else. 'Don't know why never occurred to me before. Donat and Guilabert—something worth looking into there.' "

"Keep going, Theo," said Claudia.

"'Checked into Donat's past. Born north of here, but no one knows family. Must take trip. Annoying.' He leaves a month later. Here we go: 'Found village where Donat born. Mother had gone to Toulouse, fell on hard times, prostitute. Banned from city, came back dishonored, with child. Told neighbors boy's father was married miller who promised to take care of her. Occasional visits from lover, usually cloaked on horseback. She died when Donat was small. Lover came to claim him. Baptized in village church, priest remembers mother giving him name of Donatus Guilabert! Dates are right—Arnaut's brother! Explains connection, but not why Benedictine.' And that seems to be it for Brother Donatus."

"An illegitimate Guilabert," she said.

"A bull among sheep," I said. "When we set the fire, he was the one who took charge. He may not be the abbot, but he runs Saint Sernin."

"But not the Bishop," she said. "The cathedral's not part of the Benedictine order."

"But Raimon de Rabastens was elected by the canons," I said. "Half of them are from Saint Sernin, half from the cathedral parishes. Brother Peire, the legate, said it was a close election. What if the Guilabert brothers bought the bishopric for Raimon, just like they bought the consulate?"

"Except the Bishop's an ally of the Count," she pointed out.

"The Count thinks so. But what has the Bishop been doing lately? Preaching against the Cathars. Brother Peire was surprised to hear he's doing that—he wanted him to sound the alarm about them a year ago."

"And what would preaching against the Cathars accomplish? Seizure of their lands by the Count? How would that increase the coffers of Bazacle?"

"I don't think the Count would go that far," I said. "He has allies among the Cathars as well. He wouldn't come down on them just because the Church tells him to."

"But if the Bishop of Toulouse and the Abbot of Saint Sernin both decree that he must, and he refuses?"

"Then he could be excommunicated," I said. "He's wriggled out of that before. But if this collection of names means a long-term plan by Guilabert to take control of Toulouse, then maybe the Bishop's a recent acquisition. And if the Count is weakened by another excommunication, Guilabert's forces will be ready to seize power."

"Did I just hear you agree with me?"

"You knew I would, sooner or later. Sometimes it takes me a while to catch up to you."

"Well, good," she said, rolling up Balthazar's notes and re-tying them. "Enough reading. Time to act. Where shall we start?"

"We need some proof of all this to take to the Count."

"Where do you propose we get it? I didn't notice any shops with evidence for sale."

"From Vitalis," I said. "He's been hiding the book instead of coming to the authorities. We are going to get him to tell us all about it."

CHAPTER 15

The bells rang for None, and once again we watched the ants scurry into the anthill.

I pointed out our quarry to Oliver, who stood holding tightly onto Helga's hand.

"The big one, second from the end," I said. "Do you mark him?"

"Yes," said Oliver.

"As soon as the final hymn ends, you give him this and then you leave immediately," I instructed the boy, handing him a small scroll. "Don't speak, don't answer any questions. Can you do it?"

"Yes," he said firmly.

"Good boy," I said, patting him on the back. "Now, go."

He walked across the square to the church and went inside.

"You know what to do?" I asked Claudia and Helga.

They nodded.

"Good luck," I said.

Helga vanished. Claudia turned to me.

"We still haven't figured out who killed Armand," she said. "I forgot about him in all the rush."

"I haven't," I said. "But there are things to do first. I will see you later."

She gave me a quick kiss, then left. I watched her walk away until she disappeared around the curve of the street. Then I turned and walked toward the river, muttering and humming the Office of None. I turned upriver as I passed Saint Pierre des Cuisines. Sunday afternoon, and the tanners' pits loomed on my right, their toxic waters seeping into the skins of dead things while their minders were at prayer or rest. I went through the gate. Guilabert's fortress glowered at me, but that was not my destination. I passed Bonet Borsella's sawmill, which was quiet except for the groaning of the wheels.

A stone bridge, wide enough for two wagons to pass each other without touching wheels, connected the bank to the island. I crossed it unchallenged. One mill after another lined both sides of the channel, but there were no millers at work. At the far side of the island, the Bazacle dam stretched across the Garonne. There was a single sluice gate right by the shore. It was open since the mills weren't in operation, and the water poured through in a torrent, spreading back out across the shallow riverbed. A small footbridge crossed the sluice to the dam proper. I walked over it, stepping carefully from piling to piling until I was about twenty feet from shore. The Garonne surged against the dam, occasionally sending up some frigid spray. I wrapped my cloak tightly around my motley and sat facing upstream. I watched the river as the sun set to my left, taking what little warmth there was with it.

I sensed his approach without hearing it, I'm not sure how. His footsteps made no sound, yet there was a disturbance in the world, a vast amount of air displaced by a massive body of a man. I glanced over my shoulder to see him standing at the other end of the footbridge, his face hidden in the shadows of his cowl. I looked back at the river.

"I have been thinking about water, Brother Vitalis," I said, not giving him another glance. "Where it comes from, how it gets here. It's so clean when it begins its journey, whether from the mountains or raining from God's Heaven above. It travels in brooks and streams, then small rivers, then large. And in each place where men touch it, it becomes more defiled."

I cupped my hands and dipped them into the Garonne, then sipped from them.

"This still isn't too bad right here," I said. "This is the last point before the city captures it. And just two miles downriver, I wouldn't drink it if I was dying of thirst. It becomes rank, filled with death and decay, all because it has come to Toulouse. Does that happen to people when they come here? Do they start out as pure as a mountain stream or Heaven's rain, then become corrupt when they come to this city?"

"Mountain streams aren't pure," he said.

I started, quickly getting to my feet. It wasn't Brother Vitalis's voice.

"Bears piss in them," he continued. "So do wolves. But they drink from them anyway. They have no choice. We do. We come to the city, knowing the dangers, expecting to be corrupted. We drink the water. It's our choice."

"Brother Donatus," I said. "I wasn't expecting you."

"Apparently not," he said, pulling down his cowl. He held up the scroll I had given Oliver. "This was misdelivered. That child must have been told to take it to the large monk. That happens to Brother Vitalis and me frequently. We usually get a laugh out of it."

"I'm surprised anything makes you laugh," I said.

"Nothing from you has done so," he said.

"Then I have failed in my profession," I replied. "Forgive me."

"I took the liberty of reading it," he said. "'I have what you lost. Meet me at the dam after sunset.' It looks like you have something that doesn't belong to you."

"I have many things that once belonged to others," I said. "Could you narrow it down?"

"Something that you took," he said.

"Anything I take I regard as mine," I said, smiling broadly.

"Things that are taken can be taken back," he said.

"Not everything. A life, once taken, cannot be returned."

"Are you accusing me of murder?" he said.

"As a matter of fact, no," I replied. "Not recently, anyway. But I'm new in town."

"The book," he said.

"You mean this?" I asked, pulling it out of my pouch.

"Where did you find it?"

"I took it from someone who took it from someone who took it from someone else," I said.

"I have been searching for it for some time now. Lately, I have noticed that you and your fellow fools have been popping up in the same places I've been looking. Then came that fire, and I realized in the middle of everything that there was an extra monk there, a tall man who kept his cowl up at all times. Is that when you obtained it?"

"Maybe," I said. "Is that why you were watching my place?"

"Maybe. Hand it over."

"Why should I?"

"Because I represent one who has a proper claim to it," he said.

"Your big brother?" I asked.

"Now, how did you know about that?" he asked softly.

"No shame in being a bastard," I said cheerfully. "I'm one as well. Not a whoreson like you, though I've been called one often enough, but still a bastard through and through. Why do you want this book so much? Is it really worth killing for?"

"Someone thinks so," he said, stepping forward.

I jumped over to the downstream pilings and held it over the river. He stopped.

"Not much of a reader myself," I said. "Is it worth more dry or wet?"

"I am willing to pay a fair price," he said quickly.

"But I don't even know what the market value is," I said. "Tell me why it's important so I know how much to sell it for."

"It's worth your life if you don't give it to me," he said.

"That doesn't help at all," I said. "My life is worth a great deal to me. More than I can afford most the time. But everyone else thinks I'm a worthless fool. How am I to know the truth?"

"No man is worthless in God's sight," he said, clasping his hands in mock piety.

"You sound like a monk, you look like a monk, yet you are willing to kill me," I said. "Will you shrive me first?"

"To save your soul, I would," he said.

"Thanks, but on second thought, no thanks," I said. "Want to buy a book?"

"I am a poor man," he said, holding his hands out to show they were empty. But Lord, they were large. "If you were to give it to me freely, I could arrange for an indulgence for your soul."

"From the Bishop himself, no doubt," I replied. "I saw his name at the end. Hmm, eternal Paradise in exchange for a donation to Donatus. Not a shabby offer at all. But what happens if I do that, and then your big brother's plan ends up killing people? What happens to my newly purchased soul then?"

"What plan would that be?" he asked, taking another step toward me.

"Guilabert's a miller at heart," I said. "The river runs, the wheel turns, and all manner of gears and shafts spin away, grinding and grinding until all is dust. Who will be grist for the Guilabert mill? The Cathars? Not worth the effort, if you ask me."

"I didn't ask," said Donatus, starting to walk toward me again.

"He's going after the Count, isn't he?"

He stopped.

"How did he coerce all of these men into signing their lives to him?" I asked. "Debts forgiven? Threats by you?"

"A little of each," he said. "Some came willingly. They saw which way the wind was blowing. The Count is a deeply flawed man. Left alone, he will lead us to ruination."

"And big brother will run things better, I suppose."

"He is a great man," he said. "He's been planning all of this for a very long time. And I have helped him, every step of the way."

"Very fraternal of you, Brother Donatus. When did the Bishop join the cause?"

"A few months ago," he said. "He had many debts. Arnaut bought them up and traded them for a bishop's loyalty."

"I'm surprised it was that recent," I said. "I thought your brother had bought the Bishop's election. Weren't you the canon who switched his vote to Raimon de Rabastens?"

"No," he replied.

"That was me," said Brother Vitalis.

Donatus turned, a knife suddenly in his hand. Vitalis was standing with his arms folded. He had come up quietly while we were in the middle of our conversation.

"How did you know about this?" asked Donatus. "The message was delivered to me."

Vitalis held up another scroll.

"A young lady handed me this," he said. "It said to follow you, and I would learn about the book."

"Two scrolls, two messengers, two monks," said Donatus, turning back to me. "Neatly done."

"I am something of a planner myself," I said. "Now, I could have the two of you bid against each other for the book, but an auction where the only participants are monks doesn't sound like it would be very lucrative. Therefore, I propose a contest. The champion shall win it."

"You said that you could sell tickets for a match between us," said Brother Vitalis.

"Oh, I would dearly love to see that," I said. "Alas, there was no time to advertise this battle. But the match I suggest is one of words, not blows. The best story wins. I have heard from Donatus. Now it is Vitalis's turn to tell me about the book, and why it should belong to him."

"So that it will not belong to Guilabert," he said.

"Succinctly put and a good argument," I said. "But I would like more of a story, if you please. How did you get it?"

"From Milon," he said. "Two days before he died. It was a Saturday morning. He came to services at Saint Sernin, which surprised me."

"Because he was a Cathar."

"That, and because I thought that he hated me to the depths of his corrupted soul," said Vitalis. "For which he had good reason."

"I am not interested in the reason, Brother Vitalis. What did Milon tell you about the book?"

"That it was a danger to any who held it. That the men whose names appeared in it would stop at nothing to get it back. He thought that because our mutual hatred was well known, no one would suspect me of helping him, which is why he was asking for my help. Using me was his way of—of telling me that he forgave me."

"When he was killed, why didn't you bring the book to the authorities?"

"Because I didn't know who to trust," he said. "The Count was still away, and anyone in Toulouse might have been corrupted. And I also thought that Milon had been killed by someone else, someone who had nothing to do with the book."

"Béatrix," I said. "You thought she had killed him. You were protecting her."

He bowed his head.

"She didn't do it, Vitalis," I said.

"I cannot be certain of that," he said.

"But I can," I said. "We have Milon's murderer in captivity, complete with confession. Béatrix had nothing to do with it."

"Is it true?" he cried. "God be praised!"

"This is all very touching," sneered Donatus as he started to cross the footbridge. "But I am done listening. Hand over the book or I will kill you."

"No," I said, scratching my nose.

"I swear, Fool, that—"

Vitalis suddenly dove forward, bringing him down from behind. Donatus swung his dagger blindly behind him and was rewarded by a cry of pain. Vitalis let go with one hand, but clung tightly to Donatus's cowl with the other.

With a speed and agility that defied his mass, Donatus rolled, spun, and kicked hard at the other monk's jaw. This time, Vitalis relinquished his hold as he staggered and fell backward onto the shore. Donatus straightened and turned back to me, his knife raised.

"The book, Fool!" he screamed. "Give it to me now!"

I held it high over my head.

"Let all oaths be abrogated!" I cried to Heaven. "Let all sins be washed clean in the river!"

Donatus took another step toward me, then roared with pain as an arrow hit him in the back of his thigh.

"You want it?" I yelled. "Then take it!"

I tossed the book high and to his left. He reached for it desperately, but the wounded leg gave way. With a cry, he tumbled into the sluice.

I rushed forward to help, but the current, funneled into that narrow opening, swept the monk out into the river. He struggled feebly against it, but his wet robes tangled about his body. He started to slip below the surface.

"He hit his head," called Vitalis from the other side of the bridge. "We have to go after him."

"No need," I said, pointing.

A pair of longboats launched from the small beach below the sawmill. I saw the dark forms in them lean over to grab the wounded monk and haul him to safety.

"He's alive!" one of them shouted.

"Thank God," said Vitalis. He looked over at me. "The Count's men?"

"Yes."

The book had landed on the lip of the sluice. He picked it up.

"I suppose this means I don't get it back," he said.

"Read it first," I said. "You won't find it very interesting."

He looked at me, puzzled, then held the book up to the moonlight and opened it to the first page. It was blank. So were the rest.

"Did you really think that I would risk the real book on this little production of mine?" I asked, taking it back.

"Where is it?"

"I have it," said Count Raimon, emerging from the shadow of a mill. Beside him was my wife, her bow in her hands, a second arrow nocked. "Senhor Fool, your talent for entertainment has surpassed anything I have ever seen."

"Thank you, Dominus," I said bowing.

"Brother Vitalis," said the Count. "I am curious as to one aspect of your tale, though I find that it was honestly said. Why did you change your vote for Raimon de Rabastens?"

"A certain person—urged me to," answered Vitalis. "As penance for my sins."

"Father Mascaron?" asked the Count.

"Yes," said Vitalis.

"Why did he want Raimon to be his master?"

"The other candidate, the Bishop of Comminges, is a strong man," said Vitalis. "Father Mascaron is ambitious. He couldn't control a strong man. But he thought he could control Raimon de Rabastens. Your Bishop was a deacon from a suspect family, and you've seen what a pathetic man he is."

"Your confessor put you in a perilous position," said the Count. "I do not hold your actions against you. Nevertheless, I am going to ask you to enjoy the hospitality of the Château Narbonnais until we straighten all of this out."

"The prison?" asked Brother Vitalis.

"Oh, no," said the Count. "A guest room, with all the luxuries that grateful nobility can provide. You can go back to your monastic existence and repent when you're done. Will you walk with me, Brother Vitalis?"

"With all my heart," said the monk.

"Lady Fool, your performance was equal to your husband's," said the Count as Claudia bowed. "That was a superb shot."

"It wasn't so difficult," said Claudia. "Big men make big targets."

"You will come to the Château in the morning," said the Count. "It will be my turn to entertain you."

We bowed one last time, and the two men strolled across the stone bridge to the shore, where the Count's men waited for them.

"It really was a good shot," I said.

"Thank you, husband," she replied, unstringing her bow. "Will you walk with me?"

"With all my heart," I said, offering my arm.

Soldiers had quietly taken up positions around the Château Bazacle, awaiting orders. As we passed through the bourg, we heard shouts and the sounds of mailed fists pounding on doors.

"It's going to be a bloodbath," said Claudia as we walked along the river road.

"Maybe, maybe not," I said. "But if it is, it will be nothing compared to the war that might have been. Let's get home. Helga must be dying from the suspense."

A low whistle greeted us as we reached the house of Honoret. I whistled the counter, and Pelardit stepped from the shadows.

"All is well?" I asked.

He nodded.

"Thank you. All is well with us. Stay the night, and we'll catch you up on what happened."

We went in. I climbed the steps and whistled. I heard the counter from above, then the sound of the bar sliding from the trapdoor. A moment later, Helga opened it and smiled down upon us.

The day of the Feast of Saint John the Evangelist was cold but sunny. We were meticulous with our makeup and motley. Helga scrubbed the two boys until they were practically pink, then presented them to us for inspection.

"Ever been to the Château Narbonnais?" I asked them.

They shook their heads solemnly.

"You're only going as far as the courtyard," I said. "But wait there, and I promise you there will be someone you will want to see."

Pelardit and I each carried one of the boys down the steps, while Claudia carefully held Portia, who was asleep. Helga came last, making sure the padlock was secure. Then we were off to the Château.

No less a personage than Peire Roger, the viguier, came to greet us upon our arrival.

"I'm afraid it's just the two of you he wants," he said apologetically. "But the rest may come to the kitchen for now."

Helga pouted, but Pelardit brightened at the prospect of free food, or possibly the prospect of kitchen wenches. He took the boys by the hands and led them away. Claudia handed Portia to Helga.

"Mind that she doesn't become soup, Apprentice," she instructed the girl.

"Yes, Domina," said Helga. She followed Pelardit and the boys.

"This way, Fools," said Peire.

He led us into the Grande Chambre, then pointed to the balcony.

"I believe that you will find the view from there to be quite good," he said. "The Count wishes that you be unobserved."

We bowed and climbed the steps to the balcony.

Count Raimon entered a few minutes later, accompanied by the Count of Comminges and the viguier. He carried the book in his right hand. They took their seats, then the Count looked up at the balcony.

"Good morning, Fools," he said.

We stepped into view and bowed.

"As you can see, no crossbows from on high, no guards around me," he said.

"Are we your protectors then?" I asked.

"You already have been," said the Count. "But now, I must be the protector of my realm. This will be a play in four acts."

"May I interpolate a scene of my own devising before one of them?" I asked.

"Of course," he said. "Some comic relief only enhances the tragedy. Now, stand back and listen." He turned to his viguier. "The soldiers first."

The guards brought in seven men, their hands and feet chained.

"Leave us," commanded the Count.

The guards exited the room. He stood and walked down the line of men, inspecting them.

"I am not certain if a mercenary can ever be called a traitor," he said. "But you took an oath upon entering my service, you have taken my coin ever since joining, you have accepted my hospitality in the form of food, shelter, even women on some memorable occasions. And now I find that you have thrown that aside." He held up the book and waved it at them. "If this was purely a matter of violating a contract, then I suppose that I would simply take you to the court next door and demand my money back. But this is a matter of military discipline. This is a question of sworn loyalty to my person. I will give each of you one chance to save yourselves. You are the commanders of disloyalty in my armies. Give me the names of the men who have committed to your wretched cause, and I will spare your lives and theirs. Well?"

None of the soldiers uttered a word.

"At least you are loyal to someone," sighed the Count. "Admirable behavior at the end. Guards!"

The guards reentered.

"Hang them in front of the troops," he directed.

The condemned men were led away.

"End of Act One," said the Count. "They were most eloquent in their silence, were they not, Fools?"

"It speaks well of them, Dominus," I called.

"The consuls next," he said.

The chains of office looked puny compared with the chains of captivity. Fifteen fatigued men, including Bonet Borsella, stood in a frightened bunch before the Count, who was drumming his fingers loudly on the book. Among the men guarding them was Calvet, the baile.

"Good morning, gentlemen," he said. "Thank you for responding so promptly to my invitation. I trust your accommodations were acceptable? And that the food was adequate?"

There was silence.

"I have just sentenced seven officers to death," continued the Count in a conversational tone. "Men who have in fact done me good service over the past several years. You, on the other hand, have been a constant thorn in my boot, a greedy annoyance."

He slapped his palm on the book, and the men as a group jumped, their chains rattling together. The Count smiled, and the Count of Comminges smirked at his side.

"But that isn't why I asked you here today," Raimon said. "I have come up with the most ingenious idea, and it being the Christmas season, I wanted to share it with you immediately. It occurred to me that we need to bring more of the notables of Toulouse into the court. Young people to be educated in the ways of gentility and chivalry, so that their blood, if you will, may brighten and enliven our days. Therefore, I propose that we shall select from each of your families one fortunate child to be the beneficiary of this gift of ours. People will say to you, how lucky you are to have such a generous and caring count! And as long as I am alive and safe, so will your children be, for I am a caring and loving man."

"Hostages?" blurted one of the prisoners.

"Why should I need hostages?" asked the Count, amused. "You are released. Go spend the holidays with your families. We will begin this new arrangement after Twelfth Night. Oh, Bonet, if you would be so good as to remain for a moment."

The rest of the prisoners were unchained and escorted out. Bonet stood flanked by Calvet and a guard. He could not take his eyes off the book.

"You paid that poor drunk Armand to testify at the inquest for your brother's death," said the Count. "Why did you seek to implicate the Cathars?"

Bonet threw himself prostrate before the Count. The guard started forward but was restrained by a curt order from the baile.

"Forgive me, Dominus," he said, weeping. "I was doing what I was told to do. You've seen my name in Guilabert's book. I had borrowed from him to the point of disaster for the sawmill. I had no choice."

The Count held the book up.

"Your name isn't in here," he said.

"What?" exclaimed Bonet, looking up at him.

"Honorable of you to volunteer that your name had been in here," said the Count. "Your brother tore a page out and destroyed it. I supposed he loved you enough to protect you, even though you were a traitor. Too bad you didn't love him more than you loved money. His blood is on your hands, along with everyone else in this book. You have to live with yourself. I don't. Get out of my sight."

The guard led him away.

"I was wrong," said Calvet, kneeling before the Count.

"You were too eager to be fooled," said the Count. "I know you despise the Cathars, but they harm no one. And there are too many of them for you to kill."

"Forgive me," said the baile.

"Of course," said the Count. "Stay with us for the rest."

The baile took a seat by the viguier.

"How do you like the play so far, Fools?" called the Count.

"Well-crafted and politic," I said. "Your mercy is noteworthy."

"More pragmatism than mercy," said the Count. "Were I to hang so many Toulousans, then it would be known throughout Christendom, and I will be seen as a weak man. This way, I maintain control over my own city. Is it time for your interpolation now?"

"Depends on what's coming in Act Three," I said.

"Arnaut Guilabert," he said.

"Then I will wait until you are done with him," I said.

"Bring him in," commanded the Count.

Guilabert walked in unescorted and unchained. He bowed slightly to the Count.

"I have your book," said the Count, holding it up.

"Never seen it before in my life," said Guilabert.

"Your initials appear in it," said the Count.

"Common enough in this town," said Guilabert. "I could name you a dozen men with the same."

"Your mistress, Audrica, has made a statement implicating you," continued the Count. "As has Bonet Borsella."

"A drunken slut and a man who owes me money," retorted Guilabert. "Who would believe them?"

"Perhaps no one other than me," said the Count. "Then there is your brother."

"I have no brother," said Guilabert.

"Half-brother," the Count corrected himself. "He spoke of your plot against me. He's very proud of you, you know."

"I don't know what you're talking about," said Guilabert. "I have no half-brothers, either."

"Bring him in," directed the Count.

It took several guards to move the big monk, despite his being chained and gagged. His robes were in tatters, and his leg was wrapped in bandages.

"I can certainly see the resemblance despite the tonsure," observed the Count. "Do you care to repeat your denial, Guilabert?"

"He's just a monk," said Guilabert. "Nothing to do with me."

"Then if you have no use for him, neither do I," said the Count. "Bernard, would you mind strangling him for me?"

"It would be my pleasure," said the Count of Comminges,

producing a length of cord from his sleeve. He stood behind the monk, looped the cord around his neck, then pulled it tight. Donatus's eyes turned desperately toward Guilabert. Then they began to bulge.

"He's a man of Christ," commented Raimon. "Want to deny him a third time?"

"Stop it!" shouted Guilabert.

Raimon held up his hand, and the Count of Comminges released the cord.

"I am glad to see that you care about someone," said Raimon. "It makes it easier to apply pressure. We are going to handle this quietly. You will forfeit your holdings to me. The Château Bazacle will be conveyed to the city of Toulouse for its defenses. You will discharge your soldiers immediately, and mine will occupy their barracks. When all of this has been completed, you, along with your family and your children's families will be banished from the Toulousain. On that day, I will release your brother to you. That is all. You know the way out."

Guilabert looked at his brother, then turned and walked out. The guards took Donatus away.

"Your turn, Fool," said the Count.

We came down to join them.

"By your leave, Dominus, I will take you to your dungeons," I said. "But please hang back. I wish the prisoner to believe I am alone."

"I am intrigued already," said the Count. "Lead on, Fool."

Out into the courtyard, into the Palace of Justice, and down to the dungeons. The guards on duty started to hail the Count, but he silenced them with a gesture. I walked ahead to a cell and looked inside at its occupant.

"Hello, Martine," I said.

She didn't look up.

"How was the sausage?" I asked.

She pointed to the unopened package next to her.

"Oh. Apparently not to your liking. The cheese neither? I'm so sorry. My mistake. I should have realized. Nothing that comes from coition, right?"

She picked up the package and hurled it at me with a shriek.

"Come, come, Martine." I said. "That's poor behavior even for a Cathar. Most of the ones I know are very peaceable people."

"Go away," she said.

"I should have picked up on it before," I said, ignoring her. "You refused our wonderful meal because you had a touch of the stomach, yet you ate dried fruit? Odd choice for a woman who ails so. But you turned down some very good sausage, and you didn't even eat the excellent lamb that you cooked for our arrival."

"I wish that you had never come here," she said.

"But that's all your business," I said. "I have no problem with Cathars. At least, with those who don't betray me."

"What is your meaning?"

"Armand," I said.

She buried her face in her hands.

"The day he was killed, he was supposed to meet me at the Miller's Wheel," I said. "The only person I told about that was Jordan, and he was with me the entire time until we saw Armand floating in the Garonne. But Jordan told you. And then he took me for a nice long tour of the city, while someone killed Armand in the bourg. Who was it, Martine? Who did you warn about our meeting?"

"I can't tell you," she sobbed.

"Martine, there are a pair of fine young boys waiting in the courtyard," I said. "I promised them that I would free their parents. I have cleared Jordan of both murders. But if you don't tell me who you told, then he will have to raise your boys alone."

"You wouldn't leave me here," she whispered.

"I'm the one who put you here, Martine. You were arrested at my behest. One word from me to the Count and you will either rot here or rejoin your family."

Out of the corner of my eye, I saw the Count and Claudia standing where she couldn't see them, listening intently.

"Good-bye, Martine," I said, and I turned to leave.

"It was the Bishop," she said.

I turned back.

"Tell me everything," I said.

"I was his seamstress," she said. "I repaired his vestments, his miter. Whenever he could scrape the money together, I would make him a new set. Then things began to change. Somehow, he found out that I was a Cathar. And he wanted me to come back to the Church, but I refused. Then he told me that things were going to become much worse for the Cathars soon. That if he denounced me, I would be ruined, maybe even burned as a heretic. And that my children would be burned at my side."

She started crying again.

"I didn't know why he cared so much about me. But it wasn't me that mattered to him."

"Who was it, Martine?"

"It was Jordan. Jordan and Pelardit and Balthazar, and when you arrived, he wanted to know everything about you. About what you were doing, what you were looking for."

"So, when you found out I was meeting Armand . . ."

"I told him. And he was angry at Armand, saying they should have known better than to trust him. Then he told me to leave, and I did. But I stopped to watch the cathedral, and I saw him come out. Only if I hadn't just seen him, I might never have recognized him."

"Why?"

"Because he wasn't dressed as a bishop. He was wearing ordinary clothing, with a cloak and hood that covered his face. But it was him."

"Did you follow him?"

"No," she said. "I didn't want to know. I never thought Armand would be killed."

"One last question, Martine," I said.

"What?"

"Jordan knew you were informing on us, didn't he?"

She was silent.

"I was hoping you would say no," I said.

I walked over to the Count and my wife and motioned for them to go back to the courtyard. As I followed them, I heard another woman sobbing in a nearby cell. I looked inside and saw Audrica sitting there. I tossed the package of food by her feet. She never looked up.

"Not much comedy in the interlude," I said when we were back outside.

"Did it answer all of your questions?" asked the Count.

"I'm afraid so. Thank you for agreeing to lock them up for me."

"We have dungeons," he said. "Might as well use them once in a while. Captain, bring out the fool and his wife. No chains."

Jordan and Martine soon emerged, blinking in the harsh midmorning light.

"You are no longer prisoners," said the Count.

"Bless you, Dominus," said Jordan.

"But you are banished from the Toulousain and your house is confiscated," said the Count. "You have one week. Bring them their children."

Peire Roger went to fetch them. The Count turned to Claudia and me.

"Hard work makes me hungry," he said. "I am going to have a light repast. Then we will conclude our play. I will see you shortly."

He turned and went into the Grande Chambre.

"You got us out," said Jordan. "Thank you."

"He was the one who put us in here," said Martine bitterly.

"What?" exclaimed Jordan.

"He knows," she said. "He knows everything, damn him."

The boys flew into the courtyard, screaming for their parents, Helga and Pelardit following with the baby. Jordan and Martine knelt to embrace their children.

"One more thing," I said.

"What?" asked Jordan.

"You're banished."

"I know. We have one week."

"No," I said. "He banished you from the Toulousain. I'm banishing you from the Fools' Guild."

"You can't do that!" he protested.

"I'm the Chief Fool of Toulouse," I said. "I damn well can. You betrayed us, Jordan. From now on, if any Guildmember catches you performing, your existence will be made miserable."

"But how will I live?" he asked.

"I don't care. Good-bye, Jordan. Helga, you and Pelardit wait here. We will be back soon."

Claudia and I returned to our balcony while the two counts ate.

"Last act," she whispered.

"Last act," I said.

The Count wiped his mouth with a napkin, and the servants took away the table.

"Bring them in," he said.

The Bishop of Toulouse entered in full regalia, followed by Father Mascaron.

"Greetings, Raimon," said the Count. "Take a seat. Father, you as well."

A pair of low three-legged stools were brought in. The two sat on them somewhat uncomfortably.

"I have been hearing the most interesting things about you in the last two days, Raimon," said the Count. He held up the book, opened to the last page. "There's your signature in this, for instance."

Father Mascaron leaned forward, scrutinized the signature carefully, then moved his stool a few inches away from the Bishop.

"I have meted out punishments to everyone in here but you," said the Count. "Slight question of what's appropriate. I can't hang you, can't throw you in a dungeon, can't seize the cathedral. I don't want the cathedral, to tell you the truth. It looks like a money-losing operation to me."

"Is that all?" asked the Bishop.

"I have also found out that your election was, shall we say, tainted? One of the canons was coerced into voting for you by Father Mascaron, and we have since learned that a few more were simply bribed."

"My election was approved by Rome," said the Bishop. "It is not for you to challenge it."

"Then there is the murder of Armand de Quinto," continued the Count.

Father Mascaron's mouth fell open.

"I had nothing to do with that," said the Bishop calmly.

"I have evidence to the contrary," said the Count. "But I don't intend to bring you to assizes. More trouble than it's worth. I am simply going to tell you to step down from the bishopric."

The Bishop sprang to his feet, the stool bouncing away.

"You do not have the authority!" he thundered.

"I do," said a voice to the left of us.

The Bishop turned and stared as Peire de Castelnau came into the room.

"I'd like to say I'm disappointed in you, Raimon," said the legate. "But the truth is I never had great expectations for you in the first place. You will step down, and we will give out that it was for the election. You will keep your stipend and the power to perform the sacraments. The sacraments, Raimon—remember them? What everything was supposed to be about?"

"My stipend?" laughed the Bishop. "My stipend—how could anyone possibly live on that?"

"When you have your soul back in order, come join the Cistercians and we will teach you how to live," said the legate gently.

"Sounds like a fair offer," said the Count. "I suggest you accept it."

"Enough," said the Bishop. "I am sick of this city. It will be a pleasure to leave."

He stormed out. Father Mascaron rose uncertainly.

"Father Mascaron," said the Count.

The priest turned.

"Even the Count of Toulouse must draw the line at killing

a bishop," said the Count. "Of course, anything less is fair game. Remember that."

"Yes, Dominus," said the priest, bowing respectfully. Then he followed the Bishop out.

"Come down, Fools," ordered the Count.

We did. Brother Peire winked at me.

"I thought you were spending Christmas at Fontfroide," I said.

"I changed my mind," he said. "Things were too interesting here."

"I was going to introduce you," said the Count. "I suppose I needn't bother."

"You may introduce this charming lady," said the legate.

"Then Brother Peire, may I present Domina Gile?" said the Count.

My wife and the legate bowed to each other.

"Fools, I have just acquired a house in the city," said the Count. "I am going to install you in it. Saint Cyprien is too far away."

"Very good, Dominus," I said.

"Small thanks for quashing a rebellion before it began," he said. "If there is anything else—"

"There is the matter of the Bishop's succession," said Brother Peire.

"Officially, that has nothing to do with me," said the Count. "Although I'm not sure that I trust anyone selected by the canons in this town anymore."

"My point exactly," said the legate. "I have a candidate in mind. A man from outside the Toulousain, and so unaffected by the local influences. A member of my own order."

"A Cistercian for Bishop," commented the Count. "Unusual. Who do you have in mind?"

"The Abbot of Le Thoronet," said the legate. "A pious

man. When he joined the order, he put his sons in the Abbey of Grandselves."

"I have long had a good relationship with Grandselves," said the Count.

"Your generosity to them has been noted," said the legate.

"Who is this apolitical abbot?" asked the Count.

"His name is Folc," said the legate.

The Count stared at him, then me.

"You mean Folquet, the troubadour," he said flatly.

"He was at one time known for that," admitted Brother Peire.

"He used to write songs ridiculing my father," said the Count. "And me."

"I assure you that he has repented," said the legate smoothly. "Indeed, he has written no songs of any kind in years."

"Stop pandering," said the Count. "Who does he owe?"

"Well, me," I said.

"You?" exclaimed the Count. "How so?"

"I saved his life," I said. "Long story."

"I see," said the Count. "He's a former troubadour and a Cistercian abbot. A Cistercian monk has proposed him, and he owes his life to a jester who is somehow in league with this Cistercian monk."

"Well, when you put it like that . . ." I said, trailing off.

Raimon turned to his cousin.

"What do you think, Bernard?"

"Couldn't be any worse than what we have now," said the Count of Comminges.

"Wonderful," said Raimon, turning back to us. "Fine. Send for him. I'll try to get along with him. Brother Peire, will you be my guest tonight?"

"I will, thank you," said Brother Peire. "Senhor Pierre,

Domina Gile, I look forward to making your acquaintances again."

"And yours, Brother Peire," I said.

"For you, Fools," said the Count, tossing me a purse. "Moving expenses."

We bowed to him and left.

"Up, up, up!" called Portia when we came out.

I took her from Helga and placed her on my shoulders.

"Well?" asked Helga.

"Raimon de Rabastens is out, Abbot Folc is in," I said. "There's a great deal more to it than that, but it should be told properly over a good meal. I say we repair to the Yellow Dwarf."

"Sounds good," said Claudia.

Someone cleared his throat. We turned. There was no one there but us. And Pelardit.

"Was that you?" I asked him.

Pelardit looked around to verify that no one was within earshot.

"I just wanted to tell you how glad I am that they made you Chief Fool," he said softly. "Working under Jordan would have been miserable."

We looked at him dumbfounded.

"That's it," he said. "Oh, and I'm buying."

"Then what are we waiting for?" I asked. "Let's go."

CODA

"The world is a dangerous and evil place, Theophilos," said Abbot Folc.

"Not all of it," I said. "Not all the time."

"This is what you fight against, isn't it?"

"On my good days."

"Maybe it's time for me to take part in it again. Toulouse, you said."

"Yes."

"They already have a bishop, and Count Raimon hates me. Do you really think that you can pull this off?"

"I won't know until I try."

"When you succeed, send for me. I will be ready."

Handling things quietly takes time.

Jordan, Martine, and the boys were gone by Twelfth Night. We remaining fools performed once for the town that day, then again for the Count at the Château Narbonnais. Then the four of us repaired to the Yellow Dwarf to celebrate Portia's first birthday privately. She was walking with more and more confidence. Indeed, if ever a baby could be said to swagger, it was our daughter.

The house that the Count had selected for us was near Montaygon Square, a convenient location, although I still was unhappy about living inside the city walls. Pelardit was a frequent guest, occasionally letting his guard down enough to laugh out loud as long as it was only us present.

One day in February, Claudia came home while I was preparing dinner and said, "Béatrix is gone."

"Gone? What do you mean?" I asked.

"Gone from Toulouse," she said. "She collected the last of Milon's debts, sold the house on the sly, and slipped out in the early morning with her family."

"I hope she fares well," I said.

"You haven't heard the best part," said Claudia. "Looks like Vitalis Borsella went with her."

"No!"

"Yes," she said. "Renounced one set of vows and assumed another. They were married in secret. It only came out after they left."

"We never found out why she went to Bazacle that day."

"I asked her. Guilabert was trying to find out what she knew about the book. She denied knowing anything."

"Think she was telling the truth?"

"Who knows? She had her suspicions about Vitalis, but she concealed them."

"Why?"

"Because she loved him, you dolt," said my wife. "And because she feared he might have killed Milon for her."

"They each thought the other had killed Milon to protect the other," I said. "I suppose that's love."

The Guilaberts were the next to leave, turning the Château over to the consulate in March and heading north in a grand procession. Word reached us later that they were attacked by bandits on the road. Arnaut Guilabert was killed defending his family.

I know that the Fools' Guild had nothing to do with the attack. I cannot be certain about the Count. I prefer not to know.

The removal of Bishop Raimon de Rabastens required a great deal of bureaucratic shuffling, but Rome eventually made it official with a letter from Innocent III in July. Raimon de Rabastens formally stepped down in September. The canons met with the Count before holding their election, and another papal legate monitored the proceedings. Folc, Abbot of the Cistercian abbey at Le Thoronet, ex-merchant of Marseille and formerly one of the greatest troubadours the Fools' Guild has ever known, became Bishop-elect of Toulouse.

He arrived on a Tuesday. I met him inside the cathedral as he inspected it. The Count's workmen had replastered the walls, but the place otherwise looked just as shabby as it had ever been.

"Ah, Theophilos, what have you gotten me into?" he sighed when he saw me.

"It's Tan Pierre now."

"Of course. Forgive me. This place is disgraceful. No wonder people are staying away. There is virtually no income from rents thanks to my predecessors' debts, and not one of the priests here would last a day working at my old abbey."

"Want to go home?" I asked.

"No, of course not," he said. "One saving grace is that I saw my sons at Grandselves for the first time in nine years. Awkward all around."

"How much did you tell them?"

"Everything," he said.

"That must have been hard," I said.

"Enough chitchat," he said, clapping his hands. "Father Mascaron!"

The priest entered. Folc gave him the same critical inspection he had given the cathedral.

"I understand that you are an unscrupulous, untrustworthy, underhanded scoundrel," said Folc.

"You may have understated the case slightly," said Father Mascaron, bowing his head respectfully.

"I am making you my provost," said Folc. "I want you where I can see you at all times. I expect absolute obedience. If I hear one whisper of disloyalty, I will kick you into the gutter."

"I understand entirely," murmured the priest.

"Good. Round up every priest, deacon, lay brother and servant, and have them round up every bucket and brush they can find. Send to the Abbot of Saint Sernin and tell him to lend us all of his spare monks. We are going to scrub every surface in this place until it gleams, then put a new coat of whitewash on the walls. Two coats."

"With all due respect," said Father Mascaron, "the abbot does not take orders from the Bishop."

"Then give him my compliments. Tell him that I am merely the Bishop-elect, and that I am appealing to him as one abbot to another," said Folc.

"Very well," said Father Mascaron. He glided silently out.

"How long before he turns on me, do you suppose?" asked Folc.

"Keep him on a short leash," I advised. "He may prove useful."

"I can count on your help today?"

"To whitewash the church? Why not? I like a good metaphor."

He grunted and rolled up his sleeves as priests with buckets and mops started to enter.

There was no small irony that the ceremony installing Folc as Bishop proper was presided over by none other than the Archbishop of Narbonne, the same man that the legates had sought unsuccessfully to depose. But ceremony is ceremony, and if it draws a good crowd, it serves its purpose.

Folc stood on the steps of the cathedral, Father Mascaron at his elbow, the rest of the priests and clergy gathered behind them. The Count and his retinue were seated on benches set on the top step, while the Abbot of Saint Sernin and his monks stood on the ground to the right. It was a glorious, sunny day, and it looked like half the town had turned out, the children running around screaming, the women competing in their finery, and the fools juggling in the midst of it all.

It was strange to see Folc up there, the shabby white robe of the Cistercians replaced by the opulent vestments and miter appropriate to the See of Toulouse. The Archbishop, who had the same handsome, dark complexioned looks of his Aragonese family, held up the ring for all to see.

"In accordance with the wishes of His Holiness, Pope Innocent the Third," said the Archbishop, "and with the pleasure and the favor of Emperor Frederic the Second, you have been elected Bishop of the See of Toulouse. Do you consent to this election?"

"I do," said Folc.

There were cheers, and the choir sang the *Te Deum*. They still needed work.

"Receive the ring, the sign of faith," intoned the Archbishop, placing it on Folc's finger, "so that, adorned with pure faith, you may preserve without harm your bride, the Holy Church of God."

Folc held up his arms, and Father Mascaron and another priest wrapped the pallium over his vestments. The Archbishop handed Folc the staff of office, and held his hands out in blessing.

"It is done!" he cried.

The crowd cheered as Bishop Folc turned to bless them. I held Portia high over my head so that she could see, while Helga sat on Pelardit's shoulders. Claudia wrapped her arms around me.

"We did it, Theo," she said. "We actually did it."

"Yes, we did," I said. "No time to rest on our laurels. We have a performance."

We grabbed our gear and rushed to the Château Narbonnais to set up for the dinner that the Count was having in the Bishop's honor.

In light of the occasion, we restrained ourselves, saving the bawdier material for other occasions. But we made sure that there would be one special performance. When dessert was brought in, I stepped forward and bowed to the Count and the Bishop.

"Dominus and Domina, Your Holiness and Your Other Holiness, ladies and gentlemen," I said. "In honor of the new Bishop, I would like to sing something from his past, for although he is a man of God, he is a man of Music as well. This was one of his loveliest songs."

I sang as my fellow fools accompanied me.

"Singing will expose my true hidden heart,
Saving me when words have left me alone.

Newfound joy confounds all that I have known.
Song triumphs where falls the orator's art.
Who bids me sing? Whence comes my inspiration?
Love has called, and I must take up her part.
It pleases Love for me to sing her praise,
Although I quail before her fearsome gaze.
But Love commands, and so her slave obeys."

And so on, with four more verses that sustained the rhyme scheme throughout as only Folquet of Marseille could do.

When I was done, the room burst into applause. All except for the Bishop Folc, who sat there modestly accepting it.

Or so I thought.

"A beautiful song, Your Holiness," said Count Raimon.

"I must apologize, Count," said Folc, a bitter smile on his lips. "A foolish triviality from a misspent, sinful youth. I must—forgive my departure. Thank you for the excellent dinner."

He stood abruptly and walked out of the room, followed by the astonished stares of those left behind.

"What just happened?" asked Claudia.

"Let's find out," I said, and we followed the Bishop outside.

He was standing in the courtyard, breathing hard. Then he took off his miter and placed it on the ground. He removed his vestments, folded them carefully, and set them next to the miter. From his pouch he produced a length of knotted cord tied to a short, thick leather handle. He knelt, his lips moving silently for a minute. Then he whipped the cord about so that it smacked against his bare back. He gasped, then repeated the action, each time striking harder.

"Theo," said Claudia softly. "I am starting to think that the Guild has made a terrible mistake."

I could not reply. I could only watch in horror as the blood began to drip down the Bishop's back.

"Sale of the Château Bazacle, with its outbuildings and land adjoining the city gate, made by Arnaut Guilabert and Gentille, his wife, to the consuls of Toulouse, under the consent and guarantee of the two sons of the two vendors . . ." from a Toulousan charter, March 9, 1205.

The study of medieval Toulouse must begin with the works of John Hine Mundy, who devoted much of his life to it. It was in his *Studies in the Ecclesiastical and Social History of Toulouse in the Age of the Cathars* (2006) that I learned of a pair of Toulousan jesters named Jordan and Pelardit. Their existence was documented in 1192. Little is known of either, but Pelardit ultimately had a street named after him: Carraria Pilisarditis joculatoris, part of which survives as the present Rue de Filatiers. (The Rue des Sept Troubadours dates from a later period.)

A portion of the Daurade Bridge has been preserved, jutting out from the west bank of the Garonne, just north of the Old Bridge, which was built later and is still in use today. The Bazacle Dam would continue in existence for centuries, and the mills depending on it led to the creation of one of

Europe's earliest stock companies in the mid-thirteenth century. Saint Sernin, Saint Étienne, and Saint Pierre des Cuisines all stand, the last as a museum. The two châteaux, so crucial to the defense of the city, have long since vanished.

My principal source for the life of Folc remains N. M. Schulman's *Where Troubadours Were Bishops: The Occitania of Folc of Marseille (1150–1231)*. The song in the last chapter is my verse adaptation of Folc's *Chantan volgra mon fin cor descobrir*, based in part on Ms. Schulman's literal translation. I have tried to match Folc's rhyme and rhythmic schemes.

Of particular use were Terry S. Reynolds's *Stronger Than a Hundred Men: A History of the Vertical Water Wheel* (Johns Hopkins University Press, 1983) and Robert Benson's *The Bishop-Elect* (Princeton University Press, 1968). In addition, I would like to acknowledge the work of Cyril E. Smith, Patrice Georges Rufino, Pierre Gérard, Maurice Prin, Jean Rocacher, Violet Markham, Sister Mary Ambrose Mulhulland, Laurent Macé, Élie Griffe, and M. H. Vicaire.

Finally, thanks are due to my brother Joshua Gordon, who, during a family brainstorming session, came up with the title. Runner-up was my son Robert, who came up with *To Lend Is Toulouse*. It is good to know that punning is hereditary.